I0658871

JUST LET GO

ALESSANDRA THOMAS

SIXPENCE PUBLISHING

CHAPTER 1

NATALIA

MY SISTER-IN-LAW MAY HAVE BEEN able to convince me to go to the support group, but she couldn't make me participate.

Amalia had cornered me this past weekend, at a Sunday dinner she'd haphazardly pulled together in honor of me visiting. To be fair, I'd just blown up at Sebastian for rolling the tamales the wrong way and stalked off to the kitchen.

He had done a really shitty job of rolling them but, even as I screamed at him, I knew that wasn't what I was really upset about.

It was that I missed Mamá, the only person who had ever rolled the tamales right. It was that I was really hungry, and I only wanted tamales, and I was pretty sure I would never have tamales that tasted like Mamá's ever again.

There were a lot of things that would be different now that Mamá was dead. Tamales were the least of my concerns. But that was what finally, three months after her funeral, made me scream at Sebastian, pound my fist on the table and make my 10-year-old niece cry.

That, in turn, had made me cry, which had made me storm

over to the gym and punch the bags without gloves until my knuckles bled. It didn't take long. Three days later, here I was at the Chestnut Street YMCA, sitting in a cold metal folding chair, my arms crossed, staring at my cross-trainers and scowling.

Three months later, I still struggled with a love-hate relationship with these cross-trainers. On the one hand, running was the only thing that brought me respite from constant thoughts about what I could have done differently that day. On the other, if I hadn't insisted on running that day, Mamá might still be alive.

As if she could read my mind, the group leader piped in, "So, now that introductions are out of the way, I wanted to introduce tonight's topic - guilt, and how to cope. Guilt can manifest in several different ways after a loss, and I wanted to open this space up to share our experiences of that."

"I think there's the guilt of having a less-than-great relationship before he passed away," one sniffly middle-aged woman said. "We had disagreements over so many things... politics, how to raise the kids. We never said anything nasty to each other, but..." Then she trailed off as she dissolved into tears.

My arms crossed even tighter over my waist. Politics. Fighting over politics seemed almost as stupid to me as fighting over tamales.

"For me, it's over selling his things," another middle-aged man piped up. "Going through every single hand-made fishing lure and realizing I wouldn't be able to keep what he'd spent hours working on."

"Exactly," someone sitting right next to me said. "A year after my great-aunt passed, I finally unpacked some boxes she had in storage. I found dozens of half-finished teddy bears she was crocheting for the Philly children's intensive care unit. I tried to figure out how to finish them, but I was all thumbs. I mean. Have you ever tried to crochet?" A few people chuckled. I gritted my teeth and cracked the knuckles of my index fingers. I wanted to tell her that she could just buy some fucking teddy bears. It wasn't the same as watching your father slowly implode on himself now that your mother had left a hole in the family, and being able to do nothing about it.

A guy directly behind me cleared his throat after the laughter had died down a bit. "For me, it's knowing that I was all she had, and a year before she died, I left her to go to college." He cleared his throat again, and though I still wasn't looking up, I heard him change positions in his chair, shoving his feet underneath the foldable metal, shifting his body with a sigh. He cleared his throat again. "We, uh, didn't have any other family. It was just her and me, my whole life. She was all alone. She mentioned she had a really bad chest cold, you know, was having trouble taking deep breaths. Said she was thinking about going to urgent care, but I was coming in to visit the next day, and I said I'd take her to the doctor. She went in anyway. It wasn't like her – she must have been feeling really bad. She, uh... she had a stroke on the drive there. Wrapped her car around a light pole." His voice broke on the last word, and when it did, it was like it cracked something inside me. Suddenly, I wanted to spill. Everything.

"Mamá was perfectly healthy," I said, surprised at how low and soft my voice came out. There was nothing soft about me. Not ever. "She just hated driving in the bad weather. She'd wanted me to drive her to the market. We'd just had freezing rain, but she'd promised my brother's boyfriend his favorites – tamales – and she insisted on having the husks from the specialty place. My dad was working, and my brothers were busy too. I wanted to meet a friend at the gym first. I told her to relax, and if she still felt bad after my workout, I'd take her." I swallowed, hard. The group leader stayed quiet, giving me a little nod, encouraging me to go on. And it worked.

"When I came home from the gym, she was sitting there in her favorite chair. So peaceful. She just looked like she was asleep. But, ah..." My throat was painful and tight, but I was determined to finish what I'd started. "It was two days before Christmas. Turns out, she hadn't been perfectly healthy. I think she was holding on so that she could see me, you know. When I came home for break. "

This was the part I hadn't said out loud. Not to anyone, let alone a room full of people. But it would be stupid to stop now, probably. "She didn't tell me about the cancer, because she didn't want me to change my plans. I was always away from home." As I said the words, I was transported back to that gray, icy afternoon. There was nobody and nothing except me and Mamá, the room somehow chilled by the loss of her soul in her ruined body. Everyone else's afternoon was going on exactly as they'd expected it to, and there I'd been, hopelessly trying to rouse my mother, feeling my entire world shift seismically beneath my knees where they dug into the shag.

The entire room was silent for several agonizing seconds. Then, the group leader, Maisie or Millie or something, took a long breath in through her nose. "Thank you for sharing that story. Both of you. Thanks to *all* of you." She rushed to add that last part.

"It can be helpful," she continued, "to connect with others whose experiences of guilt are similar to your own. I encourage you to do that. Meet outside of this group, or exchange numbers. Lots of people even find comfort in texting, since that's something you can do at odd times."

Thank God. It was over. I'd promised Amalia I'd come to one support group, and I had. Not only that, but I made it through the whole thing.

Here was the thing - I'd known when she first suggested it that I would hate this shit. Who really wants to talk about all the details of their heart being ripped out from different angles, week after week? Not me. Not when it was still so fresh, so raw, so devastating. Not just to me, but to our entire family. And now with the state Papá was in...

I planted my love-hate trainers on the ground and shrugged out of the flowy sweatshirt I'd brought with me. Early March in Philadelphia meant that sitting still would make goosebumps crop up on my arms, but I'd break a sweat jogging within a couple minutes.

I'd almost made it to the door when the throat-clearer did it again, this time right behind me. I froze.

"So, I don't know if you'd be up for it, but I thought I'd ask anyway. Wanna exchange numbers?"

I should have thrown a short response over my shoulder at him, reached for the door handle, and kept going right out of there. But I didn't. Instead, something in his voice sent electricity skittering down my neck and over my shoulders. I stopped and turned, and when I looked up into his eyes, it was like someone had punched me in the gut. The last time I'd looked into those eyes, I was on the edge of the best orgasm I'd ever had.

"Ethan?" I stammered. "What the hell are you doing here?"

CHAPTER 2

ETHAN

HOLY. Shit.

Emotions cross-fired through my brain, making it impossible to process a single thought. I'd been coming to this bi-weekly grief support group on and off for almost seven years, ever since Mom died and the desolate feelings threatened to drown me. I hadn't ever seen someone I knew here.

I'd never once imagined I'd see the only woman I'd never been able to get out of my head.

I lightly brushed her elbow with my fingertips, fought the urge to grab her upper arm, spin her toward me, and crush her to my chest. God, I'd remembered what it felt like to have her pressed up against me, wearing far fewer clothes than we were now, far too often for my own good. "Outside," I murmured.

Her mouth hung slightly open, but she obeyed.

In the stretch of sidewalk between the Chestnut St YMCA and McDonald's, the cold March wind howled. It was her, of that I was certain. I wouldn't ever forget that soft caramel skin, those lush lashes that curved up to frame her impossibly dark, sparkling eyes. Natalia shivered, clutching her thin sweatshirt to her body so that it stretched over her muscled shoulders.

"Natalia." Her name barely caught purchase on the heavy breath coming from my chest, like it was amorphous, like it could blow away with the wind at any moment. "Natalia, I had no idea."

She raised her eyes to mine, and the strength and fire of her personality sparkled in the trace of tears there.

"Ethan," she breathed, swallowing hard. I remembered watching her throat move when she spoke, when she moaned. These two parts of my past - Mom's death and the most intense week-and-a-half I'd ever had with a woman - were strangely, inextricably intertwining before my eyes.

She nodded, casting her eyes down to her cross trainers. Same brand, same color. Brand new pair. I used to tease her about what would happen when they stopped making them, in the haze of an afterglow or the delicious anticipation that charged the air when she first stepped into my place. "Three months ago," she clarified. "Few days before Christmas. There was nothing anyone could do. Nobody could have known."

It was obvious, even as she said the words, that she didn't believe them.

"Your birthday," I said.

"No," she said, finally giving me a soft smile. "My birthday is Christmas Eve. Remember?"

I laughed. "Now I do. Ten days wasn't exactly enough to get to know each other that well, I guess."

"Please," she said. "I've had boyfriends who didn't even remember which month my birthday is in after we'd been dating for much longer than that."

I chuckled, but it soon petered out into an awkward silence. The wind howled gently, and Natalia shivered again. "Walk?" I suggested, and she nodded.

"This way," she said, touching her fingertips to my elbow to guide me down the sidewalk from the YMCA entrance.

"What was that about in there?" she asked. "Why did we come outside to talk? Not that I mind, it's just..."

"Instinct, I guess," I said. "I've been in that group long enough to know that Maisie will discourage people who know each other from a different walk of life from attending the same group."

"And you wanted to see me again," Natalia said. Not a question, but not a confident statement, either. "After today."

"After we both spilled our guts about our dead mothers? Can you blame me for not wanting those to be the last words that we say in each others' presence?" The truth was that I never thought I'd talk to Natalia again.

Natalia was a captivating woman. Some part of that, I was sure, was contained in her penchant for drama. I'd met her last winter and we'd fallen into bed right away. I was smitten within days. She didn't seem unhappy to be around me, either. But she had plans - insane, life threatening, terrifying plans that not only threatened to make me hyperventilate from envisioning her dying all sorts of ways, but that also would take her far away from Philly.

After a few hours of sad consideration, we made the mutual decision to cut ties. She made a big deal out of erasing our numbers from each other's phones. She reminded me that not even her brothers would have her number in Pamplona, and the Alps, and wherever else she was planning to put her own life at risk for the next several months, and that this would be for the best. A clean break.

Except, at least for me, it wasn't that simple. I hadn't been able to stop thinking about her, and now, here she was. With a red nose, the same brand and style of cross-trainers, wind-swept thick dark brown waves, full lips and round eyes, all as beautiful as ever.

"I had no idea," I repeated after I realized she'd been silent for several long seconds. "I'm sorry."

"I didn't know about your mother, either. You never told me how she died. Just that she was gone. And I guess I never asked, because..."

"I know. It wasn't serious between us."

"No, but it was fun. It wasn't serious, but it felt like... I don't know. More than just passing the time. I'm glad to see you," Natalia said. In the short time we'd spent together, I'd discovered that was one of her hidden talents - anticipating what people needed to hear, and filling that need with a few short, perfect words. "Ha! Look at that," Natalia laughed, looking up. At first, I thought she was talking about the freak snowflakes that had begun to fall, swirling through the sky. But then I realized we were standing in front of The Knockout Brothers – her family's gym. I knew there was a small apartment on the top floor. That must be where she was staying. "We're all the way back already." The conversational sentence was soft, wistful-sounding on her lips.

I threaded my fingers together, quickly pulling them apart and rubbing my palms together to hide my nervous gesture. "So, what'll it be? You're not going to turn all this down, are you?" I twisted my shoulders and raised an eyebrow, like I might do if I was in a modeling shoot. My cocky act had never failed to make her laugh, and tonight was no different.

"Come up with me?" she asked, her eyes still sparkling from the laughter I'd caused. She bit her lip and looked down at her shoes again. She bounced on her toes, an adorable nervous habit that soothed her runner's twitchiness.. My head spun. "I thought you'd never ask." Ten minutes back in Natalia Ortiz's orbit had set me off course. I just wanted to be with her again. There was no point denying it.

No, this wasn't a romantic encounter, per se. But the

snowflakes were swirling in the gentle late winter breeze now, fat and beautiful. It was like we were figurines in a snow globe. It was almost perfect, except for one thing. Snow globes didn't feature couples stupidly staring at each other. So I reached down, pushing my freezing fingers into her thick mane, biting back a groan at having them buried there again, after so long. Then I leaned down and devoured her mouth with mine.

CHAPTER 3

NATALIA

I WAS STAYING in the small studio above The Knockout, what the Ortiz family all referred to as "the hotel." Mamá had loved guests. Some of my earliest memories were of Mamá making lists of who was coming for a holiday dinner and standing in the middle of our small living room, silently mapping out a seating plan. My brothers would haul folding tables out of the basement and I would set the tables with plastic plates painted to look like china, and our little North Philly four-bedroom, which could barely hold the seven of us on a normal day, suddenly held thirty or more people for dinner. Christmas Eve lunch meant that you had to suck in your stomach and move stealthily if you wanted to make it between Aunt Claribel and the Christmas tree without causing a catastrophe.

After my four brothers had all left home, Mamá and Papá had sat me down, saying they wanted to downsize. It would allow them to put more money in the gym. We moved into a two-bedroom a block away from the gym, but that didn't stop Mamá from her urge to host. There was a small studio space above The Knockout, and within a couple months, Mamá had polished it up, added some simple furniture, and begun to urge my brothers to stay there. For three weeks after Mariana was born, my brother and his wife stayed in that little studio while Mamá waited on them hand and foot.

I couldn't remember a time when she'd been happier.

My stay in The Knockout Brothers hotel this time around coincided with a four-day break in my traveling. Amalia had warned me that the gray cable-knit afghan Mamá had made still covered the bed there. I'd been careful not to let my tears be heard over the phone.

The air between Ethan and me was tight and thin as we walked around the corner, down half a block, and up the stairs to the hotel.

"You living above the gym?" Ethan asked, his voice betraying how hard he was trying to sound casual.

"I'm not living here. Just staying for a few days. I had a couple days between jobs in L.A. and Papá asked me to come in for a family meeting."

"That something you do often?"

"No. Just updating us on the financials of the gym, our shares, all that. We haven't had one since after..."

"Yeah. I can imagine the business wasn't top on everyone's list."

My heart wrenched. Ethan's mom died. She was dead, and she'd been gone from his life for years when I met him, and I never knew. If I had, would I have called him after my own mother died? I'd wanted people to call me, when I was at the bottom of the pit of the deepest grief I'd ever experience in my life. Nobody had – probably because my number had changed. A couple people, including my friend Liz who lived here in Philly, had checked in on Facebook, something I only discovered weeks after the fact. I hardly ever logged on.

"No, it wasn't," I said quietly. "But The Knockout Brothers is a family business. So here I am."

I unlocked the door to the narrow stairway that led up to the hotel. One wall was entirely glass panes, large squares separated by leaded cames. There was a large floor lamp just inside the door, but I rarely needed it. Natural light lit up the single room during the day, and at night, the fantastic view of Philly lent numerous street and building lights to the space. It was simple, but breathtaking.

Right now, especially, it felt wrong to turn it on. These few days had been a whirlwind, and the breathless giddiness of seeing Ethan again felt like stepping into the eye of a storm. The first time I'd met him, life had been easy and predictable, filled with lazy pleasure. In fact, orgasms from Ethan Anderson were one of the only things that had ever been able to distract me from my wanderlust for any length of time. The ten days I'd spent with him had felt like some sort of record of almost-commitment. When we'd been together, I hadn't fantasized about where I'd travel, or what insane things I'd do, next. I'd only fantasized about more of him.

Maybe that was why I'd been so desperate to take off, all those months ago.

Right now, I felt desperate for something completely different. Thank God, so did Ethan. He spun me around with one hand and pushed the other one through my hair again. Whether he remembered how much I loved that particular mood or he really did love my hair that much, it didn't matter. His long, strong fingers tugging so gently on my thick strands sent a jolt of pleasure straight down to my belly, and the echo of it even lower. I choked on a gasp, and before he could lean down to kiss me again, I pushed up on my toes to kiss him. My hands fell to his waist, fisting his crisp white button down with both hands, untucking it from his pants as I did. My thumbs brushed his belly, feeling the fine hairs that I knew collected there in a path, leading straight down to the very best part of him. He jerked, and the movement made his teeth scrape against my bottom lip. I pulled away and licked it, tasting the faintest trace of blood.

"Still ticklish," I teased in a whisper.

"Yeah," Ethan said, gulping in a breath while he leaned his forehead against mine. "Just try and see if that stops me."

"God, I hope it won't," I managed before he swooped down for another kiss. This time was slower, deeper. Like he was tasting me, recording my flavor and feel for posterity.

"Tali, what - what are we doing?"

"I'm here in Philly for 24 more hours. So right now, we're kissing and groping each other in the dark, but I hope before that 24 hours is up you're going to give me what I really want from you."

Ethan peered down at me. God, was he actually giving this consideration? How did he not remember how good we'd been together? My self-discipline was nearly flawless, but even so, at this moment I was about to jump on him and tackle him onto the hotel's fluffy white bedding.

But within seconds, a wicked grin pulled at his lips. "Natalia Ortiz, I thought you'd never ask."

Within a single breath, he bent down, scooped me into his arms, and dropped me onto the bed. My grin cracked wide open as I bounced on the mattress, then watched appreciatively as Ethan unbuttoned his shirt, then stepped out of his pants, laying them neatly over an arm of the single brown leather armchair that sat in the corner of the apartment. He really was beautiful. Dark hair covered a big, muscular chest, trailed lightly down his abdomen, and collected again at the top of his boxers. That was one of the reasons I loved his thick beard so much - it reminded me of what I'd discovered under his clothes.

In seconds, Ethan hovered over me, undressed except for

boxers. He kissed me again, so slowly and carefully that I barely noticed that he was tugging my shirt up as he did.

God, I'd forgotten how this man had been able to make me forget myself. The difference between the last time we'd done this and tonight was that now, just for this one night, I really, really, really wanted to forget. Not only myself - the business, the way my life was in a constant state of limbo, the nagging feeling that free spirited could turn to aimless at any moment. The grief over Mamá that sometimes felt just as sharp as it had the day after she died. I didn't want to think about any of that right now. And with Ethan's mouth sucking at my neck and my collarbone, with his thumb already flicking my left nipple into a hard peak, I didn't have any choice in the matter. I couldn't think at all.

CHAPTER 4

ETHAN

EVEN THOUGH I didn't even want to admit to myself how desperately I'd wanted to see Natalia, to be with her, again, the feeling hit me right then, hard and powerful. This was unreal, the embodiment of every daytime fantasy and white-hot dream I'd had about the two of us together again.

The first time we were together, only ten days, was magical. Perfect. I'd tried to tell myself to appreciate for what it was, to move on. It hadn't worked.

I snaked my arm underneath Natalia and flicked the clasp of her bra open, thrilling at the muscled heat of her skin. She sighed, and I wanted to taste her sweet breath, so I did, gulping as much of her as I could.

Twenty-four hours. She said she was here for just a day, and that tomorrow she had a meeting, and that meant that all we had was tonight...

I growled at my own maudlin tendencies. I couldn't slip into depression over this. Yes, Natalia was one of a kind. Yes, I only had her for this one night, then maybe never again. I still had to enjoy it, to make it a night we both would remember, instead of spending it moping.

She'd shrugged out of her bra, and now, dear Lord, she was arching her back so that her tits pushed up toward my face. Exactly where I always imagined them, high and round and big and perfect. A nipple brushed my chin and I growled, feeling a beast inside rattling at its cage.

"Go ahead, Ethan," Natalia ground out. It sounded more like a plea than an invitation. She pushed my boxers down and dug her short nails into my ass. I answered her with a growl of my own, then dipped my head and sucked a nipple into my mouth, hard and fast. It took her breath away, and as she gasped, she ground her pelvis against mine.

She craned her neck up and bit my shoulder, and I groaned, sliding my hand under the blessedly stretchy waistband. She never wore any panties, or kept any hair on that sweet little pussy. "Jesus, Natalia. Promise me that you'll never wear anything except yoga pants."

She answered with a breathy laugh. "I wasn't planning on it."

"I don't think you could manage to put panties on around me if you tried," I whispered into her skin.

"There's that cocky guy who always drove me crazy." Even her breath smelled sweet.

For weeks after the last time we'd slept together, I swore I could remember her scent. I hadn't been wrong. It was exactly as I remembered it. She was earthy and delicious and begging me to lick her until she couldn't stand it anymore.

So that's exactly what I did.

She was wet when I bent down to flick her clit with my tongue, hard and fast, and oh God, this really wasn't a daydream because I hadn't forgotten the sound of her tiny shocked moans when I did this, either. I opened my mouth and pushed two fingers inside, thrusting and curling until she screamed.

"Please tell me you have a condom," she panted as I wiped

my beard on the edge of the sheet. I'd considered shaving it these last several months, but I couldn't do it. I never shook the memory of Natalia cooing that she loved the way it felt rubbing against the inside of her thighs when I ate her.

My heart stuttered. "Fuck," I said. Did I have one? I'd only gone out with three or four women since Natalia left town, and only one of those had actually resulted in sex. It had sucked. I hadn't even stayed all night.

I sat up bolt upright, then scrambled to get off the bed and into my pants pocket. Natalia laughed. Natalia only ever laughed, deep throated and full. No giggles, no titters. She was all or nothing, in that and everything else.

I managed to wiggle my wallet out of the back pocket, and let out a long, slow sigh of relief. I'd stuffed three in there last time, and there were still two left. I strutted back over to the bed which only took three long paces, and Natalia waggled her eyebrows at me. "Thank God," she said. She was still laid out, her flawless caramel skin drawing a curved outline of the most perfect body I'd ever seen on the stark white sheets. She was art, pure and simple. And she was mine for tonight.

If I was a religious man, I would have said a prayer.

"Come here," she purred, and I obeyed. There were times for teasing, for drawing out pleasure, for touching and tasting and sucking love-bites on skin for hours on end. This was not one of those times. This was a taste of the salvation I thought I'd lost forever. Natalia was back in my life, for however short a time, and I was going to spend at least some of that time inside her.

I nuzzled my face in her neck, scraping my teeth against the tendon there, while my hand wandered down to her sweet spot. "You're so wet," I moaned in her ear, in the most unoriginal line of dirty talk any guy had ever said. I didn't care, and neither did she, because she tilted her hips up, making my cock drag through her slick folds.

"Please, Ethan. Please."

Okay, I guess neither of us got any points for originality. This was still hot as hell.

Quickly, I rolled the condom on, then lined myself up as she nibbled at my neck. With one thrust, I was deep inside her. Inside heaven.

I hadn't slept with an insane number of women, but it had been enough that I knew that one cock and one pussy did not a perfect fit make. Sometimes, the magic just didn't happen, no matter how attractive or experienced both of us were. Other times, it was awkward, but we managed to find a rhythm and have a good time.

But sex with Natalia was above and beyond all of that. She fit perfectly around me, her muscles fluttering at exactly the right place and time. She writhed and moaned and grabbed and bit in the exact perfect combination to make me feel more plea-sure than I ever thought I could during sex. She matched me thrust for thrust, no matter the pace we set. Every time Natalia and I had sex - sixteen times, before this - was more mind-blowing than the last. It was like every time I was inside her, she learned to read my mind a little more.

This was the best one yet. I drove into her, slow and hard, my pace unflagging, grinding my pelvis against her clit every time I bottomed out. The sound she made when I did that was transcendent - a sharp, shocked gasp. Each and every time.

It wasn't long before she breathlessly started to warn me. I fucking loved that - she would announce her orgasm every time. "Ethan, I'm - oh God, I'm going to - holy shit. Ethan. I'm coming!"

The sweetest sound on the planet. Only to be upstaged by the sweetest feeling on the planet - Natalia Ortiz's perfect pussy clenching around my cock. I was lost. My vision went white and I held on to her strong shoulders for dear life, losing my drive seconds later. I collapsed on top of her with an exhausted huff, which earned another full-throated laugh from her.

Another incredible thing about Natalia - even though she was smaller than me, there was no way I would ever worry about hurting her or crushing her. I was a big guy - big hands, broad shoulders, thighs I sometimes had trouble fitting into standard trousers - but she was one hundred percent pure, powerful muscle. Yeah, she had curves, but right underneath her full breasts and beautiful round ass were layers of strength she'd built up over years of training for every conceivable athletic endeavor.

I had a love-hate relationship with her tight, strong body. On the one hand, she was durable as hell in the sack and could hold her own in any other situation besides. On the other hand, her dedication to building that athleticism and using it for any new experience she could was what had broken us up in the first place.

Not that we were ever really together. But when she insisted that running with the bulls in Pamplona was a totally reasonable thing for her to be doing, and that I was the one who was being ridiculous to worry about her getting hurt, I couldn't take it. Couldn't go with her, couldn't watch. Couldn't even wait by my phone for word that she'd made it out unscathed. Life was too fragile, and I couldn't let myself get attached to someone who acted like it wasn't.

Not after what had happened to Mom.

I slumped to the side, tugging her with me so that we faced each other on the bed. Deftly, I reached down and dealt with the condom, then craned my neck to deliver an open-mouthed kiss to the underside of her jaw. She hummed happily. "Thank you," she murmured, turning her head so that it was halfway buried in the pillow. "I still can't believe I ran into you. Especially like that."

Ah, there it was. The elephant in the room. The reason she was back in Philly in the first place. Suddenly, I felt sick.

"You could have told me about your mom, you know. I would have come to the funeral. I could have helped with... something." When my mother had died, I was a freshman. My brand-new friends and professors had danced around me, mumbling "sorrys," and letting me off easy on social engagements and homework assignments alike. Seven weeks later, a new semester had started, and it was like everyone expected me to have used that time to hit the "reset" button. It was one of the reasons I started going to the grief support group. It was the one place I could talk about Mom, about how I lost her, where people would listen. Where they would understand.

The fact that I hadn't been there for Natalia to do just that made me physically ache.

She shrugged. "I didn't know. Where we stood, you know? Pamplona made you really upset."

"You know I was just afraid of you getting hurt. I didn't want to think about that."

"So you would have been okay seeing me through days of weeping, a funeral, and weeks of depression, but not stitches on a torn bellybutton?"

My eyes flared wide. "Natalia. You didn't."

"Yep," she smiled. She stretched out onto her back and raised her arms over her head, making her breasts wiggle a little as they resettled. I only watched them for a moment, though, because I was zeroed in on her navel, which now slanted slightly down and to the right, tugged there by an angry dark-pink scar, only slightly shorter than my middle finger. "The lamest thing was that it wasn't even a bull. Some asshole shoved me against the wall and it caught on one of those pointy iron fence posts," she chuckled.

I sucked in a breath, then bent over to press my lips to it. "Does it hurt?" I mumbled against her skin.

"Not at all, compared to losing my mom."

I drew back to look at her, and caught her dark eyes shining in the moonlight. "Oh, babe," I said, my heart melting. Suddenly it didn't matter that we were both naked, with not even a sheet covering us, and that my cock was already half-hard again. I tugged her into my arms and cradled her head in the crook of my neck, understanding her deep, long sigh. She couldn't do anything about this pain except try her best to get through it. I couldn't do anything but be there for her.

In this still, soft moment, it felt like enough.

"Thank you," she murmured against my skin. "I'm so glad I found you again. Even if it was just for one night."

As I held her even tighter, my heart threatened to break all over again. It didn't matter. Natalia was worth it.

CHAPTER 5

NATALIA

SOME OF MY earliest memories were set in the lounge of The Knockout Brothers gym. This pilled brown couch had been here since I was little. I remembered the day my teenaged brothers hauled it in off the street, remembered the way Mamá's eyebrows pulled together as she searched it, inch by inch, for bed bugs and mold. That was after she yelled at my brothers for bringing in furniture from an unknown family off the street. Afterward, when she sat on it and sighed into the cushiness of the couch, she grabbed their heads and kissed them. She didn't say another word about that couch, but from then on, she and my father sat there, side by side, to deliver all the important family news - the expansion of the gym into the neighboring building, Sebastian's baby with his high school girlfriend on the way, his second baby with his new wife Sarah on the way ten years later, Rodrigo and Amalia getting married. Papá giving Mamá a diamond ring on their twenty-fifth wedding anniversary.

Now we were back here again, my four brothers, Amalia, my other sister-in-law Sarah, my brother Christian's boyfriend Daniel, and Papá. And me.

My brother Alejandro had told me they were getting Mallorcas for breakfast from Freddy and Tony's in honor of me being home. I was the last one to arrive, and I stopped in my tracks at the doorway, seeing everyone, including my nieces, gathered in the break room. As promised, a white box of the pale swirled pastries sat on the coffee table. My mouth watered.

Papá had added two vending machines and a foosball table for the gym's employees, but there was still the same tube TV in the corner I'd grown up with. Papá sat on that same old couch. His eyes were deeply wrinkled now, but his eyebrows were bushy as ever. In the three months since Mamá's funeral, his thick hair had tripled its gray.

I let out a slow breath. He was getting older. So was I. My brothers definitely were.

Even though Mamá was missing, home was still the same.

Sebastian jumped up when he saw me, tilting his head as he walked over to me with open arms. "Natalia," he said. I breathed in his smell - strong coffee and the same generic laundry detergent Mamá had bought by the gallon.

"Hey," I said, squeezing his waist extra hard until he made a show of coughing at the force of it.

"Your love is dangerous, Nati," he said, stepping back and ruffling my hair so that it arced up out of the ponytail I'd thrown it into. I grumbled and took my hair down, shaking it out and pulling it into a new ponytail as I walked over to the couch.

The lounge looked so empty, with just Papá there.

I should have sat there, next to him, to bolster him. I should have pulled him into a hug too, scratched circles on his back in the way I'd done since I was little. But in front of the couch, there was a circle of folding chairs, filled by my four brothers, Christian's boyfriend Daniel, and Sebastian and Rodrigo's wives, Sarah and Amalia. There was one folding chair left empty. It had to be for me.

Carefully, I took it, grateful that Amalia was there. Neither of us had grown up with a sister, and had decided when she married Rodrigo that we must be long-lost sisters. Meant to be. She was my best friend, and if she hadn't told me what this was about, then there must be a good reason. A serious reason.

She pulled me into a hug and I just whispered, probably a tad desperately, "What's up, Amalia?"

"We just found out too," she whispered. "I'll let Papá tell you. Tell all of us."

"Hey, Nati," Papá said, his craggy face shifting into a soft smile. He reached out a hand and I reached forward and grabbed it. I'd seen him just yesterday afternoon. Before the support group. He'd wanted me to go. "That's good," he'd said. "That's good for you. To talk."

As if I needed more reminders that talking was not exactly my thing. When were they going to invent a support group where you talked while you jogged around the city? At least there would be no stale air or awkward looks.

"What's up, Papá?" I asked, my gaze darting to my nieces playing quietly in the corner. Mariana, at 10 years old, never complained about playing with Camila, 2 years old. Family was everything to us. Everything.

"A couple days ago, Christian took me to my doctor's appointment. I'd been feeling more tired than usual, some pains in my chest, but I thought it was nothing. Heartburn, the stress of the gym. You know."

I knew. Knew as soon as he said "doctor." I was going to lose Papá, too. Of course. We all were. My brothers and I were close, but our parents were what always brought us together. Their house for holidays. Their forced family gatherings. Their insistence on group video chats because family should see each other once a week, at least. "That's why Sundays were invented," as Mamá was fond of scolding.

I felt my face twist into one of disbelieving pain, and Amalia reached out and squeezed my hand. "It's okay. Deep breath. Let him talk."

"The cardiologist says I will be fine," Papá rushed to explain. "But there are things I have to do. Precautions I have to take. If I do that, I can live ten more years. Fifteen, maybe longer."

"Okay, yes," I said eagerly, checking my brothers' faces. They all still had their mouths set in hard lines, their eyes cast downward. "Whatever it is, we'll make it happen," I babbled, looking at my brothers in confusion. This was the look they got when they knew I was going to be pissed off about something, and they didn't want to tell me.

Arturo, handsome and calm in his blue police uniform, spoke up. "Medication, of course. Regular doctors' appointments and cutting way back on the exercise. Nothing too intense."

This was what baffled me about the words 'heart disease' being applied to my father. Papá was a boxer. He ran and he worked and he lifted weights three times a week. He should have had the healthiest heart out there. "This makes no sense," I blurted. "He's so healthy,"

"Sometimes it just runs in the family," Daniel said. "It did for my mother's side."

Papá nodded. "I'm going to have to change a couple other things. My diet," he said. I nodded. We could arrange to have heart-healthy meals cooked and put in Papá's freezer. Of course.

"Easy," I said quickly.

"And now comes the not-easy part, *mija*," Papá said. "The doctor says if I want to stay alive to see a dozen grandchildren, I have to cut back on work. Way back."

The Knockout Brothers gym had been my parents' dream for this family, named when Mamá had given birth to Arturo - their third son. They hadn't bothered to change the name when

I, a surprise baby and a girl, was born. Boys were the ones who boxed and lifted and ran.

They had built The Knockout Brothers from the ground up and raised all of us here. Our whole family had reaped the rewards. They'd sent three of us to college with that money, and paid off the mortgage on our house. Now that Mamá was gone, Papá was taking on most of the bookkeeping and management of the gym all by himself. In my grief, I'd jetted off to the other side of the country to distract myself. My brothers had done degrees of the same, in their own ways.

"I'm going to sell the gym," Papá said. "I didn't want to make it official until you knew. All of you."

My emotions swirled within me, making a tornado that sent nervous energy down to the tips of my fingers and toes. Before I knew it, I was out of my chair, pacing. Only one word fell from my lips. "No. No. That's not going to happen."

"Nati," Alejandro said, "We did have another suggestion." His voice was calm and cold, sleek, just like his appearance. It was his businessman voice, cultivated over years of building his own architectural firm in a New York City skyscraper office.

"We think...we could make it work. The Ortiz siblings," Alejandro said. "I have some money to invest for some extra staff, to help out."

"And Rodrigo and I can definitely teach classes, manage the free gym time," Arturo said. "Even Daniel said he would help out."

"I'm close to getting Crossfit certified. I could cover some of the trainers for no cost," Daniel said.

I nodded, slowly. The Knockout Brothers could actually be run by... brothers. Nice.

"If we bring in massage and nutritionist consults we could get some extra income that way, just for the cost of a spare room or two," Amalia said.

"This sounds great," I said, nodding enthusiastically. "Sounds like you've already talked about this. So why are you all looking at me like there's an anvil about to fall on my head?"

"Well," Alejandro said, "Because we're not sure how you're going to feel about your part in all this. Nati, we're going to need you."

"My part? But I can't..."

"You can," Alejandro said, that same cool and calm affect coating every word. "Nati, you're smart as a whip and you had a 3.8 GPA at Temple in Business Management."

"Okay, Ando, but you have actually, you know, managed a business. I have no idea what I'm doing."

I didn't *want* to know what I was doing.

"Nati, come on. You've been running classes here for years."

It was true. I'd taught Krav Maga at the gym since I was in college. "That's because I was pitching in to give you Papá a break on my *vacation*. And don't call me that little girl nickname when you're expecting me to act like a grownup, Alejandro."

Alejandro's cheeks took on a ruddy tinge. This was not good. "Well, Nati, it's about time you -"

Papá 's lip trembled. "Alejandro, enough!" he roared. Papá had seemed so small, so timid, and when he used his big voice like that it brought back memories of when I was little. The youngest of five by three years, I got in plenty of trouble, thinking I could fly under the radar of my parents' rules. Sometimes I could. Other times, Papá's big voice let me know that he hadn't missed a thing, and that I was in big trouble.

I couldn't remember a time I'd ever heard that voice used in my defense.

We all turned to Papá. I was pretty sure my jaw hung slightly open. "This is not what Mamá would have wanted, and it's not what I want. Nati is a part of this family, and she does have a business degree, and we could certainly use her help. But she is her own person. She does not have to give that help. Anyone who thinks it's a good idea to tell my daughter what she has to, or cannot do, will learn the hard way that it is *estupido*. Okay? Nati can do what she wants."

Papá 's words seemed to echo through the now completely-silent lounge. Even little Camila had gone quiet, her eyes round and big. The edges of my mouth ticked up in a smile, even as my heart twisted. I loved Papá, and felt more strengthened than I could say that he just jumped to my defense, but he was wrong. I knew it in my heart, and so did my brothers and Amalia. We all exchanged looks, Christian and Rodrigo shrugging, Alejandro and Arturo refusing to meet my eyes.

I loved my father, just as much as I knew he was utterly and completely wrong.

My mother, rest her soul, would have wanted me to do whatever I could to help him. To help the family, when she couldn't anymore.

It wasn't my fault she was gone - I knew that, logically. I also knew that if I had driven her to hospital. we might have been able to save her. I couldn't get my mom back but losing her was plenty for this family to try to survive for a good long while. We couldn't lose Papá. We couldn't lose Knockout Brothers.

I stuck my tongue in the inside of my cheek, making myself look like half a chipmunk, then switched it to the other side. Arturo grinned. They all knew what that meant. I was thinking.

Finally, I pulled in a long, slow breath, and said, "Papá, we are not selling the gym." All my brothers' faces lit up like Christmas morning. I could practically see their ten-through-sixteen year-old selves in my memories of Christmas morning, seeing the gifts they'd begged for but weren't a hundred percent sure they'd actually receive until they saw them with their own eyes. I held up my hands, palms out, and squelched any cheering or thanks that would have begun in the next breath.

"We're not selling the gym yet." I could do this. I knew I could. It didn't matter that I'd never actually run the business operations before – the most I'd ever done at Knockout Brothers was manage the class schedules and the front-of-house operations. But The question was whether I wanted to. The answer to that question didn't seem to matter too much right now. What mattered was making sure my brothers understood my terms.

"I will manage the gym for six months, as a trial. I'm hiring an office manager to do the bookkeeping, website maintenance, and some human resources stuff."

"Oh, Natalia. You're a goddess," Christian said.

"I'm not finished," I said. "All of you - all seven of you," I said, swiping an index finger around the circle of folding chairs to indicate each of my brothers, Amalia, and Sarah and Daniel, "Are going to be available to consult on a moment's notice. If you live in Philly, you'll help me cover time slots if employees call off or if I need extra hands. We can't afford to hire half the city just so our people can cover each other's lazy asses."

They all nodded. I sat up the tiniest bit straighter. I had never, not once, commanded this kind of attention and respect from my siblings. It was kind of exhilarating.

"Papá," I continued, "I know that the hotel is a source of income, but I'd love to be able to stay there for the time being, if that's okay."

Papá's eyes glistened. "Of course, *mija*. I wouldn't let you stay anywhere else."

"I promise I'm going to do my very best to make it worth it," I said, leaning over and covering his hand with mine. I squeezed and he squeezed back. That right there was worth taking six months to figure out how we could keep the gym in the family without forcing me to work there forever My father deserved to know that I would be here to support him. Nothing was worth losing my father's faith in me, not even the small movie stunt double gig I had booked back in LA for tomorrow.

"One more thing," I said, before my brothers could get up, pat me on the back, and consider The Knockout Brothers Gym no longer their problem. "Ownership of the business goes from an even percentage split between the six of us to fifty percent mine, ten percent for each of the rest of you. Of course, we'll make sure Papá's needs are covered as well, *if* I agree to do this."

This was the real gauge for how much faith they had in me. Money talked. Sebastian's jaw clenched, and Alejandro's mouth moved slightly, like he was doing some mystery calculation of the cost-benefit analysis of a deal like that in his head. Several seconds later, they were all softly agreeing, either with a nod of their head or a quiet "Okay."

Wow. Now I was shaking. More power. More respect. From my *brothers*. Not that they'd ever *dis*respected me, but they'd never once indicated that they'd be willing to trust me with anything this big. Ever.

"Oh, and finally," I said as I got up, stretching my legs, "We're not calling it The Knockout Brothers anymore. Long live The Knockout Gym."

Christian chuckled. "Can't argue with that, Nati."

I rolled my eyes at the nickname. "Natalia. And no," I said, a triumphant smile forming on my lips even as my tummy flipped and tied itself in knots. "You really can't."

CHAPTER 6

ETHAN

EVERY ONE OF my friends since I was a freshman in college had made fun of me for my career goals: Major in actuarial science, the field of study that calculated the amount of risk inherent in any business, estate, or personal life, and pass my exams with flying colors. Get a job with a good, steady firm, work good, steady hours, and make good, steady money.

None of my friends were all alone in the world, either.

I was the only person I had to count on. I'd loved my mom, so much that every time I thought of her, which was several times a day, my heart still ached. I'd admired my mom, but for my whole life, she barely held it together financially. I didn't want that to be me. Not ever. And the only person who could make that happen was...me.

Yep. All alone. I was lonely a lot, too, but I'd never be broke and panicked about my next step. Not with my job. Out of all the careers that millennials could pick up, Actuaries were one of the only ones in high demand.

Plus, I got to help people. Not in a touchy feely way, like a therapist, or even in a concrete, immediate way, like a doctor. But I helped people plan for the future, usually in the form of helping them with their insurance policies. At the risk of sounding like a sanctimonious lecturing old man or an AARP commercial, peace of mind was one of the greatest gifts you could give someone. It was something I'd never had. The least I could do, I figured, was help give it to others, while getting paid enough to give it to myself.

I got to go out on an insurance eval a couple times a week, if I was lucky. It was one of my favorite parts of the job. Meeting with clients face-to-face was usually a nice break from staring at a screen and fiddling with algorithms. Writing reports was okay, but I lived for the days one of my bosses, Mr. Kennedy or Ms. Sousa, would send me out on an assignment. I was a beginning actuary, so, like a beginning realtor, I got assigned to the lower-paying clients, meaning lower commission and longer hours for me. That was fine.

After all, I was all on my own.

Mr. Kennedy had a last-minute cancellation this morning - something to do with his daughter getting into some trouble with the sorority council at Penn State - so I got the email to cover for him at a new-client evaluation today, which was something he normally did. No problem. I'd been itching for something to take my mind off seeing Natalia four days ago. That woman was going to kill me, I was convinced of it.

Which reminded me, I should re-evaluate my life insurance.

I mapped the SEPTA route from our offices downtown to an address near Chestnut. I smiled. I loved University City, having graduated from UPenn just a couple years back. Even though I complained about it to my buddy Mark, I enjoyed the trips to the Sonic Wave Studios, where we recorded our weekly radio broadcast, the BroShow. Sometimes I even regretted buying that Brownstone downtown, even if it was the best move for Future Me. It only made Present Me more isolated.

I hopped off the train a few minutes later and strolled to the location. It was late-March, and uncharacteristically warm. The ground was wet, still damp from the frost and a light snow that had covered the ground yesterday morning. Somehow today was forecasted to be fifteen degrees warmer, and the rays of sunlight piercing the early morning air broadcast the coming Spring.

The only writing on the heavy metal door was the address numbers, and the tall windows on the all-brick corner building didn't have any advertisements or identifiers, either. Interesting. Mr. Kennedy had been so rushed this morning that I had no idea whether I was visiting a law firm or a hairdresser's studio or a bookstore. I'd just put the address in my phone and followed the GPS instructions. When the robotic voice in my phone announced I had arrived, I looked up and laughed. I was standing in front of The Knockout Brothers Gym – the place where I'd met Natalia over a year ago. Where I'd slept with her, in the upstairs apartment, just days ago.

My heart sped up. She said she was leaving town. Was it even possible she was still here?

"Fuck me," I groused under my breath as I knocked on the door. Of course, the universe would throw her back into my orbit, only to take her away and make me hang out with her brothers a few days later. Just to make sure I couldn't stop thinking about her.

Then, I heard heels clicking on the other side of the door. It wasn't a confident, steady rhythm like most women had when they walked in heels - in the few seconds I heard, there was a scrape, a stumble, and a couple of swear words. I smiled to myself. Whoever this woman was, she probably needed special insurance if she was planning to wear these shoes on a regular basis.

The door slowly pulled open, and on the other side, staring down at me from the top of the steps, with her mouth half-open, was a woman I would have known instantly even in an ill-fitting pinstriped skirt suit, teetering heels, and hair worn down and free so it tumbled over her shoulders.

"Natalia?" I stammered.

Maybe I'd been praying in my sleep. Maybe I'd wished upon a star without knowing it or maybe I was just so desperate to see Natalia again, even after all the times she'd promised me I wouldn't, that the universe had done me a solid.

Right away, though, I knew something was different. This wasn't the Natalia I'd spent those precious, sweet, wild, hot nights with - this Natalia had a hard, weary look on her face, like she was about to fall over from the strain of whatever she was going through and she probably had no plans or wherewithal to get back up again. "Is this – are you – I thought you were leaving town. I guess your plans changed?" I couldn't keep my heart from twisting painfully at the realization that she was still here in town, and hadn't bothered to clue me in.

Natalia, gorgeous, flustered Natalia, took a deep breath, and then stepped to the side, gesturing for me to come in. "Saying my plans changed is an understatement." She gestured to the familiar open gym inside, its well-worn punching bags just waiting for abuse. "I am the new owner.'"

"Holy shit," I breathed.

I walked in, surveying the place. It was all familiar, of course, but now that I wasn't here to work out, I was looking at it through new eyes. The original exposed brick stretched from wall to wall, and what looked like the original four-panel huge windows let in blocks of slightly dusty light that stretched across the floor and illuminated the whole place, throwing the center of the vast room in comparative shadow. Which wasn't bad, because the shadow gave the competition-size boxing ring just the right dramatic lighting. Brick structural support columns framed the corners of the ring, and against them leaned boxing dummies and racks holding an assortment of gloves, weights, and resistance bands. At intervals throughout the rest of the space hung punching backs, more dummies, and chin-up bars. I let out a low whistle.

"Your father handed this over to you? Tali, I had no idea that was going to happen."

She motioned for me to follow her down the hallway directly to the right, where it looked like there were several office doors. "Neither did I, last time we... um... saw each other." I loved the color of Natalia's cheeks when she blushed - dusty rose that colored her high cheekbones gorgeously. "I thought I was home for a visit, but a lot has changed. Of course, I'd worked at the gym for a week here or there, but that was only the front desk. Teaching classes. But as far as the business end, I'm lost. Which is why I'm here, dressed like an idiot, waiting for some stupid stuffy suit who's going to try to sell me millions of dollars' worth of insurance that I don't need. But I promised my brothers I'd meet with this stupid Kennedy person, so... here I am." She'd gotten so worked up saying all that I could swear I saw a sheen of sweat begin on her upper brow. God, she was gorgeous.

"So what the hell are you doing here?" Her question broke through my thoughts. "I mean... how did you find me?" she amended, sounding a little guilty. That was the Tali I knew. Abrasive, sure, but never cruel. Not to me, anyway.

"Well, as happy as I am to see you, I'm afraid that I *am* that stupid Kennedy person," I said, sheepishly. "I'm an associate at Kennedy and Sousa, and I'm here to assess your insurance policies.

The hallway was illuminated by a bare hanging Edison bulb, and I winced inwardly at the hazard that was for the people who actually had to use the hallway on a regular basis. I resisted pulling out a notepad to note it. Natalia let her head fall back at the news I'd just dealt her and her throat emitted a long, gravelly "Ugh."

"Happy to see you too," I quipped.

"I'm not sure whether I'm annoyed or relieved. Annoyed, because this is not how I'd prefer to spend my time with you, Ethan Anderson. But relieved because, if you don't mind, I'm going to get out of this stupid jacket and these torture heels."

I let out a harsh laugh. "Mind? Not in the slightest."

She nodded, stepping out of the heels and leaving them in the hallway, and shrugging out of her jacket as she walked into the first door to our left. "Step into my office, stuffy Kennedy suit who I'm very glad to see."

And, just like any other time she asked me to do something, I did exactly what Natalia Ortiz wanted.

CHAPTER 7

NATALIA

ONE OF THE reasons I loved spending time with Ethan was that he looked at me like I was a snack to be devoured while also being worthy of his worship.

Maybe he looked at every girl he'd ever slept with like that. All I knew was that when I was with him, I felt like I was the only woman he had ever had in his life. The only woman he ever wanted to have.

It turned out that even when he saw me at my most awkward, in Sarah's skirt suit and heels, trying desperately to look like I had a handle on my life, he looked at me in exactly the same way.

And now, apparently, I was supposed to have a conversation with him about insurance for my business - which still sounded completely crazy - while I had no idea what I was talking about.

"You were only here for a few days," Ethan said as I guided him into my office. It was only lit by a floor lamp and a desk lamp, the light coming from the bulbs a bit too yellow to make anyone look good or feel comfortable. The chairs were getting old, as evidenced by the cracked vinyl that let a puff of half-shredded foam escape from the pad. Ethan didn't seem to notice. God, he was so professional. So nice. So grown-up. So exactly the opposite of everything that I was.

I tried to suppress a sigh at the thought as I motioned for him to sit, then moved to the other side of the metal desk. The laptop I'd just bought myself at a shiny minimalist store down town was the first I'd had since college. That first computer I'd owned had been basically falling apart by the time I'd ditched it for my adventures traveling around the world, chasing the latest thrill. Every time I couch surfed or slept under the stars, I thought to myself how I'd probably never need a personal computer again, and felt really smug about it.

Well, it turned this wasn't the first time in the last few months my assumptions about life would smack me in the face. About how my mom would live forever, basically. About how I'd be able to do whatever I wanted, whenever I wanted it, never depending on any person, place, or thing. About how I wouldn't be tied down by responsibility. About how I'd never have to be a grown up.

If anything said grown up it was this stupid, itchy suit, combined with the fact that I was sitting across from the man who had given me the best orgasms I'd ever had, discussing insurance.

"So, I mean, if you wouldn't mind my asking," Ethan said in that infuriatingly cautious way he had of asking everything, "How exactly do you own this business when just four days ago you were still a nomad?"

I saw pain flicker in his features, and I felt bad about that. I really did. "I didn't lie to you," I rushed to explain. "Life sort of comes at you fast."

He sat back in the chair, which creaked against his weight, which just reminded me of his weight pinning me to a bed. Waiting for me to say more. Waiting like he had all the time in the world, like he'd gladly wait until I finally spilled all my closely kept secrets to him, like he knew I would.

"You know my mom passed away," I said, pushing the words out in a rush, trying to dodge the pain of them as I did. He just nodded, his mouth turning down in that soft sympathetic frown I'd grown so used to seeing from everyone I'd ever known before my mom had died. "Well, she and my dad built this gym and kept it going strong since I was little. It's what put food on our table and me and two of my brothers through college. It's everything we have. Everything he has."

"So isn't your dad the one who owns it?"

"Technically," I said, half annoyed and half embarrassed by the previous reality of this whole situation, "Only my dad and my four brothers owned it. You're looking at what was, until three days ago, 'The Knockout Brothers Gym'. Now it's just 'The Knockout.' And it's fiftypercent mine."

His eyes went wide, and I rushed to explain. "You know that I have nothing else going on. No real plans. Nothing I own. No... relationship." I let my eyes flash to his, checking for hurt there. I wasn't sure whether I saw it. "My brothers all have lives. Only three of them live here in Philly. They all have jobs, families... other things they have to do. And only one of them has a business degree. Interestingly enough, I have one too."

"That's right!" Ethan said, snapping his fingers. "I remember now."

"Yeah," I confirmed. "And you might have realized by now that I don't really half-ass anything. So I graduated cum laude. Even though I've never run a business, and the only thing I've ever accomplished is checking off destinations on a map and items on a crazy-person bucket list, my dad is really proud of that 3.8 GPA. My brothers too. They all seem to think it translates into some ability to actually run a business. So here I am."

"You don't seem so confident," Ethan said, leaning forward

in his seat. Something about the way his upper arms strained against his shirt had me feeling the slightest bit dizzy.

"Well, would *you* be?" I practically yelled at him, throwing my hands in the air. This was the first time I had let myself crack on this issue since the family sit-down three days ago. Something about being a room with Ethan made me feel open. Vulnerable.

"If I were me, no. But if I were you, having never even thought about running a business... yeah, I get it. But you're going to do great. I can just tell. "

I could have jumped across the desk to hug him in that moment. It was dumb, and he was wrong, but the fact that one person who wasn't related to me, who knew me a little bit, could say that...well, it helped. "I guess I do know enough to be alarmed at the insurance coverage this business had previously," I said, ruffling through the shallow drawer that held all my most immediately important papers. My fingers located a yellowing manila folder that held a few sheets of paper, some of them pink carbon-copies. That was how old this insurance policy was.

Ethan took the folder and gingerly flipped through the papers. He gave a low whistle. "Natalia, this insurance agency went out of business five years ago. I could probably find the original policy, but... I'm not going to lie, you seriously need an upgrade. With us, or with someone else, but your coverage is very shaky, if what I'm seeing is the whole picture."

I rolled my eyes. "Obviously. And my brother Alejandro's assistant recommended your agency, so I called you. Help." He stared at me blankly for a second, so I added, "Please," feeling my cheeks blush. The last time I had said that word to him, it had nothing to do with insurance or business arrangements or anything other than how I felt in that moment, begging him to make me come.

If he was half as good at insurance as he was at making me scream in bed, The Knockout Gym was in wonderful hands.

He spent a few more minutes looking over the papers, his lips moving gently as he read over them to himself. Watching him, I bit my lip. It was hard not to remember the expert way his mouth worked me over. How it made me feel - cherished and desired all at once. I squeezed my legs together. Of all things, I couldn't be thinking about that now.

"Okay," he nodded. "You have basic liability on the premises, which covers up to ten thousand dollars. That means if some guy clips his chin on the pull-up bar and gives himself a concussion, or one of the punching bags swings back and knocks him on the ground, or, hell, if a ceiling tile falls out and breaks his collarbone, goes to the hospital, and sues you for the bill...."

"This insurance is only covering ten grand. Which means a gurney and a bottle of water."

"And maybe an aspirin," Ethan agreed. "That is if you drive him to the hospital yourself. If he takes an ambulance, you're already halfway to ruined."

Dammit, Papá. Was it that hard to keep this stuff up to date?

I knew as soon as I thought it, though, that we probably couldn't really afford more. This gym needed more than the maintenance my parents were able to give it for the last fifteen years. Times were changing, and if I wanted to keep my family business, which was now *my* business, functional and profitable, I had to make some changes.

Just thinking about it made my neck feel hot. I was glad I'd taken the suit jacket off. My hand went to unbutton the top button - maybe two - of this ridiculous, stiff button-up.

Ethan's brows furrowed together and he stood up, wrapping the fingers of one of his big, beautiful hands around the frame of that half-ruined chair and swinging it around so that it sat next to mine.

"It's okay. This is going to be fine. Insurance has changed a lot and I think you'll be surprised at how affordable it can be. Okay? I'm just going to get my laptop and ask you some questions. We'll get through this together."

Something about the tall, steady presence of his body right across from mine actually did help to calm me. It was confusing, of course, that most other times Ethan's body made me feel anything but calm. I worried at my bottom lip between my teeth, nodding. That word echoed through my mind - together - as something I knew should have made me want to bolt, even though I knew that bolting was the absolute best thing I could do.

So, instead, summoning more strength than had ever been required to take stunt-driving lessons or go cliff diving, or even to run with the bulls, I took my seat again, smoothing my skirt, swallowing hard, and trying not to think about how my life had changed for the boring and gotten so completely terrifying all at the same time.

Ethan's computer was a heavy-duty business model, and he explained while it booted up that half of his visits were at construction sites. "This building is beautiful," he commented. "Nothing beats the old construction. Exposed brick and piping makes this a Philly treasure. Honestly."

"Are you a real-estate agent in your spare time?" I asked. Ethan's lips twitched, and I was grateful he'd understood that I was joking. At least, mostly.

"Well, actually, I got kind of obsessed with it a while back when I was buying my house."

My heart stuttered. "You bought. A house?" As simple as the concept was, my brain was having trouble putting it together with someone my age. Someone I'd had pretty inventive and very, very good sex with not too long ago. "I mean... you own that house?" Of course I knew he had a house. I'd slept with him in it. On its kitchen counter and in its shower, too.

He just smiled, then laughed gently. "How about if we talk about what a lame old geezer I am after I finish doing my lame old geezer job with you here and we get your insurance squared away, huh?"

"Point taken," I said, allowing myself a wry smile.

For the next completely exhausting half hour, Ethan fired questions at me about The Knockout. It was sort of embarrassing how many of them I had to guess the answers to, or had no answers to whatsoever. Ethan, in return, assured me that it was perfectly normal and fine for me to have no clue about anything insurance-related for my own business, even though I was pretty sure that was a lie.

Ethan wasn't a good liar. His nervous laugh gave him away every time, which I'd learned that time he said he didn't mind spicy food and then almost wept when I fed him Arturo's arroz con pollo with lots of pique and watched his eyes water and his tongue smack against the roof of his mouth. He'd nervous-laughed all the way through the half-hour recovery period for that.

We spent the next hour going through all the questions in his little insurance checklist. Everything from the cost of gym equipment and how much of it we'd need to replace in any given year to the average number of injuries sustained into the gym went into the equation. Ethan explained that because the rate at which people in this area attended gyms remained pretty steady from year to year, that would improve my rate; the fact that this was an old building, on the other hand, would increase our rates. When he started to ask me questions about business plans – our goals for advertising, possible expansion, and continuing member acquisition – I could practically feel my head start to spin.

"Not to be a pain," I said, rubbing my temples, "but maybe we could revisit these questions once I've had a chance to tackle the business plan. Right now, I just have a bunch of messy notes in my sorry excuse for a bullet journal."

The corner of his mouth tugged up. "You keep a bullet journal?"

"It sounded like a good idea, but I'm failing pretty hard at it," I admitted. "I already forgot which colors are supposed to go with which categories, and I made a mistake on the calendar page."

"Gotcha. Yes, of course. Business questions are getting tabled, which is fine. They're relatively minor. Now, the next thing we need to talk about is insurance for you."

"Me?"

"Yes. Specifically, life insurance. If something were to happen to you, it would impact the business significantly. We need to make sure that, in the event of your untimely death, the business would have enough cash coming in to mitigate the shock."

It was like he'd thrown a bucket of cold water at my face. Even more jarring was that he was just sitting there waiting for my response, like instead of talking about my gruesome, sudden death, he had asked me if I wanted fries with my order.

"I mean... I don't plan on dying," I said, throwing out a nervous chuckle.

Ethan tilted his head, looking at me like I'd just brayed like a donkey. "Nobody *plans* on dying. But you, especially..."

"What's that supposed to mean?" All of a sudden, the safe feeling he'd given me felt like it had transformed into a knife being held at my throat.

"You know what I'm saying, Natalia. It's like you're asking for it."

Tears pricked at my eyes, though for the life of me I didn't know why. He wasn't wrong. I liked to sky dive, and run with bulls, and drive cars too fast. The way he said it, though, made it sound like by doing those things I'd be trying to hurt the business.

"Okay, I'm sorry. That was rude," he said, leaning forward and covering one of my hands with one of his. "I know you're trying to get your feet under you. We'll talk about it next time we meet, okay?"

"Yeah. Okay." I shook my head, trying to re-center myself. Ethan was a professional, just trying to help me out. This was business, and it was stupid to get emotional over matter-of-fact discussions. So I took a deep breath in and closed my eyes, re-centering myself.

"I'll just start the file on you, and the gym itself then, okay? It's a few pages long, and then there are some long forms for the gym's property info like taxes, licenses, and all that. We can fill them out together, if you want." There was an apology in his voice, and I decided to accept it.

The forms were, indeed, long. We paused way too often to remember some TV show we watched or food we ate, and to detour in a discussion about my brothers, what they did, the situation we all found ourselves in now. It was all related, I knew, but it also felt intensely personal. Not only like he was getting to know me, who I was, what I wanted from life, but that he cared.

"Okay," he finally said, reaching over and squeezing my hand. I felt my body lean toward him, like a house plant toward a bright window. But one second later, he closed his laptop and stood up, then began to pack up his things. "So, I'll give you a call in a few days. This is a multifaceted situation, but it's not complicated, I don't think. If that makes sense." He smiled at me with such fondness in his eyes that I almost wanted to ask him to stay, even though I didn't know how I could, what excuse I could give him for why. I had told him that I was leaving town. We'd both treated our last night together like it was, well... our last night together.

"It'll be a few days from now. We can set up another time to meet, and as your actuary, I want to make sure you get covered sooner rather than later, especially if you're going to keep The Knockout Brothers open for business. Are you? Still open for business?"

His eyes darted around the empty gym.

"It's just The Knockout, now," I said. "No brothers involved. And yeah," I said, "It's just that ten in the morning isn't our busiest time. Things will pick up in an hour or so. If... uh... if you want to stick around. We could spar, maybe?" I shot him a little grin. He knew I'd kick his butt. I knew he'd like it.

"Gotta get back to the office," Ethan said, holding up his laptop bag and wiggling it a little. "I'll give you a call, okay?"

"Okay," I said, worrying my lip again. My breaths felt shallow in my chest. I couldn't tell whether it was panic or excitement over definitely hearing from Ethan again, but I did know one thing - I didn't love the out-of-control feeling, no matter what it was.

I hauled open the heavy metal door and blinked at the bright sunlight, which contrasted so sharply with the cool, wet Philadelphia early spring morning. I'd missed this, I realized. Everything in Philly was dynamic, the exact quality I'd run away to chase, just in its own quiet way.

"Thanks again," I said, right before Ethan caught me completely by surprise. He stepped close and slung his arm around my waist, pulling me close enough to him to feel his hard muscles through his shirt, to feel the warmth of his breath on my neck as he squeezed me into a hug. Then he stepped back just enough so that his face was in kissing distance.

"I know you called Kennedy and Sousa, and not me. But I'm glad you got me, anyway."

For the first time since that terrifying moment three days ago when my life had changed in such a big way, my mouth stretched into a grin. I was glad, too, but I wasn't sure exactly how to say it. Turned out that Ethan didn't need to hear it. He just skipped down the steps and toward the train station, waving at me over his shoulder. "See you soon, Tali. Oh, and by the way – love the gym's name change," he called.

I just stood there, smiling and waving, until he turned the corner.

CHAPTER 8

ETHAN

THE KNOCKOUT GYM was an insurance nightmare. It would take an agent three times as experienced as I was a week to figure it out.

I was going to do it as quickly as humanly – or, at least, actuarily - possible. Because once I had a proposal and some quotes for Natalia, I could see her again. Hell, I just wanted to share air with her again. Honestly, I'd been too surprised by the circumstances of seeing her again that I hadn't even been able to formulate a coherent plan for how in the world I'd get her back in my life in a serious way, now that she was planning to be in Philadelphia for the foreseeable future.

The rest of that day, I focused hard on the screen in front of me.

The rest of that day, and into the night, I worked frantically at my desk, plugging in various scenarios and variables into the system. What if The Knockout hired extra staff? What if they lost the staff they already had? If they added some classes and expanded their clientele, would they be covered? How much extra would it cost to make that happen? What investments were feeding into keeping the place up and running? Who was covering the gym's debts in case of lean times? Was their equipment up to date and safe? What budget did they have for replacement costs? Did they have an updated records and client management system? How did they keep their clients' payments secure?

And, worst, the dreaded death question - what would they do if the business completely died? Would the sale of the building bring in what it needed to in order to get them back on their feet?

Would the business be worth putting back on its feet at all?

I fell asleep at my desk, a couple hours after wolfing down a burger when my stomach protested. I couldn't have named exactly what possessed me - I only knew that Natalia's face kept haunting my vision. It wasn't the Natalia I'd gotten to know during our brief fling last year, confident and ecstatic to be alive. This Natalia looked apprehensive, unsure, and terrified. And the awful yellow lighting in the gym offices was only a small part of that.

I was overwhelmed with one simple desire - to help make it better. To comfort her. To ease her fears.

After a few hours' sleep, I roused, squinting against the barest hint of tangerine sunrise creeping over the horizon. I'd pinched something in my neck, sleeping in such a weird position, but at least I was nearing a preliminary report I could bring to Natalia as soon as I got a hold of her and worked out a time. I hoped it was soon.

Yeah, I was desperate. Normally I'd try to brush that kind of feeling off, but something about this being *Natalia* dulled that reaction.

I sent her an email from the firm, at eight o'clock sharp. I knew she was an early riser, strapping on her running shoes most mornings for the same reason most people stumbled to the coffee maker. She needed that activity to wake her up.

While we were seeing each other last year, I'd convinced her to replace running with another early morning activity a couple times, even though she groused half the time about how awful her morning breath was. It never really had been that bad.

I paced, waiting for my email to ding a response. I got my coffee, did a few jumping jacks, and halfheartedly jotted down a list of all the other crap I had to accomplish today for work. Even though part of me wanted to devote an entire second day to helping Natalia, I knew that it was foolish to rely on her reply. First, we had a history. Maybe she thought it was weird. Second, she had every right to get a second opinion, or even a third and fourth. It could take days to hear back from her on updating her insurance. Hell, it could take weeks. But the thought of that made my chest constrict. The Knockout definitely couldn't risk being uncovered for very much longer.

Since I was a little kid, I'd been anxious about pervasive dangers and impending doom of the world. Every tree was waiting to drop a branch on someone's head, every rock on the road was waiting to send a bike and its rider flipping end over end. My skill for exercising caution had carried through to my adulthood. After writing up the report of all the kinds of insurance coverage The Knockout really, definitely should have, I was envisioning every bad thing that could possibly happen there... happening. A fire. A shiny new gym that charged half as much, had twice as many classes, and was open 24 hours opening around the corner. All of Natalia's brothers moving away and leaving her without a built-in helping hand. A flood. Hell, there could be a tornado. They were rare in Philly, but theoretically, they could happen.

Or, with his heart condition, her dad could die. When Mom passed away, I was barely functional for months. Natalia talked big, but anyone could see the fear in her eyes at handling this all-consuming responsibility. And it sounded like her brothers were barely pitching in.

I stopped at the big printer around the corner where I'd sent all the documents, yawning against the realization that it was still too early for my secretary to have gotten into the office. I'd removed my belt sometime yesterday late afternoon, and shed my button-down shirt to protect it from the ketchup I knew would glop out of my hamburger bun. My beard was extra scraggly, I could tell by the slight itch that the hair curling at the ends caused.

I should go back home and take a nap, see if I could reset my neck to a position where it didn't hurt so bad. Clean up a bit. Natalia hadn't even emailed me back, but she was probably at the gym by now.

It was like there was a tiny engine in the center of myself, continually churning and saying, *Gotta see her, gotta see her, gotta see her.*

I should have walked the one and a half short blocks back to my brownstone, where my cleaner, Susan, would be arriving in the next hour. I should have taken a shower and eaten a square breakfast and read over my papers to make sure there were no glaring errors.

Instead, I turned toward the SEPTA and took the next train back to The Knockout.

I was pretty sure I dozed off on the train ride, which was only seven stops. Thankfully, when I jolted awake it was right before my stop, and I felt refreshed. It was another damn morning, although the air held the promise of warming up enough to ditch my overcoat by lunchtime. Hell, a bluebird might as well have been singing on my shoulder, given the rays of sunlight and the skip in my step. I was going to see Natalia again. I was going to help her. And I was going to figure out how "I'm only going to be here a few more days" had changed, and whether she would let me spend any of the extra days with her.

To my surprise, the top quarter of The Knockout's windows were propped open, and bass boomed out of them, shaking the glass panels slightly. I winced. That right there was something I'd already forgotten to include in the assessment. I'd considered the structural integrity and maintenance needs of the brick and the interior of the building, but somehow in my exhaustion the decades-old glass windows had escaped my consideration. Dammit. She was going to think I was an idiot.

I approached the heavy metal door, ready to knock on it, when I realized it was propped open with a child's car seat. Thankfully, there wasn't an actual kid in it, but it made me wonder -was there really no other way to prop the door open? I cursed myself for not doing a thorough walkthrough of the property, or better yet, hired a building inspector to go through it before I came to talk to Natalia. But all those things required time, and my instincts about Natalia told me that it was likely she'd be bolting, and soon. And I needed - *needed* - to see her again.

Against my better judgment, I reached up and gave the door a good solid knock, it was pointless. The sound reverberated through the door pitifully, barely making a dent against the booming music. Someone was on the floor, doing something. Maybe it was Natalia, working out. Burning off frustration. Maybe I could convince her to do that with me.

I ducked into the gym, figuring that if the door was propped open anyone was welcome. Just as I did, a muffled "oof" sounded from the boxing ring and two male voices shouted when a body hit the floor. The victor of the boxing round, shirtless and in basketball shorts and bare feet, raised his gloved hands high above his head and crowed, lisping through his mouthguard, "I AM THE BESSSSHT!"

Suddenly, the music cut off with a pop, and the guy who'd been knocked down raised his head. "Who did that?" he asked after spitting out his mouthguard. "Put it back on. It was muffling my groans."

I grinned at that, then panned over to the corner where Natalia, tall and taut and muscled, stood shaking her head next to a tiny woman at least six inches shorter. The petite woman stood there, tapping her foot, arms crossed, absolute nuclear fire shooting out of her eyes. "Rodrigo, how many times have I told you not to fight to knockdown with your *estupido* brothers? Especially with that baby girl at home? Now I have to leave Natalia and find someone for Camila and take your sorry shit-eating ass to the emergency room." As she yelled, she gestured over to the corner, where a small child, no older than two years old, played quietly with blocks.

"Amalia, *mi amor*," the guy who'd won the match said. He jogged to her side and looped an arm around her waist, planting a sweaty-faced kiss on her cheek. She made a face. "*De verdad*, it's nothing. Okay? Just a little fun and games."

"Yes, mister fun and games, I saw your brother's *cabeza estupida* bang against the floor and you did not. So I am telling you it is not okay. He has two girls to take care of." Finally, she approached the ring and glared at the guy who'd gone down until he picked himself up and walked over to her. He bent down over the ropes, sweat dripping, and reached down to give her a hug. She flinched.

"Take a shower, Sebastian. If you don't faint in there, I won't make you go to the hospital." She still sounded stern, but the barest hint of a smile played at her lips.

"Ethan!" The sound of my name pulled me out of the scene, and I looked up to see Natalia walking toward me. "Is every-thing okay?"

"Yeah, I..." I fumbled in my bag for a second and pulled out the folder I'd put together. "I brought some initial paperwork."

"That was fast," she said.

"I just wanted... uh... to get these to you as soon as possible." I was suddenly acutely aware that the other four people in the gym were staring at me as I talked to Natalia, probably standing a closer to her than mere business associates would. "Nice that the gym's this full of clients this early in the morning," I said.

Natalia threw her head back and gave me a full belly laugh. "Ethan. These are not clients. Meet my brothers."

Oh. *Brothers.* I raised my eyes to theirs and was met with a barely-concealed glare of contempt from all four of them. Even the woman, who I assumed was married to one of them, looked wary.

I swallowed. "Your family. W - wow."

"They won't bite," she said, grabbing my arm and guiding me back to the office. The brothers were only a few steps behind. "Ethan, meet Rodrigo and Sebastian, who will probably kill each other one day. Amalia, the woman you saw, is Rodrigo's wife, and she's taking care of Sebastian's little girl Camila today."

CHAPTER 9

NATALIA

MY HEART POUNDED as I led Ethan back to my office. I had no idea he'd been here after less than twenty-four hours, but I was grateful. My brothers were driving me insane. Christian and Daniel had been taking Papá to doctor's appointments, and Arturo had been cooking meals for his freezer while bossing the others about getting his car tuned up and cleaning his house. We were all busy bodies, always had been. It was in the genes. But if my brothers really were going to give me a fifty percent share in The Knockout and trust me to take care of the gym and of Papá, I kind of wished they would... just do that. Yes, I was the baby sister. Yes, I was also a grownup. They didn't have to hang around here forever. And they couldn't fool me by saying that's not why they were here, even if they disguised it with their dumb morning pissing contests that masqueraded as workouts.

Amalia didn't count in that resentment. She and I were close, and she'd already offered to take point on Papá's care. She was pursuing a master's degree in art at Drexel, and selling her pottery creations on the side to various boutiques in Philly. She was a nurturing soul, a role she enjoyed.

Ethan coming here, however scruffy he looked, could only help with my problem. When he stepped into the room, I wanted to scream, *See? I can do grownup business things, I am doing them, so just give me the benefit of the doubt and leave me be!*

Of course, my brothers did just the opposite of that. They both left the ring and followed Ethan, who was following me, back to my office. One of them was texting furiously, no doubt to Alejandro, telling him to hurry over to the gym. I glanced over my shoulder, my eyes flashing murder at them, to which Rodrigo turned his eyes to his shoes, knowing he was being dumb, and Sebastian cracked a smile.

There was barely room in my office - Papá's office, just two weeks ago - for two people and a desk, but somehow my sweaty brothers managed to cram their reeking bodies in there. As a gross bonus, they were both still shirtless. Amalia, who had finally caught up with the baby slung on her hip, squeezed in too. She wrinkled her nose. "Ay," she said. "What were you Neanderthals thinking?" She reached up and gave Sebastian's head a light smack, despite having been apparently so concerned about it having a concussion just a few minutes ago. "Everyone out, to the lounge."

"Or you could just get out, and let me conduct my own damn business meeting with the insurance guy."

"It's a family business, Nati." Rodrigo's voice was quiet, but testy.

"I told you not to call me that," I barely kept myself from growling. "Excuse me, Mr. Anderson. My brothers seem to think that I am still seven years old."

Ethan briefly quirked an eyebrow at that before apparently realizing I was in no mood for jokes. I knew what he was thinking. I was most definitely not a little kid, at least as he knew me.

As much as I would have liked to dwell on those happier, more carefree memories right now, I couldn't. Not with a pack of my stupid brute brothers fighting for space in my stupid tiny office.

"Give us a break, Natalia. We just want to participate while we can," Sebastian said. He had taken time off work to help me for a few days. As much as it annoyed me, I supposed I should have been grateful.

Ethan chimed in, holding up the sheaf of papers. "Might be helpful for them to see what we're working with, here. Do you have a copier?"

Amalia snagged his wrist and tugged him briefly toward the door, chatting about how she'd show him where it was, and it was better for her to be there just in case, since the copier often broke down. His eyebrows furrowed together at that, and he quickly pulled out his phone, tapping something into it.

There was silence in the room for a few seconds while I took the time to glare at all my brothers in turn. "You give me fifty percent," I growled, sweeping my eyes across the room, "You give me freedom and your trust that I can run this." None of them said anything, which I took to mean that they really did understand they'd gone about this the wrong way. "Got it?"

"Yes, Nati," they chorused.

I'd let that nickname slide. This time.

We circled up in the break room, just like we had four days ago, now, when Papá had given us the bad news. It was bad news, of course, because of his health. I'd been surprised over the last few days to discover that it hadn't been the worst news for me. I was impressed with myself at how much of my business degree education came flooding back to me, as I'd gone over financials and reached out to clients. I couldn't deny that the meeting with Ethan had raised some important questions for me. But all in all, I'd been feeling more confident. I could do this. I could get The Knockout to a stable place, keep my share in it, use some of the income to hire a director for the whole facility, and use the money to resume traveling the world and pursuing my real dream - to be a stunt woman in Los Angeles.

Yeah. That was what I really wanted, after all, I'd realized. I needed my blood to pump hard and fast through my body. Nothing at The Knockout could do that for me. No matter what I did with it.

Ethan re-entered the room, now having a soft conversation with Amalia as they walked. "So are you really the only one who can make that printer behave?" Ethan asked her, and she smiled at him, taking the question as flattery. I knew what he meant. He was really asking how close the copier/printer machine was to death.

I stood, only regretting the stupid formality of my action once I realized how awkward it must have looked. But Ethan just beamed at me. The brightness of his smile almost hid the dark circles under his eyes. "You said it'd take a while," I blurted. "Not that I'm not glad to see you, I just -"

"Just wanted to get you the numbers as quickly as I could," he said. "Now, I made copies for everyone. The first page is a breakdown of the insurance you currently have...."

"Thank you," Rodrigo interrupted. "If we could wait until my brothers could get here, though, that would be best. At least Alejandro, Christian might be a little harder to bring in." I glared. Christian would be impossible to bring in. He was a middle school math teacher.

"You won't get Christian or Arturo. They're both working. And we do not have to wait," I growled at Rodrigo through my teeth. "In fact, my brothers are welcome to leave."

"It's okay," Ethan said with a soft smile. "I don't mind waiting."

. . .

I fought the instinct to roll my eyes. He hadn't gotten my meaning at all. Either that, or he was ignoring it. Both possibilities were annoying. One was infuriating.

Alejandro showed up ten minutes later, with Federal donuts in hand. I rolled my eyes at him. I was sure it was delicious, but my body was a machine. I hated putting trash in it.

Ethan led the four of us through the pages for the next twenty minutes or so, carefully explaining his findings and his recommendations for the business. I was no insurance professional, and neither were my brothers, but it was pretty clear from the expressions we shared that we all realized one thing - this news wasn't the best.

Alejandro cleared his throat when Ethan was done glossing over the papers he'd brought, claiming the first question. Asshole. "First, I want to say thank you for taking on this case. I asked Kennedy for the best guy he had available, and obviously that was who he sent."

Wait a minute. I had been the one to call Kennedy and Sousa. I had no idea that Alejandro talked to them on the side.

Ethan just nodded. "Honestly, I think Mr. Kennedy meant to take on the case, but he had some things come up. But obviously, I'm glad to help."

I jumped in. "It looks like, from all this, that we have some changes to make around here."

"Not necessarily," Ethan said. "Just some choices to make. I am concerned about the level of coverage you have versus the level of security should the market change or the building, security and communication systems, or equipment fail en masse. But there are things we can do to mitigate those risks."

I couldn't help it. A small, unrecognizable thrill went through my body at hearing Ethan say "we" while he was sitting in my business. My space. My home, sort of. It was exciting and comforting all at once, knowing he was in my corner. "Yes, but from what I've seen, your main recommendations are either to diversify and expand the business or to sell some of it off."

"That's right," Ethan said, dipping his head.

"Well, neither of those is acceptable to me." I might as well tell him the truth. I didn't want to give up any share of this business. But adding and changing and implementing whole new layers of stuff to be in charge of wasn't going to work either.

"Nati, if you'd just -" Rodrigo broke in, while Sebastian contributed his own unintelligible argument.

"Enough," I roared. "Shut. Up. Do you boys trust me, or do you not? Did you tell me I could be in charge of this, or did you not?"

There was a beat of silence, and then Alejandro's mouth curved up into a wide smile. "We did, Mamá."

The rest of my brothers laughed. Laughed. And my heart twisted. I knew what they meant. I sounded like our mother when she was frustrated, when she was on the brink of going nuclear- angry at all of us. And I just... missed her. I didn't know what she would do in this situation, but I did know - I could *feel* - that she would not have wanted all these stupid voices trying to crowd out my own instincts.

"Ethan," I said, "Please excuse me."

"I love you guys," I said to my brothers, "But I absolutely cannot do this with you here. Ethan is going to help me go through this step by step," I continued, then snuck a look at him. "I-If you can, that is," I added, realizing I'd just assumed that he'd help me however, whenever I wanted. It had felt natural, somehow. "Ethan will send you weekly updates, and we'll keep paying him for his work until I reach a proposal for how to move forward with The Knockout – all of it, including insurance and the future vision – that we can all live with. Does that work?" I shot them a look that said it had better work for them, or we were going to have a problem.

Now my brothers were finally silent. Alejandro had his mouth half-ajar. "Yeah, Natalia. Yes." It sounded like he barely held back a 'Ma'am.' I smiled softly. "Thank you."

CHAPTER 10

ETHAN

I HADN'T EXPECTED to see over half Natalia's family at the gym that morning, but as they walked me back to the front door, I was almost glad I had. Scratch that - I absolutely loved meeting them. Yes, they all had strong personalities, just like their sister. Yes, they could be a little domineering. But they also radiated absolute love and concern for each other. All it took was that one short meeting for me to understand that Natalia's brothers would do anything for her, and she would do anything for them.

I would have killed to have family like that in my life.

Walking beside me, Natalia leaned into me and said, so quietly only I could hear, "I'm sorry about them."

"Don't be," I said. Then, thanking the gears in my head for turning as quickly as they did, I added, "Watch your phone."

Natalia's brows pulled together, and just as her tallest and most hulking brother opened the door, I reached down and gave her fingers a short squeeze. I could have sworn I felt her relax, just the slightest bit. "I'll see you soon, okay?"

"Ethan, I -"

"We'll look forward to your updates," one of her brothers said, watching me with a polite smile. It was clear I was supposed to get out now. So that's what I did. But not before registering the adorable look of annoyed disappointment on Natalia's face as I walked back toward the train station.

I didn't really know whether Natalia wanted personal communications from me, but she had put her cell phone number on the paperwork she provided for our agency, and she hadn't spooked when I'd grabbed her hand earlier. So I tested my luck and punched it into a text box.

One of the reasons that I'd been interested in doing insurance work with my actuary degree, instead of just behind-the-screen analysis, was that I loved people. I loved meeting them, reading them, figuring out the best way to interact with them. Sussing out what made them tick. That challenge of discovery had never felt more important to me than it did with Natalia. I couldn't put my finger on exactly why, and that was what I was determined to do.

I took a deep breath and tapped out a message:

Ethan: Hello, Miss Knockout

I set my phone down and paced my office, stopping at my desk to shuffle papers or brush a non-existent speck of dust off one of the two armchairs settled opposite my desk. The phone pinged with a new message, and I practically pounced on it.

Natalia: I'm so sorry, again.

I shook my head while my fingers flew.

Ethan: Don't be. Can you get away for dinner?

Natalia: Are you asking me out on a date?

Ethan: No.

I smiled to myself. That would catch her off guard.

Natalia: ...wow. Didn't expect that.

A laugh burst out of my mouth.

Ethan: I'm not sure you'd say 'yes' to a date with me now, and I don't want to ask unless I know it'll be a yes.

Natalia: Not taking any risks, Insurance Man, huh?

Ethan: Not with you. Never.

I grinned at my phone, satisfied with the level of flirtation I'd put in, then started tapping out one last message.

Ethan: I have a dinner place I want to show you. New to Philly since you grew up here. It'll be quiet and we can talk and plan our next moves.

Natalia: :) Sounds good. When and where?

Ethan: It's close to The Knockout. On my way from home. Can I pick you up there? Around 7?

Natalia: Well, since I have no other plans....

Ethan: C'mon. Say yes. To a business meeting.

Natalia: Yes. To a business meeting.

Ethan: Thank you. I'll see you then.

I set my phone face-down on my desk, took a seat, and cracked my knuckles. I had a bunch of stuff to pull together before I saw Natalia in a little less than six hours, and I also had to sleep and shower before then. There was no way I was meeting her at less than my best.

Six hours later, I stood in front of the same dingy red-painted metal door that seemed to have completely kick started my life over the last couple days. I'd slept for a solid 90 minutes, jogged on my minimalist fold-out treadmill for 15, showered, shaved, and splashed on the fresh-smelling cologne with a hint of woodsiness Catharine, the girl I'd sort-of dated few months ago, had given me for Christmas. I wasn't vain or anything, but as I looked in the mirror, I confirmed that I looked about as good as I could. Every single girl I'd ever dated had called me tall, dark, and handsome, and I never argued.

"Handsome" was going a bit far, I thought, but I was also the guy who'd grown out his beard because I didn't have the strong jaw that every woman seemed to crave since reading 50 Shades of Gray. I thought about shaving it, but never got up the nerve. The only time I'd come close, actually, was when one girl I was dating referred to it as "lumbersexual." I still cringed when I thought of that.

Not that I had anything against lumberjacks. I just had somewhat more... urban sensibilities. I liked things that involved fewer bugs and less humidity.

I knocked on the door, hard, and stepped back. I reminded myself to include this dangerous entrance arrangement in the list of things we needed to address, and as I was brainstorming solutions, the door opened with a heavy whoosh.

"Oh. Hi." The tiny woman with the dark bob from earlier today looked me up and down. "Did you leave something here?"

"Ugh, Amalia!" In a second, Natalia stood next to her. She was absolutely fucking radiant. Form-fitting jeans with scattered rips, revealing precious inches of her skin, a baggy white tank top, and a flowing sweater cardigan made her look comfortable. The peach color of the sweater seemed to make her skin glow, and her glossy hair was pulled into a simple high ponytail that made it swish around her shoulders.

The style was also perfect for grabbing during less public activities. I scolded myself for letting the thought slip through and making my dick stir with interest. This wasn't a date. I didn't know exactly what there was between me and Natalia, but I knew it was fragile, and I knew she spooked easily. That meant that this wasn't a date, because it couldn't be. It was more like... me auditioning to date Natalia. Maybe. If she wanted to.

Amalia's eyes darted down to Natalia's shoes. Pristine white

Adidas sneakers with black stripes. "You want some heels?" Amalia asked quietly.

Natalia just glared at her, and I tried to hold back a laugh.

"Some earrings, maybe?" Amalia pressed. "Lip gloss? Stay here. I'll go get "

"No!" Natalia said, her tone so harsh it made the other woman stop and stare at her. "It's not... this isn't... I don't need heels and jewelry to have a meeting with Ethan."

"A... meeting," Amalia said, her eyebrow raised. This was a woman who, just like Natalia, took zero bullshit from anyone, who was always ready for someone to try to pull the wool over her eyes. Good. I guessed you needed that in a family with five brothers, who grew up pranking and teasing and wrestling and one-upping each other.

"Yep," Natalia said, grabbing a big black bag next to the door. "See? I'm even taking my laptop along. *Bueno?*"

Natalia didn't wait for Amalia's answer. She just stepped out the door, angling her shoulder to slide past me and hurry down the steps.

"I won't wait up!" Amalia called as we started down the sidewalk.

"You don't live here!" Natalia shot back. "But please *lock* up, okay?"

Amalia's mouth stretched into a grin. "Of course! Have fun!"

She looked so happy, and she waved so frantically at us, that it would have been hilarious if it wasn't so sweet. Just another part of Natalia's family that loved her and wanted to take care of her, more than she seemed to want to take care of herself.

"Okay," Natalia said, blowing out a long breath and looking up at me, her eyes round and searching. "Where to?"

CHAPTER 11

NATALIA

"SO," I said after several long, agonizing seconds of Ethan and I walking down the quiet Philadelphia street in silence. Monday and Tuesday nights were always quiet in this little neighborhood. The college kids that lived close by were recovering from their first day of classes after a weekend of hard partying. Restaurants were recovering from the weekend, too, anticipating empty tables by hiring fewer waitstaff. Sometimes it seemed like Philadelphia only had two modes: lit up and crazy, or almost totally quiet.

That was one reason I loved LA and New York. They were always crazy. They kept me occupied. In LA and New York, I was never alone with my thoughts.

"So," Ethan responded, dipping down to nudge his shoulder against mine gently. "We have a lot of work to do, huh? Figured we might as well do it over dinner."

"To a place I've never been?"

"Well, I didn't know that for sure, but I was trying to entice you. I know you like adventures, which is why you were so annoyed when your brothers were trying to drown you in business talk."

"I wasn't -"

"You were. And that's okay. They are annoying."

"Yeah, and you're trying to tell me what I'm thinking and feeling just like they do." Exactly what I needed - another man pretending he could ready my mind, tell me what was best for me. God, would it never stop?

Ethan stopped dead in his tracks, which made me do the same. He pressed his lips together and pulled in a deep breath through his nose.

"You're right," he said. "I'm sorry."

"Just like that," I said, deadpanning. Didn't believe him for a second.

"I was wrong," he shrugged. "I have no idea what you were thinking or feeling when your brothers were all trying to take over your business while you were standing right there. Maybe you'll tell me, and maybe you won't, but that would be the only way I'd find out. I'm sorry for the assumption."

"O-okay," I said, cautiously, trying not to look into his eyes for so long. Those eyes were the initial reason I'd slept with Ethan all those months ago, after a lazy night at a bar I'd never been to, and they were the reason I kept coming back to him. They held such fire when he spoke, when he studied my face, when he thrust into me. I'd never been able to resist getting as close as possible to fire.

"Okay," he said. "We're here, if you're still willing to have dinner with me."

I looked up at a simple placard above what looked like a hole-in-the-wall restaurant. It was done in a stark contrast of white, turquoise, and red. Joey and Hawk's, est. 2013. Just a spoon and fork and some random wings.

I gave it the side-eye. "That sign tells me nothing about what this place is," I said.

"Thinking like a businesswoman," Ethan said as he held the

door open for me. "You're right, the signage is kind of shit. But it doesn't matter, because word of mouth does all the advertising for these guys. You'll see why in a second."

He guided us to a small table in the corner, pulling out a chair for me. The smallest tables were a hodgepodge of repurposed furniture, and the larger ones looked like the one in Abuela's kitchen, covered with coupon clippings, a pile of washcloths mid-folding, and a bowl of apples. I ran my hand over the surface of our table, painted in matte turquoise and decorated with a single daisy in a bud vase. Every table in the place – only a few others occupied – were painted in different bright colors.

"Hey! Ethan!" A voice called from the back. "I'm dealing with a wonky fridge in the back. Slow night."

"Yeah, I see," he replied to the voice. "Hawk could have hired people to do a bunch of stuff around here," Ethan explained. "I interviewed him for one of my final projects in college and we've been buddies ever since. His dad left him this restaurant."

"Is that why you brought me here?" I asked suspiciously. "As kind of a case study or something? Are you, like, lecturing me on how to revamp a business?"

"No!" Ethan said, genuine surprise in his voice. "I swear, I genuinely brought you here so I could evangelize about the bacon mac and cheese."

I relaxed a little. There were far worse motivations than marginally fancy macaroni and cheese.

"It used to be a dump," Ethan continued, loudly enough for Hawk to hear as he set something down on the table beside us. "Now it's one of the trendiest places in Philly. They just opened up another location on the other side of town."

"That's thanks to the missus," Hawk said. "I'll send her out to take your order," he said as he ducked back into the kitchen. He was intercepted by a blond-headed whirlwind of a woman two heads shorter than he was, who smacked him on his tattooed arm as she passed out the doorway he was entering.

"William Hawkins, how many times have I told you, if I hear you call me that one more time..." a woman with bouncy blond curls said as she walked out of the kitchen.

He held up both hands, palms out. "Okay, okay. I just really like the idea of it. You. My missus."

Joey just stood there with hands on hips, trying to keep her smile reined in. "Okay, but you're going to pay."

"Gladly," Hawk said, taking the towel he had slung over his shoulder and smacking her ass with it.

Ugh. Love.

It wasn't that I didn't *want* to love someone and it wasn't that I hadn't ever had feelings for a guy beyond wanting to sleep with him. It was just that the way of the world seemed to be this - boy meets girl, girl and boy fall in love, boy locks girl into a bond of inescapable marriage hell. Or was it supposed to be bliss?

Why in the world would I tie my future to some guy just because of a feeling I had for him? There were things I wanted to do, places I wanted to see, stupid decisions I wanted to be free to make. I knew how Mamá and Papá always consulted each other on every little decision. I saw how my brothers sacrificed things for their spouses, made decisions with their help they never would have made otherwise. Love was great, but chasing the thrill of base jumping or hang gliding or deep water snorkeling or even just driving a car really, really fast? That was something otherworldly. That stuff made me feel invincible. Larger than life. I couldn't get enough.

If things got more serious between Ethan and me, how could I ever tell him that chasing a thrill was just as important to me, just as vital to my well-being, as staying in one place and loving him?

Luckily, I didn't have to ponder that too long. Ethan and I spent a few minutes chatting, then a live band started, and we let the music fill the air between us.

"So, you helped him figure his shit out?" I asked, gesturing around the restaurant, which was filling up at an impressive rate for a Monday night.

Ethan coughed in response. "Me? *No.* No, absolutely not. I was only a senior in college. He and Joey were in their second year of business, and maybe I asked him one or two questions he hadn't thought to ask himself, just because they were on my checklist. But no, these two have been a pretty dynamic team since they started this whole operation, as long as they could quit arguing long enough to talk something out."

I smiled a little at that. Mamá and Papá had fights sometimes, I remembered, but it was only because they were both so passionate about something that they had to stand up for what they thought was right, whether it was the hours the gym was open or which equipment most needed updating or how they were going to stretch our budget to pay for college for all six of us.

"That's kind of cute," I mused, stopping to smile at Joey as she brought us glasses of water.

"Hi, Ethan," she chirped, her blond curls bouncing as she fumbled for something in her pocket. Eventually she came up with a thin stack of post-it notes, smiling at me. "Sorry, I didn't introduce myself before. I'm not supposed to be doing anything with the restaurant tonight. It's supposed to be my night off, but... anyway. Who's this?" She shot me a brilliant, genuine smile.

"This is Natalia. She's the owner of The Knockout Gym, and my firm is handling a small insurance update for them," Ethan replied. The way he said it made me sound like I was mature, organized, responsible, and driven in running my business. It made me sound like a grownup. Settled, with a strong head on my shoulders. No, I was none of those things.

"It's a total mess right now," I rushed to explain.

"You're talking about that old boxing gym a couple blocks east? Wasn't there a self-defense class there, free for the college girls? I remember Hawk wanting Olivia to go to something like that..."

Not that I knew of. "Well, I actually just took it over. Family issues." Joey's mouth turned down into a frown, and I rushed to fill the awkwardness. "It's fine, I'm just trying to get my bearings now that I'm officially running the place."

"Well, good luck. Ethan, you going to order? Or you want me to pick for you?"

"You have the bacon mac?"

"Yep. And potato broccoli soup, wonton soup, sweet potato spring rolls, classic meatloaf, and tortilla soup with a chicken grilled cheese."

"Tortilla soup, please," I blurted, only realizing that I was chilly with the deep shiver that ran through my body.

"Okay. Well, you two kids get to work," Joey said, disappearing into the background. My gaze turned to Ethan. He was studying me like I was a fascinating puzzle he needed a strategy for before he started to assemble it.

"So, what are you really doing with the gym?" he asked. Wow. Okay. He was serious about this 'business meeting' thing. "I can't get a read on you. I thought that night we spent together was going to be the last time I saw you. So when you showed up at the door yesterday, I was shocked, or something, at seeing you again. You'd told me you were going to leave."

"I don't want to be here," I blurted. My hand clapped over my mouth, and my heart sped up. "I did not mean to say that," I said, my voice muffled.

Ethan reached across the table and, gingerly, pulled my fingers away from my mouth.

"What were you doing all that time you were gone?" he asked. Maybe he was trying a new tactic. "Besides your crazy bull-running and getting gored and whatnot."

I smiled, my heart warming. "I didn't get gored," I reminded him.

Ethan's eyes went wide and he turned green just at the sound of the word. I tried to hold back a laugh.

"'Gored' is a stupid word for it, anyway. It makes me think of, like, intestines hanging out. It just means that the bull's horn gets your body in some way. Didn't happen to me. It was actually a little boring." Now Ethan looked sick. I grinned. "Anyway, I was in LA trying to get into movies, I guess."

"I didn't know you were an actress."

"I'm not. But my body is."

"Um..."

"I want to be a stunt double. You know. Drive cars fast. Motorcycles, too. Jump out windows, get blown up, leap off buildings, all that. I was here on a break from shooting and, well. Then Papá broke the news. I went straight from jumping off five-story buildings to combing through spreadsheets. So, you know, that might help you understand how I feel about being just locked down here.?"

CHAPTER 12

ETHAN

"I'M SORRY, before you came here, you had been in the middle of doing *what?*" I could barely get the words out. I wasn't Natalia's boyfriend or anything. Still, I liked her. A lot. And thinking of anyone, let alone a girl I liked on more than one level, putting their body in that much danger in that short of a time frame made my heart stop.

Not to mention that my mother had died in a horrific car accident. The idea of anyone else I cared about dying the same way, except this time on purpose, was too much to bear.

I was an actuary. I had practically memorized the cost of the risk of doing each one of the things Natalia mentioned, and offhandedly at that. As if stunt driving and bungee jumping were as normal as going to the grocery store. It was like Natalia was trying to become the most expensive person to any insurance company ever.

"I was working as a professional stunt double," she said, more slowly. Like maybe she had suddenly started to speak a foreign language I didn't quite understand. "I was free to do what I wanted, you know? My mom and dad always ran the gym. It was, like, their thing. My brothers all have real jobs. Or, real enough anyway. I never thought anything would happen to Mamá..."

She trailed off there, and I watched as she paused to pull in a breath, swallow down something - tears or emotions, or both.

"Yeah. I know. We never do."

She pressed her lips together and nodded. "But," she continued, "I guess in the back of my mind I assumed that one of my brothers, or a couple of them, would deal with The Knockout if it came to that. Turns out that Papá can't run it like he used to, and they all assumed I'd be the one. Because of my business degree."

My brain literally ached, in the front corner. "I'm still trying to process that you have a business degree, from where? Penn?, And you were jumping through windows instead."

She snorted, wiping under her nose and setting her glass back down after she'd tried, and failed to take a drink. "From Temple. Please. I'm the sixth child in my family. And I'm smart, but not full-scholarship-to-an-Ivy-smart."

"Okay, but that's damn good still," I said.

"Good for someone, maybe. I'm not made to sit in a cubicle. Or to wear heels. Or to be a yes-woman."

My brain may have had trouble wrapping around the idea of anyone abandoning a steady promising business career to fling herself off buildings and recklessly ride motorcycles for a career, but as I watched Natalia, I knew she was speaking the absolute, immutable truth. She was right. Managing a business - not even a higher risk, rough and tumble one like a boxing gym - wouldn't give her the crazy adventure she craved. Even though I could barely bring myself to think of Natalia, with this body that I'd worshiped so many times and never quite been able to forget, hurtling down a road in some vehicle and putting herself at risk of -

Well, of exactly what had happened to my mom.

I'd made the mistake of looking at the police photos from her accident. I'd decided to make her funeral closed-casket after I'd seen them, and I hadn't ever seen her face again. I hadn't wanted to. There'd been too much blood pooling on the street and smeared on the windows.

"Okay," I said, eyeing the mac and cheese that Joey set before me in a steaming crock. I had suddenly lost my appetite. "So, um," I choked out. "What are your goals for The Knockout, then? Your brothers sounded pretty confident you were just going to... manage it. Forever."

"Yeah, they did," she said. She bit her lip and looked up at me through her lashes. Damn, but I loved when she did that. "I haven't exactly told them that yet. The truth is, I was kind of stuck in the whole stunt career thing."

GOOD.

"I wanted to get un-stuck. But I would need to take lots of classes on technique, travel to some locations on my own and piece together some training to really become marketable for the things I want to do. I didn't have the money and I was barely making ends meet waitressing. My brothers offered me 50% of the gym and... I don't know. I guess I figured eventually I could turn enough of a profit to hire someone else and take the remainder and make a life for myself out there. Doing stunt work. "

"And so *that's* what you want me to help you do?"

"As soon as you came to see me, and started asking all those questions about our future plans," Natalia said, leaning over her tortilla soup, "I knew I was in over my head. But you're so smart. You sounded like you knew so much about this, and my brothers know nothing. They just want to think they do. I hope you don't mind that I put you on retainer. Just... when you're around, I feel like I can handle it. And I want to handle it. I really, really want to handle it, like my mom did." After she said that, her eyes grew wistful, and she focused on the pockmarked tabletop for a few seconds. Then she took a long breath in, and continued with a steely look in her eye. "This could be a way for me to prove myself to my brothers, pull The Knockout together for my family, and make enough money to live the life I really want. You know? And I just... I'm clueless. Or at least I felt that way, until you rolled along. So..."

"Thank you," I said, puffing out my chest, loving the roll of her eyes when I did. Loving that she laughed at me when I was cocky, both finding me amusing and putting me in my place. I loved my job. I really did. But the truth was that I didn't feel like anyone in the world really needed me. Not at the insurance agency, not on the Bro Show with Mark, not in one of the handful of bars and restaurants I frequented. My entire life was lived as something auxiliary to everyone else. I was a friend, someone a girl dated, but never settled down with, an employee – but never someone's everything. Ever since Mom died, I had been simply an accessory in everyone's life. I wasn't necessary to anyone. So, for Natalia to say that she needed me to feel like she had a handle on her business, it was the best thing I'd heard in a really, really long time.

Because, yeah. Sex with her had been good. Really, really good. That was why I'd acquiesced to a fling with her in the first place. But I hated flings. I hated short term. Short term was the opposite of a sure thing. Not to mention that it just made me an accessory in one more way.

Slowly, watching Natalia eat and make commentary on her food - how Joey and Hawk's was good, but her brother's boyfriend Daniel could add just the right combination of spices to make it truly addictive, trust her - a sort of peace settled in me. She fascinated me. She was smart as a whip. I didn't think I'd ever get enough of being with her.

I'd be lying if I said I hadn't thought about the possibility that Natalia would be staying in Philly now. These past three days had been crazy, and I knew Natalia had to be swimming in a quagmire of complicated emotions, but I'd loved - LOVED - reconnecting with her. Not only in the obvious way, but on a more personal level, too. She gave me an energy that I honestly couldn't describe and had never gotten anywhere else.

"So, you really are planning to build the business and then hand over the reins?"

"Yep." Natalia let the "p" pop as she said it, then stuck a forkful of the turtle cheesecake Joey had slid onto the table at some point in her mouth, pulling it out slowly and then licking her lips with that clever tongue of hers. Jesus. She made it hard to stay focused. She had to know it.

"So that you can go bungee jumping and shit."

She raised a shoulder and looked right into my eyes. "I don't have to explain myself."

"Of course not," I jumped in, wishing like hell she just... would. I seriously wanted to know what would possess someone to risk her life as a job. Over and over again. Especially not when so many people cared about her.

"But I like you. Like... I like this. Talking to you. Spending time with you." She turned her head a bit and shook her head once, like she had just surprised herself. "So, I will. Explain myself. It's just... the adrenaline rush. It makes me feel power-ful. Invincible. And, this is going to sound crazy, but I feel, like... secure. In the world. Like nothing can shake me." She shrugged again. "I don't know. Maybe that sounds stupid."

"Wanting to feel that way? After what both of us have been through?" Her eyes caught mine, and they were shining with the beginnings of tears. "Absolutely not crazy. I could even see how it could make sense. Wanting to feel alive. Wanting to feel like we have control over our lives." Her eyebrows shot up. Maybe she was surprised that I understood her, even a little. Understanding, though, didn't equal agreement. "I think my reaction to those experiences explains my outlook, too. I like to be safe. To know what's coming, and to plan for it."

"Obviously," Natalia laughed, sweeping her hand in the air in some vague gesture to indicate... me.

"What I'm saying is... I don't know. If your dad is entrusting the whole business to you - like, not just in name, but in actuality - do you really want to put that at risk by trying to kill yourself every day?"

"First," Natalia said, shoving her fork back into the cheesecake, "It's not as dangerous as it sounds. Otherwise you would be reading all the time about how this stunt guy got decapitated or that stunt girl had her face pulled off."

My stomach turned. I reached for my phone. "I mean, I'm sure there are plenty of - "

"No phone at the table," Natalia said as she dropped her fork and reached out, swatting my hand away from my iPhone. It was strange, but I hadn't actually touched the thing the entire dinner until now. I'd been enjoying talking to her too much, and only felt like I needed it when I wanted to prove her wrong on something.

"I didn't know that was a rule of yours," I said. When I thought back on it, every meal Natalia and I had shared months ago was either in bed or in pajamas at my kitchen table while we were half dressed. If you had asked me where my phone was at pretty much any of those times, I wouldn't have known. Or cared. Natalia had a way of making me forget my current reality.

"It's not mine," she said. "It's my mother's. Well," she said, stopping with the fork almost at her mouth, "I guess it's mine now."

Natalia's brow furrowed, and it made my heart pinch. I'd been to dozens of support group sessions for people who'd lost their parents. I'd learned to identify when I'd taken on a behavior of my mom's in her memory. It was why I always kept peppermint tea – her favorite – in the house, and why I went ice skating once every winter. Likely, Natalia had a handful of such behaviors that she hadn't even acknowledged to herself yet. "That's my point," I said. "She's not here anymore. Your dad can't really handle things. Your brothers are here because they trust you to do what you need to do."

"And that's what I've been telling you, Ethan." The way she said my name had a bite to it. One that made the skin on my shoulders crawl just a tiny bit. I didn't like it. "That's what I'm going to do."

"Well, if you're going to run around trying to kill yourself," I said, only slightly amused by her glare, "You at least need to have life insurance. And really, really good accident and liability insurance. You need to protect your family in the event that you... you know... kill yourself."

"Do you have any idea life insurance for me would cost? With all the crazy things I do in a year? Hell, in a month?"

I threw my hands in the air. "Yes, actually, I know exactly what it would cost! And with the plans you have for your life, it's more than the combined operating costs of the gym all added together."

Her eyes flew open wide before transforming to cold, hard orbs seconds later. "Of course you do. Tell me, Ethan, did my brothers hire you to tame me?"

Quick as a flash, Natalia picked up her napkin and dropped it on the table. She dug in her pocket and pulled out a couple twenties and dropped them on the table, too. "We're getting out of here," she said, and then stood up and started walking toward the exit while I just sat there, my mouth hanging open.

Did she... want me to follow her? She was pissed off, obviously, but she had said *we* were getting out of here. And she'd paid. I'd just decided that I should at least stand up when she reached the door. She whirled around on one sneakered heel and looked at me. "Well? Are you coming?"

When she said it like that, with expectation and urgency in her voice, how could I say no?

I called goodbye to Joey over my shoulder and hoped the forty bucks was enough to cover the food. I could always come back and -

"Oomph!" I managed as Natalia's hand locked like a vice around my wrist. She tugged me away from Joey and Hawk's. Even at my height, half a foot taller than her at least, the force and speed of the tug made me trip over my own shoes. She snorted out a laugh as I caught up.

"Is everything okay?" I asked, completely confused.

"Everything's fine. I just want you to take me home," she said, reaching down for my hand. She twined her fingers with mine and yep, there was that energy zipping through my veins again. God, if she made me feel like this, I might agree to anything she asked of me.

Which was exactly what I was afraid of.

I was afraid to ask any more questions and ruin it - the good luck I had to be walking down a Philly street with Natalia, holding her hand. The good luck that she hadn't left me alone in the restaurant after I'd so obviously said something that upset her. She still wasn't talking. She didn't say a word until we were back at the gym.

"Are we.... working out?" I asked, my voice going to a whisper when I realized how close Natalia stood to me now. We were both a little short of breath from walking so fast - her more so than me - and our breaths made clouds in the air between us.

Natalia gave a throaty laugh. "That might be a healthier solution. But no. We're going all the way upstairs."

I nodded dumbly. Her jaw had a hard set, and I wasn't sure

if I should be thrilled or terrified by all the things I imagined her doing in bed when she was this angry.

"Natalia, I know you find it nearly impossible to resist me, but I'm working for you," I attempted, a lame excuse. My risk alarms were going off left and right. Yes, I worked for her, but I also wasn't sure that this particular cocktail of emotions was a good one to start sex with.

My cock, however, was very sure. It strained painfully against my zipper, a condition only made worse by the way Natalia pressed her body to mine.

"You're off the clock," she said, tilting her hips forward slightly. The head pressed against the top of her pubis, separated by a few thin layers of cloth. I wanted to shred them.

"Who punches that clock?" I asked, inwardly hating myself for continuing to talk when Natalia's lips began a path from my ear to my Adam's apple.

"How about if I punch it by undoing the lock on this door," she said, raising her big doe-eyes to mine, "And you punch it by undoing my pants?"

I wheezed out a laugh of disbelief, and the next thing I knew, her arms were around my neck. She pressed her lips to mine in a pillow-soft, slow, utterly persuasive kiss. Her tongue flicked against the seam over my mouth only the slightest bit, but somehow, I could taste her. That was all I needed to know I couldn't refuse.

"Deal," I said, smiling against her mouth. Without overthinking it - a feat for me - I bent my knees, hooked my hands around the backs of her thighs, and hoisted her up in the air, swinging her so that her ankles locked around the small of my back.

She screeched, not seeming to care whether anyone heard or saw us. Wait. *Could people see us?* Were there cameras outside the gym? No, she'd said there was just one in the locker room when we'd talked about it a couple days ago.

It didn't matter. My body was acting independently of my brain, it seemed.

The hard-on in my pants, for one, but also the confident way my legs carried the both of us up those big concrete stairs, the way my arms braced Natalia against the brick and held her close to me as she fumbled with the old key in the lock, and the laugh that resonated from deep inside me when we got inside and she tried to kiss me, but failed because of the hair covering her face. My thighs burned by the time I got the both of us up the stairs to the third floor. Natalia was all muscle with a small amount of padding, and now I knew from practical experience that muscle was heavier than fat. I panted with relief when I spotted her bed, a simple platform construction with pure white bedding, facing the wall of floor to ceiling windows. I dropped her on the bed and stood there, drinking in her beauty. She was stunning in the moonlight that flooded the room. Golden skin, mussed hair, absolutely wild. And, for this night at least, she was all mine. Suddenly, I just wanted to be close to her, more than I wanted anything else - including being inside her. I flopped down next to her so that our faces were even and looked at her with a grin.

"You really want to?" I asked, giving her one last chance to back out of this. Whatever this was.

She answered me by sitting up, flinging one leg over my waist, and kissing me long and hard.

Okay then. We were doing this.

God, she was breathtaking. I wanted to burn the sight of her, hair tousled, chest heaving, smile beaming, into my memory. Her camisole edged up just enough for me to see the waistband of her jeans digging into the curve of her hip.

"Oh, baby," I crooned. I leaned down to kiss the skin there, groaning quietly as my tongue swept out, seemingly of its own volition, picking up her warm, sweet taste.

I knew, I *remembered*, that the area below her waistband only intensified that taste. She was hot and musky and salty with an edge of sweet. Last time I'd been desperate to make her come, to hear her scream. This time, I didn't know what to make of her - didn't know what we were or how we would end up. I did know I would be seeing her for the next few weeks, at least, though, which made me want to savor her.

So that's exactly what I did.

We spent a lot of time that night with my face buried between Natalia's legs - licking at her slick, dripping pussy, until she screamed my name, biting at the tendons on the inside of her thighs as she drew deep breaths in the aftermath of her orgasm. I sucked love bites on her perfectly smooth, round ass. I rasped my beard against the base of her spine and held her ankles down while I did it. I knew from memory that she was severely ticklish there. I took full advantage, relishing her laughing screeches.

I adored every inch of Natalia. In all the years I'd been romantically involved with women, she was unique. There was sex for maintenance, sex for fun, and then there was Natalia.

Sex with Natalia was a life-changing experience. As she flipped over beneath me and cupped my jaws with both hands, then devoured my mouth, licking into it slowly, like she had an eternity to do so. I shivered. She owned me. And she knew it.

Her thighs locked around my hips, and with a small grunt, she flipped me over. My cock badly needed attention, and brushing against the insides of her thighs wasn't quite doing it. She smirked down at me, as though she could read my thoughts, before leaning forward. Her tits swayed in my face while she fumbled in a nightstand drawer. I wasn't sure whether I believed in heaven, but if I did, this would certainly be part of it.

"I love how hard you get," she murmured, righting herself. "It makes a woman feel good, you know, when a man gets hard as soon as he kisses her."

"I was hard long before that, honey. It doesn't take much when I'm with you."

She smirked. I smoothed my palm over her hip, then down between her legs. Her eyes rolled back a little, in time with the slight arching of her back. I shot her a smirk in return as my fingers glided through her slick lips. I used two of them to trace a lazy circle at her opening, and when she tried to raise up to take me inside, I pushed them in farther, crooking them against her front wall. There was a dime-sized patch of flesh inside that would make her tremble, and before I thrust inside her, I wanted her to feel it.

She let out a long, full-throated moan, and I mentally fist-pumped. There it was. Now that I'd given her one orgasm and the promise of another, I could take what I'd been dreaming about for days. I pulled my fingers from her channel, using her slippery juices to run my hand down my cock, and nodded at her to roll the condom on. She did, then grabbed at the base. "Open up for me, honey," I murmured, knowing that she'd tensed around my fingers.

She did, allowing me to sink into her instead of pushing my way in. And, oh Lord, was she heaven. She lazily rocked her hips forward and back, slicking my cock through her channel even though she barely let it slip out of her. Warmth crept up my body at the lazy intensity of it all, and within minutes, that warmth turned to fire. When she dug her fingernails into my pecs, I locked her hips in a vice-tight grip, and thrust up into her as hard as I could manage. She moaned, arching her back, which gave my thrusts a new angle. Before I knew it, we were moaning our release together.

She collapsed on top of me, and we puffed out exhausted

laughter for a few seconds before she swung her leg up and over my torso. Then I eased her down to the bed, wiped her slightly sweaty brow, and ran my fingers through her hair, slowly. She nuzzled into my neck as her fingers ran up and down my torso.

"You've been working out since the last time I saw you," she hummed.

"Remember my buddy Mark?"

She tilted her head back and I barely made out her scrunched brows in the dim blue city light as she considered. "Mister blondie with the beard? A little... round? Here?" Her fingers danced over my abs and I jerked as a rogue ticklish nerve jumped.

"Yeah," I chuckled. "Well, he was." Then his girlfriend broke up with him - totally shocked him - and he was a fucking mess. I made him do couch to 5k just to keep his mind off it. Didn't hurt me, either."

"I remember him," Natalia said. "He was working on it. Looked good by the time I saw him at Knockout Brothers last year. All that because of a shocking breakup," Natalia mused. "It's only ever a shock to one person, isn't it?"

"It was a shock to all of us," I replied, remembering. "Mark and Kylie were a sure thing. As sure as sure gets."

"Nothing is for sure," Natalia said. I thought of our moms, knew she was thinking of them too.

"Guess you're right," I replied. "Except... I'm pretty sure of one thing."

"Hmm?" Natalia asked, her hand stilling on its idle path.

"I'm absolutely certain that I will be extremely disappointed if I don't get inside you again before the sun comes up."

"Is that so? Well, I guess, if you think you can - oh!"

Natalia's hand had made its way down underneath the sheet covering my crotch and found me rock hard again. Already.

"I can," I growled, and flipped her onto her back. I dropped a kiss on her perfect mouth. Yeah, she looked gorgeous when she bothered with an occasional swipe of lipstick, but I loved her lips best just like I loved the rest of her. Naked. Soft and relaxed. Ready. She was even relaxed when she rolled the condom onto me.

There was no riding or frantic roughness this time around - there was just me and Natalia, pressed against each other, moving together like we breathed - heavy, slow, easy, peaceful. Natural. Without overthinking or rushing or chasing something we knew was coming. I bottomed out inside her and she craned her neck up to kiss me. Her fingers twined in my hair as I pulled out, quietly beckoning me back to her. We took our time. We savored each other. I half-forgot myself - who I was, why I existed, outside of this moment.

It was only when Natalia said my name in a choked gasp - "Ethannn!" - and her hips arched off the bed, her pussy pulsing around my cock, that I came back to myself, only to be swept away again by my own orgasm. I growled adoration and praise for her into her neck, and found the same sentiments in her eyes when I finally pulled away to give her one last kiss before taking care of the condom.

She cradled my head against the pillow of her breast afterward, and my hand found a perfect resting spot gently cupping the curve of her ass. Suddenly, I had a flash of a vision - these thighs that I'd just licked every inch of straddling a motorcycle seat, or hemmed in by a climbing harness. Her beautiful breasts encased in Kevlar. The sinews in her neck straining as she fired a gun or crouched to jump off a building. A small groan escaped me as I involuntarily grabbed her butt and pulled her closer to me.

She chuckled. "You cannot be ready to go again. You are human, right?"

I shook my head, then took in a long, slow breath, thinking I could suffocate in her breasts and I probably wouldn't even mind that much.

"That wasn't it."

"Well, what then?" Her voice was low, soft, her words slow to come. She was on the edge of sleep.

"I don't want - you're just - God, Natalia, are you sure?"

"About having sex with you?" She laughed, sounding a little more awake now. "Pretty sure. I think."

"Not that. It's just... you're perfect."

She snorted, but I stayed quiet.

"Ethan. You sound so upset. What's going on?"

"I..." I let out a long sigh, loathe to say the words but knowing I had to. "I don't know if I can stand it."

She propped herself up on one elbow, peered into my eyes. I tried to keep my own eyes from tracing the shape her breasts took – one resting on top of the other, their heavy curves taking on new shape. "Can't stand what?" She was genuinely confused, which worried me. How was she possibly going to understand?

"Can't stand you putting yourself in danger. Like you've described. Hell, it was hard enough to know you were running with the bulls last year, and we'd said goodbye at that point." I touched her shoulder, let my fingers brush down over her upper arm. Her eyelids fluttered with pleasure. "You seriously want to go back to leading the crazy dangerous life?"

She looked down, staring at the sheets bunched up between us. "It's who I am."

"Have you ever tried being... you know. Normal?"

"I'm trying it now," she replied. "Running the gym. Owning the gym. Being pinned down by the gym. And I can already see all the ways I'm going to be bored out of my mind."

It felt like I'd been punched in the gut. Automatically, my hold on her ass tightened. "Thanks."

"I wasn't saying I was bored with you, Ethan." Natalia snuggled back up against me, and fleetingly, I wished I could keep her this way always. Snuggly and content just to be near me. I knew I couldn't. "You're great, but you know what I mean. This life. The whole thing - going to work at the same place. Doing the same thing, over and over. Never leaving, because I can't. Everything I do, everything I have, everything I am -It's all here. Forever." She groaned. "See? I'm dying inside just talking about it."

"Well, that's because you're not looking at it the right way. Let me help."

She raised an eyebrow at me. "What does that mean?"

"Well, obviously, I'm going to help you with The Knockout." I leaned in and tilted my face up, planting a soft kiss right behind her ear. She groaned, and I laughed, blowing air against the skin there, which made her squirm. "Let me show you," I said, "how good it can be to have a life that's... calm. Normal."

Natalia shoved me gently with one hand. "Calm and normal. Why in the world would I want –"

"Because people love you," I said, unable to stop myself. I loved being with Natalia, and I could already feel myself slipping down the slope into loving her, but obviously there were other people in the equation. Her dad. Her brothers and their families. "And," I said, "as your business consultant, I have to remind you that it's cheaper. Better for the gym. You all want that. You all need that."

"So, you're going to show me... how?" Something had changed in her voice. It was somehow... thinner. Like she was now only eighty percent there.

"Dinners and movies. Walks through the city. Quick trips to a bed and breakfast. Maybe we'll even get crazy and run a 5k or go biking. Lots more of this," I said, snaking my arm around her waist, letting my hand rest on the upper curve of her perfect ass.

"If you hate it – if you really, truly miss jumping off of buildings and out of airplanes, and dodging angry bulls, then –"

"Then what? I can go back to doing them?"

I should have heard the edge in her voice. Should have realized she was leading me right into a trap with her incredible hair and delicious-looking tits and general air of teasing. I was half teasing her. She wasn't joking at all.

"Yeah," I said, leaning in to kiss her on the mouth. Her fingers laced through my hair and blood rushed back down to my cock.

That was when it all went to hell.

Her fingers tightened, wrapping my just-long-enough-for-serious-grabbing hair in a death lock. She wrenched my head back and glared into my eyes. "Listen to me, Ethan Anderson, and listen carefully, because I'm only going to say this once."

I winced, sucking in a breath when she tugged my hair again. This would be kind of sexy if there wasn't rage radiating from Natalia's gaze. I squeezed my eyes shut and managed a tight, "Oh-okay."

"Nobody – not my brothers, not my father, and especially not *you*, tells Natalia Ortiz what she can or cannot do. I do what I want, when I want, for the reasons I want. If I want your opinion about it, I will ask you. Do you understand me?"

I nodded, just a tiny bit. "Yep," I choked out.

Just like that, she released my hair. My scalp throbbed, and I dropped back onto my pillow. "Jesus, Tali."

Leaning over me, she considered my face for a moment, then dropped a long, hard kiss on my mouth. "Now," she said, trailing an index finger along my jaw, "Get the fuck out of here."

"What?!" I choked on my own shock. I was hoping to get in at least one more round, and then spend the night with Natalia in my arms.

"Get. Out," she said. Her voice was even as she stretched

out on her back and pulled a crisp white sheet up to cover those perfect breasts. "I need to sleep. You need to leave."

I lay there stock still for a moment, trying to process what she was saying. "Look, Natalia. I'm sorry. That was out of line."

"Yes, it was. But you said you understood, and I believed you. You're forgiven. Now get out. I will see you tomorrow." Her voice gentled at that, and something like relief fell over me. This was Natalia angry. If I wanted to keep seeing her, apparently, I was going to have to learn things like this.

But it was clear that she was done talking, so I silently slid out of bed, pulled my pants back on, tugged my shirt over my head, and stepped into my shoes. I walked around to Natalia's side of the bed, kissed her forehead, prayed she wouldn't head-butt me while I was at it. And then I did exactly as she asked. Aching with every step, I left. Growling into the chilly night sky, I left.

As I walked away from her, and thought of all the ways I could have lost her, I realized that this way felt the shittiest.

CHAPTER 13

NATALIA

WHAT THE HELL? He'd actually *left*?

Of course, I'd told him to, but... you couldn't just leave in the middle of an argument like that. Acceptable actions for Ethan at that moment included: arguing that I was being ridiculous (that wouldn't have gone over well), groveling at my feet (I found it hard to respect that), holding me down and kissing me until I let him fuck me again (though I didn't love the blurred lines of consent there), and begging me for forgiveness. Probably the only one that would have worked.

Instead, he'd just... gone. Without a word. With a gentle kiss on my forehead. Like he barely cared at all.

Since we'd first seen each other again, the connection between us had been so clear – whatever it was. It wasn't love – not yet, anyway. Just the idea of falling in love on a short trip home to Philly had the potential to send me into a panic attack. It wasn't just friendship, either, or focus on the job of the gym. No, whatever was between Ethan and I was elemental – strong enough to have drawn us back together and flexible enough to let us go on a date directly after a grief support group meeting.

And it was big enough that I couldn't bear it being ruined by him acting like a stupid macho Neanderthal idiot and telling me what I could and could not do with my free time, my career, my life, or my body.

Damn right. I crossed my arms and huffed at nobody in the suddenly very dark, very empty air of my apartment. My room, more like. Just me in a room. A big, dark, quiet room. And I'd just kicked out the person who probably believed in my ability to get the gym back on track more than anyone else.

So why had he been such a dick?

I spent the next six hours trying to find sleep, and failing miserably at it. Dammit. I couldn't sleep with Ethan here, after the way he'd pissed me off, and I couldn't sleep without him here, either. Apparently.

If he hadn't been such an idiot, and just stayed and fought with me like I'd wanted him to, everything would be fine right now. Beyond fine.

I rolled over, punched my pillow, then buried my face in it and screamed.

Well. I wouldn't give him the satisfaction of calling him. And if I couldn't sleep, I would make the free time work to my advantage. Just like I did with everything else.

I hadn't even bothered to get dressed after he left. The space between my thighs was still slightly sticky from where I'd come, and I groused at the reminder of how mind-blowing the sex was with him. Why did it have to be so good, when he was so annoying? So boring? So demanding of me, and of a future I didn't even feel ready to define for myself yet, let alone anyone else?

That same space ached, too, and I basically growled against the feeling, half-spent and half disappointingly empty, as I dug through my suitcase – I still hadn't fully unpacked, damn it all – to find some compression shorts and a workout tank. I stepped into the shorts and tugged on the sports bra I'd been wearing yesterday, which I found behind the bathroom door. Then the tank and a pair of brand new socks. There was nothing better in life than new socks. That was a belief I'd held since I was little.

I snagged my boxing gloves from the bedposts where I'd left them after yesterday morning's workout to air out, and smirked at the memory of me and Ethan in bed last night, fucking like our lives depended on it. With all the craziness going on around me these past few days, it sort of felt like the truth. My life did depend on doing things that made me feel... well... alive. And Ethan made me feel that way like nobody else ever had.

Something about that thought bugged me, and a crankiness infused my blood as I dumped some ground coffee in the press and hit the button on the electric kettle. Five minutes later, I took a couple scalding gulps from the cup and felt the caffeine chase that edge away for something fiercer, more focused. Instead of stewing, like I had done for the past several stupid sleepless hours, now I just wanted to fight.

The sun was just starting to come up over the city's jagged horizon, winking bright orange through the crack between the buildings across the street from The Knockout. I flipped on the big industrial lights that hung from wires screwed into the ceiling a decade ago and took a deep breath, letting my eyes flutter closed as they flickered to life.

More than the sunrise, more than the scent of hot coffee or the buzz of an alarm clock, the flicker of those lights and an empty, echoing gym meant the beginning of the day.

I stared at the big empty boxing ring as I put some heavy metal music on over the speakers, then jogged in place for a few seconds, then bounced up and down on my toes, trying to coax some warmth into my stiff calves. My memory flashed to the way I'd wrapped them around Ethan's waist last night, desperate to pull him closer to me, needing his hot muscle to force my body to mold to it.

That was one thing Ethan brought out in me that no person

ever had before – need. As the youngest of six children, often ignored, sometimes forgotten, I had rarely felt need for anyone besides my parents. I was Natalia, and I could get by all on my own. Could do it well, thank you very much.

I eyed a punching bag a few dozen feet away and charged at it, launching my shoulders and abs and snarling yell into an assault on the poor thing that would have alarmed anyone else working out here, had I not been completely alone. I attacked the column of vinyl and until my shoulders burned, then backed off.

Of course, I didn't need Ethan. Not any more than I needed high-end boxing gloves or the rush of jumping off a cliff holding only the metal bar of a hang-glider. Not any more than I needed my mother's empanadas. I may have valued those things, and they may have made my life better in immeasurable ways, and I may have been indescribably sad at the thought of never having them again, but I didn't *need* them.

Ethan would help me with the gym and then I would pass it off to the next person and we would part ways and we would all be fine. Just fine.

Satisfied with this newfound resolve, I set my jaw and charged at the bag again. With the first smack, my knuckle burned satisfyingly, and the sensation raced up my arm, like it was charging me up for another swing. I railed on that bag, punishing it, bouncing around like I was in the professional ring when it swung back and launching forward to meet it every time. A memory flashed through my mind – Arturo teaching me to punch when I was fifteen, after I'd told him about a boy at school who kept snapping my bra strap in the middle of algebra class. Mamá, working on the books at the front desk, shaking her head and *tsk*ing at him, sneaking me a secret, slightly sad smile here and there.

Mamá never commented on my boxing, on the extreme-sporting or the wanderlust. Every single time she saw me, she asked if I was happy and told me she was glad I was home. My eyes burned and, when the bag swung back this time, I dropped to the ground and launched into a round of pushups. I groaned at the top of the tenth and launched myself back up to my feet, side-stepping to one of the equipment racks. I grabbed a two-pound jump rope and swung it over my head, sighing with a strained smile as my leg muscles started burning to match my arms.

This was it – this was why I loved working out, this life – the feeling of pushing my body to the limit and knowing that I could still do more. Yes, I was starting to struggle for breath. Yes, my body was starting to whine. No, I wasn't going to break. Not now, and not ever. Certainly, nobody could tell me to stop. With that thought, I tossed the rope to the side and squinted against the sun, which was now fully up and glinting in my eyes.

Good. It would make landing a punch on the bag that much harder I charged at it hard then, pummeling it again and again, savoring the feel of the vibrations through my fists in time with Metallica's ATLAS, which charged through the speakers seemingly in time with my steps. Not the other way around.

And then, on one punch, instead of my knuckles slamming into the bag's typical easy give, they smacked into it instead, solid and unyielding.

I jumped back, stood stock-still, my heart pounding. A split second later, I was staring at a pair of perfectly-tailored pants and scuff-free shoes. The hands that held the bag still were unmistakable – they'd haunted my memories, very pleasantly, since the first time I'd encountered them.

"Ethan," I panted, unsure which emotion to pick from the several warring ones fighting within me. Pro – he wasn't a burglar or a rapist. Con – he'd just scared the shit out of me. Pro

– something inside me eased a bit at seeing him. Con – I wasn't very good at expressing that. I didn't think.

"What the *fuck* are you doing?" I growled.

"You said we'd get back to work today. I assumed that meant this morning. Like, when people typically start work." Yep. Here it was. Cocky Ethan

"I locked the door, Ethan! What the *fuck*?" I repeated.

The confident features that shined out of his face seconds ago melted for a second, then recovered. For the most part. Cocky Ethan held up something that looked like a skinny screwdriver handle with a thick, stiff metal wire emerging from the tip. "You locked the door, but your lock sucks. I picked it in ten seconds."

My eyes flared. "Why would you do that? Holy *shit!*" The curses were falling out of my mouth now, and the ghost of my mother glared at me from the front desk. It barely registered, though. My heart was still pounding and my brain was trying to make sense of why in the world Ethan would pick the lock to my gym.

"To show you that your lock sucks," he said, still cocky, but with a slightly softer tone. "Tali. I'm sorry."

"Don't call me Tali when you just picked my lock – on purpose – and scared the hell out of me!"

"Hey. Don't yell at me when you're working out all alone, blasting music so you can't hear a damn thing, with only a standard lock to keep you safe!" Something about Ethan's mouth had stiffened and his shoulders were high. Whoa. He was actually pissed off. An emotion I was pretty sure I'd never seen coming from him before.

I put my hands up in the air, still in my gloves, in an "I surrender" gesture. "Okay," I said, swallowing against the dryness in my throat. "I get it. I'll replace the lock."

"Okay," Ethan said. "And, um..." He set his briefcase down

on the floor and took a tentative step closer to me. "I'm sorry. I didn't think...it's just that I've never seen you like that. I didn't think..."

"That I could get scared? Well, congratulations, Mr. Insurance Man. You terrified me."

His eyebrows pulled together. "Okay. I'm sorry," he repeated. This time, it sounded a little like begging. Just enough that I took a deep breath and closed my eyes, collecting myself.

"So," I said, modulating my tone so Confident Natalia was back. "You came back. I wasn't sure if you would." I hadn't even admitted that worry to myself until I spoke it aloud, just then.

Ethan swallowed hard but he stood his ground. "I'll leave if you want. I just sort of figured... I don't know. Last night was last night. That was... us. But this morning, I brought my briefcase." He held it up in demonstration. "This is The Knockout. I really can help with the gym," he continued, his voice deepening as his shoulders squared. "You will be happy with the work I do for you, I promiseNo judgment on whatever happens after I help you get it up and running."

My heart sank. I thought I'd wanted him to leave. And I had, last night, when he was bossing me around. But I did want him here – in The Knockout, and in my bed. In my life. Something about his presence was uplifting and grounding at the same time.

"I mean, it is my assignment," he said, interrupting my train of thought. Ruining everything. "For work. You know. But then there's that whole part about how you're actually not planning to stay on, running this place."

"Yeah," I agreed. His reminding me of that was a nudge back into a reality that I didn't really want to keep at the forefront of my mind right now. Right now, I wanted to be the good daughter. Later on, I could be the daughter who abandoned her family. Who broke her promises.

But dammit, as Ethan stood there offering his help to me, even knowing what he knew, even after I had kicked him out of my place last night after the best sex I had ever had, I realized that the cocky Ethan whose big, confident personality had reeled me in the first time I met him was once again melting away.

Yeah. I liked cocky Ethan, the one who brought his peacocking A-game to dates and workouts and business interactions. But, I realized as I stood there watching a relieved smile settle over his face, I liked this Ethan too. The one who wanted to spend time with me, even if it meant he had to apologize to do it. The one who was standing here, now, waiting for a decision from me, his arms hanging at his sides.

"Which is what I really wanted to talk to you about today, whether you wanted to keep me on the project or not. We have to talk about life insurance, for you. Since you're the technical owner now, it'll be important that you protect the business in the event of your death."

The last word came out softly, like Ethan thought that by lowering his volume he would tempt death into our presence that much less. I knew this conversation was hard for him. Still, I rolled my eyes. "I'm not going to die. That's why we train before we do stunts. That's why I prepare for everything that I –"

"Is that why women are at a much greater risk doing stunt work? Because as a rule they're generally less protected than men since they need to wear skimpy costumes? Is that why there are hardly any industry standards for keeping any stunt people safe and protected on the job? Or why –"

Geez, Ethan was making my heart rate tick up just with the pace of his words. Or maybe it was the palpable stress in his voice, in the way his eyebrows crinkled together as he said them, like he was envisioning all the awful things that could happen to me.

"It's why I have to get a lot more experience before I get the really serious jobs in film, Ethan," I said, forcing my voice to stay calm and measured. "It's why I don't want to let this gym take over my life while I'm young enough to get the experience down."

He sighed, not saying anything.

"Take off your shirt," I blurted, secretly thrilling at his shocked expression when I did. I turned and walked over to the boxing ring, then hoisted myself up into it, ducking under the ropes. I started a little bob-and-weave and turned back to look at Ethan. To my surprise, he'd done what I told him to. I grinned.

"Your shoes and socks too," I called, gesturing with a gloved hand. He never took his eyes off me, just toed out of his shoes and then pulled off his socks. "Then c'mere."

"What's going on?" He still looked slightly confused, even though he did as I'd asked. I jogged over to the ropes and bent over them, my feet lifting off the mat, to reach the rack with gloves Ethan's size. When I turned back, there he was. Inside the ropes with me, his face looking skeptical.

"This is your punishment," I said smoothly. "For picking the lock and scaring me, just because you could."

His mouth dropped open but I held my finger up to his lips before he could get a word out. Then, with a heavy sigh, he reached a hand out and fitted the gloves on each hand. "I don't really know how to box," he said.

I narrowed my eyes and cocked my head. "But you were working out here, a little. Last year, when I was in town."

"I was using the weights, and mostly running the rest of the time."

.   .   .

Now that I thought of it, he was right. I couldn't remember seeing him in the ring for any significant amount of time.

"It's not science, Runner Boy. It's an art. Follow me." I started to bounce from foot to foot. He copied me, and I tried to suppress an "I told you so" smile when his arms naturally pulled into a fighting stance. "Good," I praised, pretending not to notice how pleased he seemed at my words. I turned to the side, letting my body go into a fighting stance. "One foot in front of the other now," I said. I paused and nudged his pant leg with the toe of my shoe. "Pull this one out front."

He did as I told him, which pulled his body forward about four feet – making him just a few inches away from me. His eyes never left mine, and I'd be damned if I didn't want to kiss him. Just the memory of his lips covering every inch of my body was enough to distract me – which it would have, if I was ever anything less than focused in the ring. Good thing I wasn't. "Front arm jab, back arm cross," I told him in a much softer voice than I'd ever used in the ring before in my life. He nodded with a small jerk down of his chin, his eyes still not leaving mine. I swallowed hard. "Show me," I said. "Jab." His left fist darted out aimlessly in front of him, and I laughed. Quickly, I ducked to his side and stood behind him, positioning my body behind his. No wonder guys liked to have sex like this – as the big spoon. The feeling of control, of surrounding and encompassing someone you found attractive, was highly intoxicating. I had to try not to think about that right now, though. I rested my bulbous gloved hand on his left shoulder.

"Punch from the shoulder," I said, inches from his ear. Then I held my glove up and demonstrated. "Like this," I said as I let kinetic energy explode from my shoulder and propel my glove forward. "Now you."

Ethan did what I asked, and I watched the muscles of his arms twitch and flex as he did. "Not bad," I murmured. "Now,"

I said, bouncing on my toes and changing my position so I was facing him again, holding my gloves up to my face so only my eyes were showing, "Hit me."

"What?" Ethan sputtered, and I giggled. "Natalia, I am not – I can't – "

"You can, and you are. C'mon," I encouraged. "I'll call the punches and you practice them. Okay?"

Ethan looked queasy. Looked like we were enjoying this activity in perfectly correlated amounts – as my amusement increased, his took a nosedive.

"Jab," I called, and like Ethan was a puppet and my voice controlled his strings, his arm shut out. It was aimless, but at least his fist came out relatively close to my face and the power was coming from the right place. I threw my glove up to block him. "Good!" I crowed, then a second later, "Cross!" This hit needed work too, but I was patient. I dipped and move with each punch I called out, making sure that his glove hit mine with a satisfying deep smack every time. "Really good," I repeated. He wasn't used to this kind of exercise – his breath was getting short and a sheen of sweat had started to form across his brow after only a couple minutes.

"Okay," I said, loud enough to grab his attention. His focus, which was adorable, broke then. I let my gloves drop and he did the same.

"Nope," I said, stepping into his space and nudging his arms back up. "Now it's my turn to hit and your turn to block."

"Natalia, why are we –"

"Just. Block," I said. Back in fighting stance, I started to bounce, and Ethan sighed as he raised his gloves back up. I kept calling the punches, announcing "Jab!" or "Cross" a good second or so before I actually threw a hit. Of course, my aim was much better than Ethan's, so even though he was an inexperienced blocker, he wasn't in any danger of actually being hit.

But who knew that he could keep up with my bobbing and weaving? He seemed to catch a second wind as his steps around the ring perfectly paced to mirror mine, until we were both panting and sweating. I stopped for a second and let my arms drop, feeling full and triumphant. Ethan's stayed up, guarding his face. "Doesn't that feel better? Now, do you believe me that I can take care of myself?"

He sighed, and fixed his eyes on me over the top of his gloves, which he still held up. Guess he wasn't ready for a breather. "Natalia, I –" But just the tone of his voice was a buzzkill. Apparently, I'd tried cutting off our session too soon, so I blurted "Jab!" and lunged toward him – just as he let his gloves drop.

In slow motion, I watched my glove connect to the side of his face with a sick smack. I hadn't taught him how to slip, or even to roll with a punch. It was like I was seeing it in slow motion – his head slid to the side, the skin rippling across his cheeks, his lips moving into an unrecognizable shape. For a second, I thought he'd stay standing, that he had been surprised but not unprepared – but, nope. Down Ethan went.

A burning sensation flooded through my chest, and in half a second, I had dropped to my knees next to him. To his credit, he'd recovered somewhat – he was propped up on one elbow, gloves still on, the cool vinyl of one of them pressed to his cheek.

I shucked my gloves off, and as I did I realized that my breath was coming short in my chest. With anyone else, I would have found this hilarious, but instead, I felt mild panic at the prospect that I'd somehow broken Ethan. That this (accidental!) punch would scare him away from all this.

I had no idea what 'this' was, mind you. I just knew I didn't want to stop seeing Ethan. And apparently that's the feeling that led to punching me in the face. Nice work, Natalia.

I scooted over to him on my knees, my hands outstretched,

and moved to cup his jaws with them, just to get a better look. He flinched away from my touch, and I frowned. "Ethan," I crooned, shocking myself with my own nurturing tone. "God, I'm sorry." I bent down and tried to touch him again, and this time he let me, letting out a sad attempt at a chuckle.

He cracked his eyes open and peered at me. "Sorry, I'm just having a little trouble understanding what you were trying to accomplish by punching me in the face."

"Accomplish? I – Ethan, I wasn't trying to *accomplish* anything," I protested, leaning forward and shoving my forearms under his arms, pulling him up to sitting. At least now he looked a little less injured, but I was the one who was out of breath. He was heavier than he looked. Unconsciously, I licked my lips at the thought that muscle was much heavier than fat. And I knew exactly how much muscle was under those clothes. How it looked. How it felt. How it tasted.

Slowly, still wincing against the sting on his cheek, Ethan shifted his legs so he was sitting with his ankles crossed. He pulled off his gloves, one with his teeth, then the other with his freed fingers. I leaned in to look more closely at his cheek. It was swelling, that was for sure – not quickly enough that I thought his cheekbone was broken, but he definitely would have some explaining to do to his bosses.

Not to my brothers or my dad, though. They would know exactly what had happened. Now it was my turn to groan.

"Hey," he said, his expression shifting from pain to pity. "No, no. It's okay. Really."

"I was just trying to prove to you that I knew what the hell I was doing. I swear, it's not –"

"Oh," Ethan laughed. "If there was any way for you to effectively demonstrate that you know how to throw a punch, it's that. Believe me. But, Natalia," he said, more quietly now. His hands reached out for mine, and I let him take them. He tugged me gently toward him. This was the not-cocky Ethan. Forgiving. Gentle. Kind. I knee crawled forward until my legs bumped against his. Then he dropped my hand and wrapped his free one around my waist, pulling me down to his lap. I squeaked in surprise at being suddenly so helpless, so wrapped up in him. Especially since about ten minutes ago he'd been so unsure, so guarded. Now he was back to taking charge.

Strange sensations sizzled through every one of my cells. I couldn't tell whether I liked this...or whether I really liked it. The closeness. The intimacy. Ethan taking charge, even in this small way, even if I knew I could take control back in an instant.

"Natalia," he continued. "I believe that you can do this stunt career thing, as safely as anyone can. I'm just saying... it's not really safe for anyone. And that makes it not safe for your business. And believe me, it's not the only way to enjoy life. "

I frowned at that. I hadn't told Ethan *everything* about why I was so set on this career, but what he'd just said hit dangerously close to my biggest fear – that I'd go through life like a zombie, going through the motions, doing exactly what everyone expected of me and never what I really wanted to be doing. There was more to it, but –

"I know," I muttered.

"I want to spend more time with you. And I want to help you with The Knockout. I know I probably can't convince you to give up the stunt stuff."

I frowned. It was so much more than just "stunt stuff." I desperately wanted him to understand that, even if I knew he wasn't ready to hear my explanation. Even if I knew I wasn't ready to give it.

"But I want to show you that it's maybe not as bad as you think." Hesitantly, millimeter by millimeter, he moved his face closer to mine. "If I'm asking a girl to let me date her after she punched me in the face, it means I really want it. Right?"

"Right," I laughed softly. "I just –"

Then, he planted the softest of soft kisses on my lips. It was so sweet, so tender, and unexpectedly slow. Every one of his kisses up to now had been seductive, desperate. This felt so caring it made my heart want to burst.

"Let me date you," he said when he pulled away, only just enough for his lips to move. I could taste his sweet breath, and I wanted more. "Let me show you that calm, and slow-paced, and even boring, isn't awful. Then you can re-evaluate. After, I don't know, ten dates, you can decide to say fuck the calm life, and I'll write up the insurance and... I'll get you a big discount on your insurance."

My eyebrows shot up. "Really. How big?" This was such a shocking proposition, I was willing to ignore the swear word.

"I'll... I don't know." He shrugged, and I could tell he was getting frustrated, even though he mostly just looked sad. "But I will. I'll figure it out. If you still want to live like a crazy woman when I'm done with you, I'll write up the policy myself and make sure The Knockout and your family is protected. It'll still be more expensive than the quiet life. I'm not a miracle worker."

"I understand," I said quietly, biting my lip.

"But if you come around, The Knockout saves that money."

Well, I did want to spend more time with Ethan. There was no point in denying that.

"Okay," I said, in almost a whisper.

Ethan's eyebrows arched up almost to his hairline. Goodness, he was cute. "Okay?" he asked, smiling hopefully.

I just nodded and leaned down again to mold my lips to his.

CHAPTER 14

ETHAN

I'D CREATED A MONSTER, and his name was Hot Mark Mahler. My best friend had gone from sad sack to model-material in a few short months, and it was all my fault.

Nobody else was calling him that, of course. But I was man enough to understand that my radio show co-host had gone from schlub to serious catch when he'd had that makeover his twin sister Hannah had pushed on him. I should have known that pushing Mark into a weekly segment for the Bro Show where we followed his search for a girlfriend – which he'd never really wanted to undertake in the first place – would end with him falling in love.

I could not have predicted it would have happened this fast. And with the sound girl on our show, Toby, no less. Shit, everything seemed to fall into this dude's lap. Figuratively and literally – apparently the yoga glass she had taken Mark to last night had involved her straddling him and wrapping her legs around his waist.

I made a mental note to get the name of that yoga studio from Mark. Yoga seemed like a nice, safe activity that Natalia might also really like. Unlike Mark's girl, I'd have to convince her that an hour spent in silent, sexy meditation could be just as thrilling as base jumping.

I knew I should have been jealous of him, but I loved Mark like a brother.

I was starting to like Toby a whole hell of a lot, too. And right this moment she was looking stressed. She didn't know that I knew that she was Mark's new girl. More importantly, she didn't want me to know.

Break the ice, Anderson.

Mark was saying something about the yoga class feeling like it had been pulled straight from *The Lion King*. So I interrupted him, "Toby, we've gotta get that sound on my grid. You know the one. At the beginning of the lion movie?"

Her face changed from slightly open-mouthed shock to relaxed relief. "On it, Bro," she said, and I grinned at how she'd adapted to Mark's and my greetings for each other. I flashed her a smile, trying to convince her that I was completely clueless about her and Mark with a single look.

It had been a week since Natalia and I made our deal – for every safe, normal date I took her on, I would agree to do something insane and/or dangerous of her choosing.

This was how I knew Natalia was different. I wouldn't agree to that for literally any other girl on the planet.

I'd only seen her twice this week, one of those times being when I broke into her very un-secure gym and struck that very deal with her. I was distancing myself, and I knew exactly why. Agreeing to do insane dangerous things was very different than...actually doing them.

Natalia had acquiesced and let me choose the first date. It was dinner at Morimoto's sushi, famous not only in Philly, but worldwide. The food was exquisite, the atmosphere was perfection, and Natalia was the best dinner companion I'd ever sat down to eat with.

Seriously. She took in every detail of our surroundings, actually pored over the menu and had a lively conversation with the waiter before she ordered, and once the food came, she savored every bite like it could have been her last. I had to seriously restrain myself from joking that it could very well be that if Natalia actually planned to go skydiving a few days later, like she said she did.

She was ethereal. She told me about an MMA competition she'd unknowingly gotten herself into in LA, and how there were scouts there, and how she'd finished in 5th place, which was actually pretty damn good. Not good enough to get noticed by the scouts, but good enough to get her first background stunt-acting gig. I told her about the Bro Show and the segment I'd cornered Mark into, thinking it'd be this big hilarious entertaining process, when really it was just turning out to be pretty boring, with him already going goo-goo eyed for Toby.

"Sounds boring," Natalia said. "But isn't that what you want?"

"Only for myself," I chuckled. "No rollercoasters for me. Or tilt-a-whirls. Or even teacups."

"So, you just want to stand on the sidelines and watch other people experience all those crazy thrills."

I shrugged. "I guess. If it means I can avoid the sheer terror that comes before it."

Natalia shoved her tongue into her cheek pocket, nodding slowly, thinking. Never breaking eye contact with me, she pulled her phone from somewhere – under her thigh, maybe, God – and started to type something.

I narrowed my eyes. "What are you doing?"

"Making notes," she said calmly. "R-O-L-L-E-R-C-O-A-S-T-E-R," she said. "Filed in 'dates with Mark.'"

I groaned, tipping my head back. The waiter came and refilled our sake cups, and I barely noticed. Natalia got up from the table and walked over to my side. She bent down and whispered in my ear, and I bit back a moan as her breath ruffled the hair there. "You go on a rollercoaster with me," she said, "and I will fuck you in our car in the parking lot afterward."

I froze, then felt my eyes flutter shut at the feeling of her hair brushing my shoulder as she stood up again. She murmured something about going to the ladies' room and I sat there, stock-still, trying to collect myself so that we could pay the check and get out of there as soon as possible.

When she came slinking back to the table in her clingy black dress, which made me damn glad she'd been sitting down the whole dinner so that that gorgeous swell of her hips wouldn't distract me from conversation, I didn't even let her sit down. I practically jumped to my feet and hauled her out of there by one arm, loving the way she giggled on the way.

I was still half-expecting sex with Natalia to get a little more resistible. Instead, I found it harder and harder to keep my hands off of her with every passing day. At my place, she made fun of my leather couch with the nail head trim on the arms, asking how old I really was if I had a sofa that looked like it belonged in a sitcom grandfather's den. I shut her up but bunching that stretchy dress up over her curvy, sweet ass and sucking her tits while she rode me hard. After, while we lay there recovering, she named the sofa Old Will. "That can be our code word," she purred, trailing a finger down the middle of my chest as she snuggled into me.

"Code word? Like, for when things get too crazy in bed?" I hummed in pleasure as she hitched her leg up over mine, twisting our lower halves together, and reached up to grab the throw blanket at the back of the couch.

Natalia laughed that full-throated way that always made me itch to have her again. "No, that's a safe word. And don't worry, Mr. Safety, I don't anticipate you'll ever agree to kinky enough sex for us to have a safe word."

I bristled at that, but didn't disagree. I'd never had kinky sex – honestly, I'd always been plenty satisfied with all the regular types of sex. So far, at least.

"No," she continued. "Like when we *want* to. You know. Then, if we're watching Monday night football or something, I don't have to jump you in front of Papá. I'll just say, 'Hey Ethan, do you think the Packers WILL get the third down?'" She frowned as soon as she said it, and her thoughtful look was so adorable that I paid attention to her face instead of her still-naked body. "That sounds like something I'd say way too often. I'll just ask if you wanna visit Old Will. Easy." She smacked her hand on the leather, and the sound had me half-hard again already.

"Monday night football with Papá, huh?" I asked as my heart warmed at the thought.

"Of course, and Arturo. And Sebastian, and Christian. Rodrigo is always there because Amalia is obsessed with football. You don't want to get near her when Denver is even possibly going to lose. Alejandro even comes sometimes."

"I thought Sunday night was your family's thing," I said, softly kissing her hair. I hadn't forgotten what it was like to have a place I would always belong – home. Conversations like this always brought a small ache to my chest. Natalia had a family. I didn't. Not anymore.

"Always Sunday dinner, which is more like a late lunch," she said. "But that was... well, never mind."

I pulled her in a little closer to me, then tucked a rogue

strand of hair over her ear. I kissed the soft shell of her ear and felt her shiver. "Not 'never mind'. What?"

She sighed, long and hard. "Just that Sunday dinner was Mamá's. She lived for that all week, you know? Or at least Friday and Saturday, shopping and preparing. Now it's... well, it's not that none of us wants to do it. It's just that we really can't. You know?"

"Can't deal with remembering her?" I asked, anticipating this answer. Of course it would be painful for Natalia to remember her mom by repeating that dinner every single week. It had only been four months or so since she'd passed away.

But Natalia lifted up on an elbow, looking at me with confusion. "No. Not that. Like, we actually can't. The cooking, the cleaning, the shopping, the inviting. She was the only one who could pull everything together like that, every week. She made magic happen. It was an art that I – well, honestly, I never really showed any interest in learning. No matter how hard Mamá tried."

Natalia's voice broke at that, and I just let her do whatever crying her body wanted to do. I kissed her hairline in a soft, slow pattern. I felt a few tears, heard a couple slow, deliberate breaths in. But then it ended. "Anyway," Natalia said on a sigh, "We always did Monday night football, too. In the lounge of The Knockout. And that was just easier than Sunday dinners, after she died. Both because all we needed was some chips and a veggie tray, and because it wasn't there. At the house. Next to the kitchen where she stood cooking and cleaning all damn weekend, until it was time for Mass." As those last words came out, Natalia's voice went soft and quiet, like she'd suddenly grown too exhausted to go on talking.

I understood that. I did. The difference between Natalia

and me was that once I got started talking about Mom, I never shut up.

That's why I tried not to get started. It had scared more than one girl away and only made me sadder in the process.

Because I understood Natalia, better in this moment than I thought I ever had, I slid off the couch, scooped her up, and bundled her into my bed. Then I made her log into her YouTube account and we played every silly video from the last two weeks of her watch history. She sniffled and smiled now and then at a girl beating her boyfriend at powerlifting or a talking dog. I was happy just being able to squeeze her now and then.

She fell asleep there, bundled in the blanket, her skin not even touching mine.

I didn't count that as a date, and she didn't ask me to later. Even though she could have traded in our YouTube cuddle for another insanely dangerous date, she didn't.

That was on Monday. We talked on the phone once, and I ran into her at Federal Donuts another time, chatting with her for precious few seconds before I had to get to a meeting. We hadn't had any couple time together, though. I was too acutely aware that I'd just given Mark the same advice that any sane guy would give to any love-sick guy: don't text her like a crazy person. Instead, I worked late hours. I binge-watched a stupid vampire show and I cleaned my apartment top to bottom, but I did. Not. Call.

Early Thursday evening, I was so close to breaking, I could taste it. That was when I heard a sharp, yet measured knock on the door that could only be Natalia's. Forceful and purposeful, just like the rest of her. I pulled open the door with a sigh of relief, only to see Natalia there in what looked like riot gear – tight black leggings, combat boots, and a running jacket – her hair pulled into a severe ponytail, fingerless leather gloves on her hands.

Oh, man. This did not look good.

"Come on, loser," she said with a sparkle in her eye. "We're going on one of *my* dates."

CHAPTER 15

NATALIA

LATELY, I'd seen Ethan far more than I'd expected to when he first walked back into my life. The city was huge, but it was like all its bustling energy and random occurrences just wanted to pull Ethan and I back together again. Yes, he took me out, and we had one phone consultation a couple days after that night - and that following morning. We also ran into each other at Federal Donuts, where Amalia had sent me because she was having period cravings, not because I would ever eat that trash.

Well, I thought I'd never eat it. All it took was one soft-eyed look from Ethan to convince me to try a bite of his blueberry mascarpone cake donut. I could taste the grease it was fried in, yes, but that hardly mattered because the combination of the craggy crust and rich, sweet, yet slightly salty cake inside was to die for. His self-satisfied smile when I moaned at the taste was infuriating and sexy all at the same time.

It unsettled me when Ethan was right. About anything. I knew deep down it was because I was afraid he was right about my stunt double career. More than that, I knew myself. I knew that, if I was faced with it, I would do anything for my family, if I knew deep down it was best for them.

I was almost too busy to think about it, though. Whether The Knockout was my number one passion or not, the challenge of making it the best it could be was like pushing an "on" button inside me. Lessons I'd learned in business school came flooding back, lining themselves up and just waiting for me to implement them. I worked hard writing up business profiles for all the independent gyms within fifteen miles of ours, and noticed that we were one of only three traditional-style gyms in Philly. We had an open floor, racks of hand weights, equipment, a rudimentary track, punching bags and a single ring. That was it. Other gyms featured rows of ellipticals and treadmills, still more specialized weight training machines, boutique features like smoothie bars, and classes. So many classes.

There was also a freakish divide between the two types of gyms - gender. Women didn't belong to traditional gyms, by and large. Heck, I wouldn't belong to a traditional gym back in LA. A male-only membership might work for some of the other sweatboxes in Philly, but we had the space to expand. Our building was almost too large, and it could benefit from an expanded clientele. The Knockout was getting old - a collection of aging men who still thought that they could fight like boys. Our area was chock-full of college students, though, thanks to a location that had seen so many universities grow up around it. I knew we should take advantage of them – run a class or two geared toward them, and hire some of them, too. At that, my thoughts turned to Mariana, Sebastian's oldest girl. It would be cool, I decided, for teenage girls to have a place where they could learn to box.

A couple days after my first "normal person" date with Ethan, I was exhausted. Not from the incredible sex we'd had that night, but from working. I'd pulled two fourteen-hour days now, much of them spent in a flurry of texts and questions to Ethan. For every observation I had about our business, Ethan had an extra point to consider, something to temper a bad assumption I was making, or even just a word of encouragement.

At this pace, I knew, I'd burn out. This was my M.O. - go at something hard and fast until I couldn't do it anymore. Pick something new. Rinse and repeat. But I couldn't afford to do that with The Knockout. It was different. It was responsibility. It couldn't just wait for me to pick up my own shattered pieces after I'd broken myself. I needed to do the grownup thing - I needed to take a break.

And I wanted to make Ethan go on one of the dates he'd promised me. It had to be something insane and dangerous - a phrase he kept repeating with disdain and a hint of fear, and one that made my blood go singing through my veins. Insane and dangerous. It had to be fun, too, but not so insane, dangerous, or, from my perspective, fun that it made Ethan never want to see me again. Even though something deep down inside told me that would never happen, I still knew I didn't want to scare him away.

That meant base jumping was out. Skydiving, too. Anything with a parachute, probably. Was hang-gliding technically a parachute? Best to leave that out too, I guessed. For the first date. Race-car driving felt too loud. Running one of those muddy obstacle courses? Maybe save that one for later, when I didn't care quite so much about looking like shit in front of him. Then it came to me. Guns.

Guns were something of a divisor in my family. Sebastian had, sadly, seen enough of the devastation guns could cause on a human body and community in his role as a middle school teacher that he didn't want any of us ever to touch them, get near them, buy them, even think about them. It was one of the only things he ever fought with Arturo about. Arturo hated how brutal guns were too, which was why he was committed to carefully training recruits to the police department to use them safely and accurately, and why he spent so much time trying to get tighter controls on who could buy guns in the first place.

I sent Arturo a quick text to check his schedule, and grinned when he said that the Academy indoor range would be clear of students for an hour this afternoon. He even said he could be there to show us the ropes and then supervise to make sure we didn't blow our heads off. I laughed, knowing his offer was most likely reflective of Academy policy and not how little he trusted me.

I tugged on tight black leggings and boots with just a little bit of a wide heel, for sturdiness and, of course, sex appeal. Then I grabbed my keys and jumped in the car. "Come on, loser," I said when Ethan opened up his door, looking happy to see me if not a bit stunned. "We're going on one of *my* dates."

"I didn't know you had a car," Ethan said as he slid into the passenger seat. Cocky Ethan was here, grinning ear to ear, fully confident that he was going to blow me away on this date. I smiled to myself at the pun as I thought it.

"It's not technically mine." I screwed up my nose, thinking. "Well, actually, maybe it is now. I'm not sure if it belongs to my dad or the gym. Or whether that matters."

Ethan chuckled. "The car belongs to the LLC. You own the LLC. So, yeah. The car is yours."

He nodded down at my hand wrapped around the gearshift. "It suits you. The car."

I smiled softly, thinking about the Jeep I drove. "I know it's kind of a ridiculous car to have in Philly. We all know it. But Rodrigo wanted to go off-roading and spent weeks constructing his case to Papá."

"Let me guess," Ethan said with a smile, "He told your dad you could use a Jeep Cherokee to haul stuff for the gym."

I chuckled. "Yeah. Exactly. It guzzles gas, but we live in the city, so we never drive it that far."

"It wouldn't even fit all eight of you inside," Ethan said, shaking his head.

No, but Mamá had her van for that. And besides, if we had two cars instead of one, he could drive me to school or back home sometimes, too. As soon as he mentioned that, I argued the case with him. I begged him to let me drive it."

"Did he?"

"Eventually," I said softly. "They all tried to teach me to drive a stick shift, but none of them had the patience. In the end, Mama taught me to drive it."

I remembered the day we brought it home. I was thirteen. It wasn't brand new – we'd found one that was two years old – but it was shiny and black and to me, it was more gorgeous than a diamond. Alejandro perched me on the hood and gathered our brothers around the jeep. Abuela had snapped a picture, shaking her head and clucking at how silly this whole thing was.

We were at cruising speed on the Schuykill Expressway, and my hand rested loosely on the gearshift, not needing to change until we slowed down some. He placed his hand over mine, gentle and warm, and moved his thumb over the place where my pinky finger joined my hand. "That's you," Ethan said. "You decide what you want and go after it headlong. It's amazing that you were the same when you were in junior high."

"I'm not the same," I told him, surprised at how quickly the words flew out. "I used to want what other people told me to want. Now I want what I want. And I go after it."

"Yeah," Ethan said. "You sure do." He said the words softly, but they came with a strange tension I couldn't name.

The last ten minutes of the car ride were pretty quiet. That was one thing I'd always liked about Ethan – his ability to sit with me quietly. He didn't need me to talk to him to feel self-assured.

As we pulled off the highway, though, he did start to fidget. "So... I prepared myself for every eventuality here, Natalia. I just want you to know that not a single one of them filled me with excitement, but I am still really damn happy to see you. To spend time with you. So, you know... do your worst."

I smirked. "That's why you came out with me, huh?"

"That's why I came," he said resolutely. I turned onto the street Arturo had told me to, and the long, flat roof of the Philadelphia Police Training center came into view.

"Not because we made a deal, huh?"

"No. Well, yes. But mostly no. It's mostly you."

I switched off the engine, and something about the sudden silence in the car made my senses go into overdrive. The day was overcast, chilly, and something about the pervasive gray made the space here inside the Jeep feel like it was charged with wild color. Ethan was here, with me, about to do something dangerous. And suddenly, all I wanted to do was to put my mouth all over him. I looked over at him slowly, only to find his eyes fixed on me.

His voice came out slow, deep, and gravely. "I'm sure you have an awesome date here planned for us, and as terrified as I am of what it involves, I think we should step out of the car before we spend the entire time we have here in... here."

I blinked, trying to process the fact that Ethan had just basically read my mind. I stammered and nodded my head, not missing the quirk in his lips when I did. I bit my lip and nodded, turning in a whirl to open the car door.

He did the same, and we met out in front of the car, face to face, mouths inches away from each other. Ethan dragged in a shuddering breath, which pleased me. He was affected by being close to me, just as I was with him.

"While, as you know, I'm always up for sparring with you, I have to admit I'm hoping this isn't a self-defense class. I just keep thinking about the poor son of a bitch who has to get dressed in that padded suit, and the pissed off German Shepherd they always have charging him in those police academy videos. We're not doing that, are we? I mean, I don't even like dogs, and I don't think we have to let one of them attack me to prove -"

By now I was grinning at this random distaste for dogs that I hadn't even been aware Ethan had, while simultaneously wanting to calm his nerves. So I pushed up on my tiptoes and smashed my mouth to his. The electricity that had surrounded us in the car remained with our bodies, intensifying at the connection, and I suddenly wished very, very much that Arturo was not waiting inside for me. Even moreso as Ethan did that thing where he slid his tongue ever-so-slightly over my lower lip, then drew back just enough to suck it between his lips.

But in the next instant, he was rocking back, smiling at me. "Like I said," he chuckled softly. "Don't wanna miss that date."

I dipped my head in a nod and started to walk toward the unassuming building, stretched out tan and low against the drab sky. Ethan followed. I realized I liked this feeling, of Ethan playing the game, going along with what I wanted. It was more than him trying to make me happy. He was respecting a part of me, even if we didn't have that thing in common.

We walked with enough distance between us to prevent comfortable hand-holding. No matter what our previous relationship had been, Ethan still technically worked for The Knockout, which was really mostly working for me and working for my brothers only a little bit. Still, I knew at least one of them would have an Issue with Ethan and I seeing each other, even if I couldn't predict which one it would be. Best to avoid problems while I still could.

"It's closed," Ethan said, confusion wrinkling his forehead, when we arrived at the front doors and saw the darkened interior of the academy.

"Mmmhm," I agreed. "Closed to cadets, but Arturo is a more senior officer and decided to help us out. Today you'll be firing a Glock .22."

I swore I saw Ethan's Adam's apple bob - just enough of a sign that I'd planned a date with sufficient safety shock value. I grinned at him, then turned to greet Arturo, who was approaching from down the hall.

CHAPTER 16

ETHAN

WHAT THE FUCK? Guns? Was Natalia completely crazy? Did she know the statistics on how many people died accidentally from guns in this insane country every year? Even when you took away the examples of insane serial killers, it was still hundreds. No, thousands. In fact, the mass murderers got all our attention, or whatever little attention our country was willing to give them, at least, but most people in our day and age didn't kill each other on purpose. No. It was the kid shooting his cousin with the loaded gun he'd found under his mother's mattress. It was the dude whose camouflage blended into the brush just a little too well when he was out hunting with his buddies. It was the poor kid waiting in a convenience store line when a robber who never intended to shoot a soul, so long as he got his money, mishandled his weapon.

And I couldn't stop seeing one of us making a mistake here, today, and shooting the other.

That would be an awful fucking end to this whole crazy romance, wouldn't it?

I swallowed hard, hoping Natalia didn't notice, for some reason trying hard to hide my hesitation. Guns were nothing to mess around with. Aside from the danger, I'd never even felt the slightest desire to hold one of the things.

But Natalia was already strides ahead of me, chattering up a storm to her brother in Spanish, her infectious energy bubbling out of her as she punched him on the arm in one second and swung her arm around his neck to pull him into a hug the next. You could see it in his face - he was a sucker for her. Natalia, apparently, could put you under a spell, and I wasn't the only guy who was susceptible to falling for it.

Arturo let us into the gun range, handed each of us a weapon, and then, after tossing me a look of half-sympathy, half-apology, left, leaving us alone in the stark white cavernous shooter's area.

"He said they're loaded," Natalia explained, in a tone that suggested that would put me more at ease. It did not. Instead I was now thinking about all the pre-loaded weapons that must just be laying around the police academy, waiting for someone to do something stupid and fuck up and hurt someone at the academy without even realizing what they were doing.

But Natalia handled her weapon like a pro, and I stood there watching her, mesmerized by the sure movements of her fingers, the coolly confident way they wrapped around the weapon. The next thing I knew, she was fitting a solid black handle into my hand, and I forced myself to pay attention as she explained the controls. It wasn't easy. As surprisingly fascinating as it had been to watch her with her own gun, feeling the movements against my own hands threatened to drive me wild.

"Just make sure that any time you are going to let down your concentration - whenever you're not ready to one hundred percent focus on your weapon and its target - you flip up this safety. The number one thing we're concerned about is having a hot weapon pointed at something living and breathing. Or, you know, something easily destroyed by a bullet."

Natalia had been sweet and playful and, with that kiss, just plain hot since she'd picked me up in her old Jeep almost an hour ago. But now she'd morphed into Business Natalia, Teaching Natalia, the Natalia who put up with zero shit and expected zero shit to have to contend with. And, I realized, she was right. Every anxiety I had over guns had been overshadowed by my nearly uncontrollable boner for her, but she was putting the scared right back into me.

I nodded, licked my lips, swallowed my pride, and asked her to go over everything one more time. Just to be safe.

She cracked a stunning smile and did as I asked.

"Now, watch how I stand. Legs far enough apart to hold my body steady, one foot in front of the other. If your feet aren't planted, the kickback can make you stumble. If you stumble," she said, stepping back from me and holding the gun out in front of her, "Your body tilts back, your arms tilt up, your aim goes completely off, and suddenly you're shooting into the sky. And that's best-case scenario. You could shoot a bird, your neighbor's cat hiding in a tree, a power line, or even a person, I guess. Anyway, plant your feet."

I tried to mimic her stance, but with the height of my athleticism being taking a jog now and then, I just didn't have a feel for it. Natalia crouched down at my side and moved my legs into place with her hands. Damn. Any part of me that doubted how being at the shooting range could be an incredible date was being proven wrong.

Same thing with the way I held the gun. I loved the feel of Natalia's small, tight body standing behind mine, settling the earmuffs on my head, her arms framing mine, guiding me into exactly the right stance. Just when I was thinking that my attitude toward this stance was about to turn from savoring to ditching the gun and ravaging her, she backed away, squeezed my ass, and stepped to my side. "Pull your ass in, too," she whispered in my ear before nipping at it.

"I think we're ready," Natalia said, stepping over to the shelf in her lane and picking up her gun. She hit a large black button to make two paper targets come down the track and approach us.

"I gave yours the beginners setting," she said, giving me a smirking side eye.

"What is that, twice as close as yours?" I asked, generally not minding at all. I realized my hands had started to shake just a little, holding this weapon that was so small and compact but could also cause such devastating damage. I'd read more than most people about what bullets did when they penetrated a human body, and I tried not to think of it any more than I absolutely had to.

Strangely, though, a sense of calm sort of draped over me now, watching Natalia fit headphones over her ears, take her stance, aim, and fire. The muffled sound and the bright white worked together to paint her in a dramatic silhouette, and for a few seconds I noticed every single aspect of her - her solid legs, her mouth pressed into a hard line of concentration, the powerful, muscular arms bucking against each shot. She was doing something incredibly dangerous, at least it would be outside these walls, and she was unspeakably gorgeous.

Part of me wanted to step back and watch her for the rest of the time we were supposed to be here. But that wasn't the deal, and I knew it. I clenched my jaw and turned to my target, still pristine. I raised the gun, preemptively flexing the muscles that I knew would be required to make it fire. I took in a slow breath through my nose and let it out through 'o' shaped lips, just like Natalia had told me when her soft breasts and slim body had stood behind me, bracing me, teaching me. She was so expert. Knew exactly what she was doing.

Suddenly, there wasn't a shred of worry left in me.

I slowly pulled my finger back against the tight, cold trigger, and a millisecond later, the bullet was rocketing out of my weapon and toward the target.

And barely grazing the edge.

It was only then that I realized that Natalia had turned toward me and was watching me with a face that could only be interpreted as proud.

And my cheeks heated to blazing red.

"Obviously, I'm shit at this," I said, lowering my gun after making it clear that I was flipping on the safety.

"No, no," Natalia said, setting her own gun down and then crossing over to me. "That is actually, really, really good."

I raised my eyebrow and made a show of looking over at her target. There were no less than a dozen bullet holes, all solidly within the inner three rings of the target.

"No," Natalia said, setting her gun down and walking up to me. She cupped my face in her hand and said, "Do you have any idea how long I've been training to do this?"

I really didn't. I swallowed again. "You're twenty-six. How long can you have been doing this for? "

"Twelve years," she replied, jutting her hip and resting her hand there. "I was fourteen when Arturo let me come to the shooting range with him. He was just a cadet then. Took a few weeks of relentless begging, but I wore him down. I was addicted from the first time. And that first time I fired probably three rounds and hit the target three times."

"So you're saying I'm just as good at this as an average middle school girl."

"No," she said, stepping close to me, her eyebrows furrowed, the mixed signals between her stance and her face driving me wild. "I'm saying you're just as good as a freaking badassed stunt woman in the earliest days of her career. I am raw, incredible talent, Ethan Anderson, and don't you forget it. There are actresses out there who wish they were as good at shooting as 14-year-old me."

She was so close to me now that every fiber of my being just wanted to hoist her up, throw her over my shoulder, drive her home, and get her into bed. I leaned down and, fighting the raging desire coursing through my veins, kissed her as gently as I could. Then I pulled back just enough to murmur hot against her lips, "I never will. Forget it. You are incredible."

"Take me home," she breathed, curling her fingers into my shirt. In the next breath, she used that hand to push me away, so that I stumbled back on my heels. I caught myself and chuckled. "Yes, ma'am."

And that's exactly what I did.

CHAPTER 17

NATALIA

I DIDN'T KNOW exactly what it had been about the gun range, but holy hell, Ethan was fired up. And by Ethan, I mean Ethan's package. It must have been the sheer power he felt reverberating through his body, the awesomeness of holding such a powerful weapon in his hands. His hand covered my knee as I squealed out of the parking lot, and he only murmured, "be careful" instead of freaking out about my fast driving like I would have expected him to. Luckily, the Schuylkill was actually moving today, and not like molasses, either. We barely spoke as I pushed down on the pedal, speeding a little bit more with every mile that passed. I tried to cut off some cars, but Ethan made clear that he was not okay with that by digging his fingertips into my thigh, something that earned him a breathless chuckle from me.

Pulling off the highway, Ethan's fingers started to drum against his knee. A pleased flush spread through my chest. This was what he did when he was impatient, I now realized. Maybe I was glad that I'd started to work with him as well as date him, because this was good to know. Those hands I'd adored since the first day I'd encountered him, giving away that Ethan was absolutely impatient to get home.

If I was more anxious, or less sure of how he felt about me, or less accustomed to his body language, it might have worried me. But I knew damn well that Ethan didn't want to get home so he could get away from me. No. He wanted to get home so he could get me in bed.

There was no way on earth I was going to argue.

By the time we'd pulled onto Chestnut, Ethan's entire hand had started to tap on the armrest of the Jeep, and my small, private smile had stretched into a full-on grin. I leaned out the window to punch my code into the panel outside the garage door. The door protested with a squeak as it rolled up on its gears, badly in need of oiling, and I tried to calm the butterflies that had just appeared in my stomach. Because Ethan's strong, broad hand had slid from mine, which rested on the gearshift, all the way up my arm, to gently grasp my neck. I pulled into the small garage as quickly as was reasonable, then tugged the clutch into neutral and twisted the key decisively. I turned to Ethan to find his other hand, the far one, pulling up the parking brake, making the muscles in his forearm flex and twitch. In a flash, that hand moved to cup the side of my face, turning me toward him, while the one that had been resting on my neck moved down just far enough for his fingers to dig into the muscles between my shoulder and neck. The delicious pressure sent relaxation bleeding down my arms, softening my entire body into a lump of clay ready to be handled and formed exactly the way Ethan wanted me.

His mouth claimed mine as soon as my lips parted for him, just one sign of my entire body ready and willing to submit to whatever he wanted to do with it.

Yes, I was almost always more guarded with my personal space than I was in this moment. I hardly ever just offered myself up to someone in the way that my own body was begging me to do. I told myself it was because I trusted Ethan, that we had a little bit of a history, that he was working for my family and he had a thousand reasons to not hurt me or take advantage of me.

But the way my heart leapt at the groan that came out of his throat when our tongues met, the way heat pooled in between my thighs at the mere memory of what it felt like the last time he thrusted strong and insistent between them, told me that something more than implicit trust was driving our whole interaction.

I didn't really care what it was, though. I just knew at this moment that I needed Ethan, and needed him badly.

My torso twisted toward him in the most awkward way, and as amazing as it felt when his hand moved from cupping my cheek to brushing my collarbone to cupping my breast, squeezing it just right, none of it was enough.

I planted my palm on his thigh, lifted myself up, and swung my leg over his waist, so that I was straddling him in the passenger seat.

At least this big old Jeep gave us a little more room than his car would have. Securely perched on top of him, I ground my center down over his cock, which was already rock-hard and begging to get out of his jeans. I broke off our kiss, only to have Ethan start sucking at my neck in a way that made me feel close to coming right then and there. "Do you want to go upstairs?" I panted, giving in and letting my head loll back as soon as the words were out.

Ethan gripped the zipper of my jacket and wrenched it down, then tugged at the deep V of my t-shirt, pulling it away from my breast and moving his sucking kisses down past my collarbone to the swell of my cleavage. "No," he grunted before his lips surrounded my nipple, then pulled my breast deep into his mouth. An eternity of delicious seconds later, he pulled off with a loud pop, and I barely registered his words through the haze of lust that particular move had dredged up in me. "Can't wait. Need you now."

I barely managed a moan as he pushed the arms of my jacket down, then tugged my t-shirt over my head, then ripped the straps of my shelf bra off my shoulders, leaving it loosely circling my waist. Cool air kissed my shoulders and turned the wet remnants of Ethan's kisses into goosebumps. Sensory overload had never felt so sweet.

My hands fisted in his shirt and he leaned forward just enough for me to tug it over his head. I caught a glimpse of his face framed in the ridiculously tousled hair, eyes glazed over, lips swollen, and felt like my heart would burst. Then, his lips were on mine again, making my head spin, but not too much to start work on his pants. His hands were inside my pants, cupping my ass, and I thanked Past Me copiously for choosing stretchy pants instead of the tight, inflexible jeans that held my lower half in a vise.

Our mouths kept up the sloppy attack on each other, tongues darting and teeth grazing, as I wrenched my feet out of my shoes and pulled one leg out of my pants. Within a few more fumbling seconds, the button to his jeans was undone, his boxers pulled to the side, his cock hard, hot and heavy in my hand.

"Condom?" I managed breathlessly, and he groaned in response, digging one out of his back pocket. While I rolled it over him, two of those thick, strong fingers plunged right inside me, making me gasp. His thumb wasn't wasting time either, pressing hard on my clit and moving in tight, insistent circles.

I planted one foot on the inside door jamb, lifted up, and lowered myself onto Ethan. A deep groan of satisfied relief eked its way out of my throat, filling the small space that surrounded us. Dammit, this was heaven.

I loved Ethan's cock. Would have worshiped it if it wasn't sacrilegious. It was just long enough to touch, but not bruise, my cervix, nice and thick, with a slight curve upward at the end. This cock did things to me that no other man's had been able to do, and I every time we had sex, I felt myself slipping a little further into fully addicted territory.

The only thing I loved almost as much was his hands, which had left my clit and moved to a strong grip on my hips. Every inch of him was solid, muscular confidence, and I gave myself over to the pace he set, lifting my hips so they slid off his length and then tugging me back down onto his lap, hard. My hip joints strained, warning me of the pain I was just asking for a few hours and days down the road. I didn't care. Ethan's body joined with mine so automatically, mouth meeting neck, his hard chest cradling my soft breasts, his big hands flaring out perfectly from my waist down over my curvy hips, that a little strain hardly seemed to matter.

He set a punishing pace, and a small corner of my brain marveled that he could thrust into me so powerfully when he was under me. But the rest of my brain was occupied by the pull of his cock against that spot inside me that sent me barreling faster than anything else toward orgasm. And not just any orgasm - the kind that turned you inside out and upside down, the kind that took over every one of your brain cells and did a full-consciousness reset, the kind that made you never want to do anything other than this for the rest of your life.

The hot itch of pleasure moved from my center up to my stomach, down my thighs, made my shoulders raise up in anticipation, racing through every sinew and cell of my body. Incredibly, I felt Ethan get even harder inside me, and he let out a low groan that sounded like a man on the brink of losing control completely.

"Tali," he growled, and I whimpered his name in answer.

The hot race toward complete release edged out every other feeling, every other thought, except how desperately thankful I was for Ethan beneath me. He gripped my hips even tighter, holding me flush to him while still thrusting wildly, the pace exchanging depth for speed. His cock pushed insistently against that spot inside me, and in one sudden, spectacular moment, I went over the edge of bliss, screaming his name and gasping strings of nonsense words over and over again until he finally stilled inside me.

Breathless, I let my head fall forward until my forehead rested in the nest of thick hair on top of his head.

I'd never been so thankful that we had a single-car garage in my life.

Ethan was busy recovering, dragging in deep breaths punctuated by soft brushing kisses against my hot skin. As my breathing slowed, the chill came back to the air around us, and I shuddered once.

"Oh, babe," Ethan said, finally looking into my eyes once again. "I'm so sorry, I just -"

I pressed a finger to his lips. "Do I look upset? Does this," I leaned down to kiss him, full and soft, "*feel* bothered by the amazing sex we just had?"

"I couldn't wait," Ethan whined. "I don't know what happened, but... I couldn't."

"Again. Not complaining." I actually loved it. I didn't know what to call the kind of energy between us that made the air pop and fizz with every breath, every look. I just knew I liked it.

For the next few minutes, Ethan and I detached from each other and cleaned up as best we could. I found my shirt and tugged it back over my head, laughing at the pout on Ethan's face as he watched me. Finally, I plopped back into my seat, squirming a little at the soreness already forming at my hip joints. "So," I said, trying my very best to sound detached, "Guess that ends the date, then."

Ethan's head snapped to the side, his questioning look both hilarious and adorable. "You guess wrong. I mean, unless *you* want to end it."

"Not really, I just... danger. You know? The gun range, sex in a car.... ? Checks two boxes."

"Oh, I'm sorry. I thought the sex in the car thing constituted one of my dates. Fun, safe, one hundred percent private?"

I cocked my head and studied his face, trying to figure out whether he was joking. "Um... sure? Though I could have been, like, impaled by the shifter."

With that, Ethan burst out laughing. "Well, I felt one hundred percent comfortable and delighted to have sex with you in this semi-vintage Jeep. So, I think this can only mean that now we are officially on one of my dates. That is, if you're not opposed to a double header. "

"I am not." I said.

"But?"

"But... we're here. At my place. Exhausted and sweaty."

"Yup. Which makes this the perfect opportunity to do the bubble bath, movie, and pizza date."

My mouth dropped open, and I was suddenly at a loss for words. When Ethan had suggested safe, normal, low risk dates, I thought he'd had something different in mind. "I thought your safe dates would be like... going to the movie theater. Trying a new restaurant."

"Those too," Ethan said. "But this one on the list. I ranked them, in case you decided you wanted to be done trying the safe-date thing with me after just one. Bubble bath, movie, and pizza is my number one choice. So, what do you say?"

His voice dropped off, and I swore I heard a little bit of shake to his voice. He was nervous. Maybe most people wouldn't hear it, but I did. It was kind of hard to believe that someone could be nervous about asking you to stay in and watch a movie with him after he'd just fucked you senseless in the front seat of your car, but this was Ethan Anderson. Ethan, who I was quickly learning was not your normal, often-cocky, post-grad bro. He was complicated. In an entirely different way than I was, but complicated all the same.

"I say yes, please," I said, my heart warming at the flicker of happiness that danced through his eyes. "I just had kind of an unexpected workout," I said, reaching in the back seat to grab my bag. I stuffed my keys in it and then squeezed Ethan's hand. "I expected my shoulders to be sore, but it's more my lower half, now."

There was that beautiful, self-confident smile. "Next time I'll try to warn you."

"Oh no," I said as I opened the door. "Don't. It's more fun that way, don't you think?"

He didn't have a chance to respond before I got out of the car and headed toward my stairs. He caught up to me in a few seconds, grabbed my hand, and leaned down to smack a big, wet kiss on my cheek.

Despite a date at the shooting range, walking to the stairs, my fingers intertwined with Ethan's, watching the single caged incandescent lightbulb flicker slightly above us - all the factors made the aftermath of this date so non-thrilling, so normal. It didn't matter. My heart was still beating even faster than it had been with that Glock .22 in my hand.

CHAPTER 18

ETHAN

ONE OF THE benefits of Natalia's room having previously been an Air B&B was that it had a big tub tucked into the corner of her little bathroom, and it even featured a couple of high-powered jets. Within 20 minutes, we'd changed out of our clothes, which now smelled like the cool outside air mixed with sweat and sex with the slightest hint of gunpowder, and slipped into a steaming hot tub. The bubbles all came from the jets - Natalia reminded me that if we put even a little soap in this tub with the jets on, tomorrow there would be a puddle somewhere in The Knockout that would make her very cranky.

Obviously, cranky Natalia was something that I wanted to avoid at any cost.

Bubbles were out, but she did let me rub conditioner through her long, thick waves as she sat between my legs. Yeah, my dick was already hard again nestled between her gorgeous curvy ass cheeks with only a whisper of water between them. But the way her head lolled back and her throat made quiet, happy moans when my fingers worked through her strands made ignoring the bastard the obvious choice. I wasn't going to interrupt this quiet stillness. Not for anything.

"So, what did you think about the shooting range?' Natalia asked.

"Well," I said, leaning forward and planting another kiss on her neck. "I've got to be honest, I don't love guns. They're dangerous and the leading cause of death in the United States." With just those words, I felt her tense under my hands.

"Gun *violence* is the leading cause of death in the United States," she grumbled. I had to give it to her. She was right. For all her tough façade, Natalia didn't take criticism well. I wasn't criticizing her, but to her, it sounded like it. I needed to work on that.

"I'm glad Arturo was there," I continued. "It was good to know we were safe."

"We were safe because I knew what I was doing, Ethan. I don't need my brother to watch me all the time in order to be safe."

Oh, shit. I was just digging myself into a deeper hole now. "That's not what I meant. I just... it was good that it was in an official place. I meant I'm glad we had access to a safer range."

She nodded quietly. "You know, all the stunts I ever do are as safe as possible."

I wanted to say something about how "safe as possible" is still not really that safe for the vast majority of stunts she was doing. I watched enough movies to know that a body flying through the air is still a body flying through the air, even if it's going to land on a cushion. Add heavy machinery like cars, and projectiles like bullets, and... yeah. But I took a deep breath. This was not the time. This was my date, and I wasn't going to start a fight I couldn't win with words. That much, I'd learned.

I didn't want to fight at all, actually. I hadn't planned on turning tonight into one of "my" dates, but I just liked being with her too damn much. That, and after I literally couldn't control myself and took her in her car, it felt like kind of a dick move to have the date end there.

"And, you know," I continued, just trying to keep the conversation going, "I liked how I felt, doing it. It made my body feel powerful in a different way than, like, running. Or lifting weights."

"Right?" Natalia said, her voice a little higher and more awake than it had been just moments ago. "I mean, it's so much potential energy, just held there in your hand. You know? Any weapon will do that – swords, bo staffs – and all in completely different ways. You feel like nothing could touch you."

"Mmm," I hummed into her hair. "You looked like nothing could touch you, too. I think that's why I wanted to so badly. Watching you shoot that, I felt kind of..."

"Terrified?" she supplied, her head turned half-back, waiting for an answer. I brushed a kiss on her temple and moved my hands to her shoulders, rubbing circles deep into her muscles with my thumbs.

"No," I said. "I guess... proud? Does that make sense? That you looked so sure of yourself, and strong."

That was when she sat up, turned to look me fully in the eye. "Seriously, Ethan? That's the sweetest thing anyone's said to me in a really long time."

I let out a brief chuckle. "Most girls want to hear how cute their shoes are or how I love their haircut. This girl wants to know that I think she looks hot holding a gun."

She arched an eyebrow at me. "Don't say 'most girls,' Ethan. This society, this *world*, was built around what men think, and the way they want girls to be. I would be willing to bet that a lot of women would love to know that their strength and confidence was a turn-on."

I'd been dating for a while. And in my twenty-seven years, I'd had a lot of fun with a lot of different types of women. I'd been friends with a few women, too – mostly ones I couldn't date, like my best friends' sisters - and not a single one of them had ever taken me to task on the way I complimented her and all womankind.

Instead of feeling chastised, I felt incredible. I felt energized, surprised, and challenged by the new and unexpected things that came out of Natalia's mouth every single day. All of a sudden, the most overwhelming feeling washed over me - I wanted more from her. I wanted tomorrow, and the day after that, and the one after that. My arms tightened around Natalia, pulling her close to me.

"Mmm," she said, her voice all relaxed pleasure. "I've gotta say, I'm surprised you're not grabbing my boobs. I'd say ninety-eight percent of straight men would be going in for round two right about now. While we were already both naked."

"Then you know that I'm not most men," I countered, barely finding words in time to avoid sounding like a stammering idiot. "This is 'my' date, and it is not time for round two. It is time to cuddle up and watch a movie with you in fluffy pajamas."

"And then round two?" I couldn't tell if she sounded teasing or hopeful.

"Maybe. Depends how you're feeling after my choice of film."

"And what might that be?"

I gripped her waist and hoisted her a little off my lap, moving her to another side of the tub so I could climb out, grab us towels, and offer her my hand. When we were both wrapped up, she wrung out her hair, plopping a fat stream of rapidly chilling water on my foot. I yelped, sounding horribly like a middle-aged lady, then pulled her laughing body to me. God, I just wanted her in my arms. I hadn't felt like this with a girl in as long as I could remember. But I resisted, holding her out at arm's length for dramatic effect. "I'm shocked you haven't guessed, given the earlier events of our date."

She groaned. "We're not watching a porn."

"Of course not," I said. "We're watching Police Academy."

"Why are we watching Police Academy 3?" Natalia groused. As if she'd seen any of them. As if the actual movie mattered when we were snuggled up under a blanket like this, exchanging light kisses, letting our hands wander over each other's bodies.

The Pizzeria Capelli box lay askew on the floor, with only a single piece left. Natalia had housed at least three slices, and watched me do the same plus one more. Then she'd kissed me, long and hard, and declared a new rule that if one of us was going to eat garlicky food the other had to as well, because she wanted "full tongue-use privileges." The expression had drawn a laugh from deep inside me, and I felt more wholly myself than I had for a long time.

I'd notched myself into a corner of the couch and spread my legs wide enough to cradle her muscled curves between them. It was simply incredible to hold her like this, touching all of her with all of me, all at once. I could take my time appreciating her, run my fingertips over the skin of her waist or wind a strand of her hair around my finger in the same moment I thought of it. I'd never been a possessive guy – I'd liked dating other women, but never before felt this peace while holding them in the circle of my arms. Never once had this urge to wrap one of them in my embrace and call them mine.

Natalia was different, in every way.

I nestled my nose behind her ear, letting my lips brush her neck and breathing in the scent of her shampoo. Her hair was thick and soft, with huge, gentle waves. "Because I am only bringing the best to the dates I plan for us. And it's common knowledge that Police Academy 3 is the best Police Academy."

Natalia snorted and scooted her butt further back, craning her neck so she could brush a kiss along my jaw. God, this was heaven.

"So you're telling me that this incredibly long motorboat chase with ridiculous music is the best this movie series has to offer? Out of all, what? Four of them?"

"Please, Natalia. You wound me," I said, curling my fingers into her side and tickling her gently. She squeaked and nestled further back into me. "There are seven, and yes, this is the best one. That doesn't mean any of them are good."

She groaned into a laugh, which made me grin. "The motorboat scene," I continued, "has the very specific purpose of giving us a window to graduate from light kissing to full-on making out. And whatever else you may request."

"You make this sound like a restaurant, where I can order up anything I want from you," she replied. I didn't miss that her voice had gone deeper, a little breathless. That feeling, of being able to do that to her – I wished I could bottle it. Being with her like this made me feel invincible.

"That's exactly what this is," I said, chancing an open-mouthed kiss at the juncture of her neck and shoulder. "Tell me what you want."

Natalia laughed softly. "I don't think you're going to like this," she said.

"Of course I will. I'm with you." Cheesy, but I meant every word.

"Well, I don't necessarily want to, but my body wants to sleep," she said, followed by a perfectly timed jaw stretching yawn. "My shoulders are sore," she said. She turned her torso to watch my reaction.

"Okay," I said, moving my hands from her waist to her shoulders and giving them a long, slow rub down her arms. She moaned in a way that sounded almost identical to the first sounds she made when I kissed my way down her body. Sexy as hell, but I was tired too. I only felt the smallest stirring in nether regions at the sound. "So, let's get you to bed, and maybe a back rub?"

"Ethan, you don't have to," Natalia said, even as her eyebrows pulled up hopefully.

I gripped her waist again and hoisted her up and over to the other couch cushion, swung my legs down, and in one fluid motion, scooped her off the couch and strode to the bed, where I laid her down. Natalia sank into the comforter and moaned again, flipping over and muffling the sound in the pillow. Her round ass curved up tantalizingly, and I wanted my body to be flush with hers again more than anything in the world. I climbed over her, straddling her back, and readied my hands for a massage.

"Ethan," she whined, "What are you *doing*?"

"Giving you a shoulder massage?" I ventured.

"In jeans? For goodness' sake, take them off."

"Tali," I said, my voice gruff with warning, "if I take these jeans off and get in this bed, it's going to be very, very hard for me to leave."

"Oh. Right." She swallowed and studied my face. "I get it if you don't want to stay –"

"Oh, babe, I want to. The only thing I don't want is to presume things."

"I like having you here," she said softly. She shrugged with one of her sore shoulders. "It was a nice date. Will you stay?"

She hadn't even gotten the last word out before I'd jumped out of bed and yanked my jeans off. I'd never been a stupid man. I didn't need to be asked twice.

"This doesn't mean you've changed my mind," she said, moaning again when my hands covered her naked shoulders.

"About what?" I asked innocently, smirking at how happy Natalia seemed to be having a night in, watching a stupid movie, and eating pizza. Ending with a backrub in bed, I couldn't think of a more normal, safe way to date someone you were interested in. Someone you wanted to spend a lot more dates with.

"If you want to keep dating me," she grunted as I dug a thumb into her trapezius, "the next date is mine. That means big adventure. It's going to be more intense than shooting guns at the Academy," she warned, punctuating it with a whimper when I flattened my palms and swept them from her neck to below her shoulder blades. "I love your hands," she said. That simple sentiment had my heart clenching, then bleeding warmth through my chest.

"Yes, I know," I said. I squeezed her shoulders a few more times for good measure. Her eyelids were drooping, the pauses between blinks getting longer and longer. Slowly, I moved out of my straddle to lay beside her, sliding my body under the covers and then gently tugging them from under her limp body and over her. I pulled her to me, and she practically purred as she let her limbs mold to mine.

"You know what?" she asked, her words heavy and slow with fatigue. "That I love your hands or that the next date is a crazy one?"

"Both," I said. I brushed a kiss across her forehead. I actually hadn't known that she loved my hands, but I was damn overjoyed to hear it. Maybe, somewhere, I loved that she was getting attached to me, any part.

"And you still wanna stay the night?" she mumbled into my chest.

"There's nothing in the world I want more," I said, only lying a little bit as I pulled her even closer. Her body grew heavy with sleep, and for that one moment, I was the most hopeful man in the world.

CHAPTER 19

NATALIA

I TOLD myself that this would be the last time Ethan would stay over for a long, long while. This relationship was, by definition, in a testing phase. The morning after our Police Academy date, I woke with the warm, reassuring weight of Ethan's body stretched out behind mine, fitted to it like a custom mouthguard, his arm draped over my waist, his fingers just barely brushing my belly under the camisole I'd fallen asleep in.

I never slept in. I wanted to get up, to train, to learn, to grow, to accomplish something while the sun was up. Every day. I was that annoying morning person who never hit snooze. In my whole life, I hadn't really even taken much care to pick out bedding. I didn't care, because I wasn't going to spend much time in my bed, anyway.

I'd only ever had two other boyfriends I allowed to sleep in the same bed as me. One of them snored, and the other kicked. But Ethan... Ethan. Ethan just fit. Perfectly. He wasn't snoring, wasn't making it hard for me to breathe. I wasn't covered in sweat. He hadn't hogged the blankets. The best – or worst – part was that his skin against mine sent my brain into overdrive, remembering what it was like to have him inside me, within seconds.

Yep. There it was. He was quicksand and I was putting myself in very serious danger of getting trapped for good. Being trapped meant I'd stay with him – for months, or maybe years – and that meant I'd have to change my goals, give up my dreams. Being at The Knockout had already derailed that enough. That was enough to get me out of bed.

With every cell of my skin protesting against the chill that detaching from Ethan caused, I slid out of bed and stood there, arms crossed, watching him. The muscles in his forearm flexed lazily as he slid it over the sheet where I'd just been laying, and his eyebrows furrowed when he didn't find me. His fists clenched around my pillow and he pulled it to him, sniffing what would have been my head. I smiled. My shampoo must really have had a distinctive scent.

But a smell wasn't enough to satisfy Ethan, apparently, because after a couple seconds, he shoved the pillow back to its spot and felt around for a few more futile seconds before dragging his eyes open. His lids, with their thick black lashes, looked like they weighed ten pounds each. The effort he seemed to be using to open them made me pity him; I bent down and rested my hand against his cheek, running my thumb gently over his eyelid. "Hey, sleepyhead, I've gotta get down to the gym. Client," I lied swiftly, knowing that the class schedule was online.

I bit my lip, hoping my voice didn't betray that I was trying like hell to get away from him right now. If I got back in bed with him, which my body wanted to do so very badly, I might never get out. Well, not for a few days. And by then I might be completely, hopelessly in love with this guy who was convinced he could get me to live a safe, calm life after a few dates and some sex.

Some incredible sex. But still, just sex. *Get your head on straight, Natalia Ortiz. You are not back here in Philly to settle down. You're not even here to have sex, as good as it may be. You're here to take care of business, do right by your family, and get on with your life.*

"I've gotta get to work anyway," Ethan mumbled. He rolled over and I fought against a whimper. His torso, dusted in dark hair, showed every beautiful muscle in the golden morning sunlight. The arm that had been protectively slung around my waist now laid on his abs, drawing attention to how very, very much I would like to suck love bites all over them. Then he sat up, and I was in even more trouble. His shoulders flexed, and his arms wrapped around his knees.

I really did love his hands.

"Meet you at noon?"

"Ethan, I – I mean, another date like four hours after the first one?"

"Second and third," he corrected. "Remember? Morimoto's?"

"Whatever," I said. My mind raced. I did want to go on more dates with Ethan. Didn't I? But this was soon. Too soon for me to talk sense back into myself, to steel myself against falling over the edge of this strange ground I suddenly found myself on. Wanting him. Not wanting to live the life he lived. The life he would ask of me, if I was his. "Maybe we should wait a few days to go on another date. Give me some time to get something good planned."

"Agreed," he said. "I was talking about the meeting we have scheduled today with the contractor to look at the basement storage area. A foundation assessment is on the checklist, remember?"

Instantly, heat flooded my face. "Oh. Right. Yes. Of course."

His soft smile wasn't fooling me. I knew he was highly amused by my being flustered by him.

He scooted to the edge of the bed, planted his feet on the floor, and stood before me. I thanked God, Jesus, and all the angels that he was wearing boxer shorts. If he'd been naked, I didn't think I'd have been able to leave him.

He held out his hands, and like magnets, mine gravitated to them. He folded them gently together. Big. Warm. Solid. That was Ethan. Something guaranteed. Something that knew what it was, what it would be twenty years from now, something that would always be there. He leaned down and dropped a soft, chaste kiss on my lips. I only got the faintest taste of him before he pulled away. "Go ahead and do your thing. I'll see you later."

It took less than five minutes for him to pull his jeans back on, grab his keys and his wallet, and leave the apartment. I plopped down on my couch and let out a long, slow breath. With Ethan gone, this space had changed. Last night, it was a cocoon buzzing with soft, happy energy. I looked at my rumpled bed and the pizza box still on the floor from last night. The morning sunlight had grown harsh, highlighting the sterile, sharp lines of my table and chairs.

I reminded myself that this had been what amounted to a hotel room up until a few weeks ago. I reminded myself that was why I'd liked it, back then.

What did I like now?

Maybe that was what I was here to figure out. Maybe Ethan was here to help me do it.

Four hours later, I'd worked out (in the gym, just in case Ethan looked around for signs that there had actually been someone using it this morning,) showered, and blow dried my hair straight and sleek. I tugged on a pinstriped pencil skirt and a white button-down; I had exactly eight pieces of clothing to wear when I needed to be anywhere but at home, training, or in the gym. All black and white, all coordinating. It was a wardrobe I'd acquired since taking over The Knockout, simple and portable. It was also a damn good look on me.

I probably could have met with Ethan and whichever contractor he'd decided to bring along today wearing my yoga pants and a sweatshirt, but something made me want to look damn good when I saw Ethan today. Even though I knew he already wanted me, wanted *more* of me. Even though I had a sinking fear that I'd eventually have to let him down.

So here we were. Back to business. Which was probably for the best.

The meeting was scheduled for noon sharp, and Ethan walked in at 11:59, with the basement inspector in tow. Ethan looked delicious in his suit, even though what really had my mouth watering was the memory of what every sinew and muscle looked like underneath it. How it had felt to press my skin up against his. *Focus, Natalia.*

The inspector took his sweet time walking the perimeter of our damp basement, and delivered the news at the end of the meeting – there were some cracks in the foundation, and even though the waterproofing we'd done fifteen years ago was more or less sound, the basement was still getting water in it. I tried to keep a professional, positive face, but once the contractor left, I buried my head in my arms.

I heard Ethan take a deep breath on the other side of the desk. "I know it's frustrating," he said, "But I'm honestly pretty pleased with how that went."

"How is that even possible?" I groaned into the nest of my folded arms. "He said the foundation is cracking. We have a mortgage that isn't paid off yet and a cracking foundation, Ethan! Not to mention old creaky windows, a HVAC system running up on twenty years, and old-school lockers and a skimpy schedule of classes that don't even come close to competing with the other gyms in Philly."

"That's right," Ethan said. "But I did some preliminary work with my real estate contacts this morning. You might still owe a not-small amount on this property, but what I don't think any of you realize is how the property in this area has skyrocketed in value."

"Ethan," I said as I raised my head, completely aware that my voice had taken on a murderous tone. I didn't care if I looked or sounded like I was going to kill him right now. He needed to understand this one thing. "I. Am. Not. Selling. The Knockout. My parents worked their entire lives to keep this gym up and running, and I'm not letting my mom's freak accident and Papá's cholesterol take it down."

"No, no, no," Ethan rushed in. "I mean... okay. How much is this building worth, do you think?"

I half-rolled my eyes. It wasn't worth much – I'd gotten that impression loud and clear from my brothers and Papá. I couldn't even bring myself to say it. Instead, I reached over to the post-it dispenser, adorably shaped like a ninja holding a board. I yanked a sticky note out of the top and scribbled the approximate figure, then smacked it down on the desk facing Ethan.

He glanced at it, then pressed his lips together. Slowly, deliberately, he reached across the desk to gently lift the pen from my fingers. When his skin brushed mine, I wished for a brief moment we really had been able to freeze time in the golden moments of this morning, sleepy and warm and tangled up in a cocoon of our own making.

He put the pen to the paper and scribbled out one thing, then wrote a couple more. Then he gently set the pen down, peeled up the note, and repositioned it in front of me. "That," he said, his eyes kind and patient, "is what I'm talking about. Yes, you owe some money on it, but it's worth a lot more than what you thought. Add together what the contractor from today quoted, what it'll cost to redo the electrical, windows, and insulation, maybe build a couple of rooms for classes and buy some new equipment, and you're still in a better position than you thought you were in a couple weeks ago."

"I don't want to add to the mortgage," I said, wringing my hands. I'd been there for every moment of the work my parents and, later, my brothers had put into the gym. "Taking out credit based on the value of this place is just like erasing all those mortgage payments they worked their butts off to make."

Ethan shook his head. "Not at all. You take out that credit, you make the improvements, you increase the resale value *if* you decide to sell it, and best of all, you make it much easier for me to give you a much lower insurance rate."

My eyes went wide at that mention. "Meaning I could still do my dangerous stuff that requires the more expensive personal insurance?"

"Well, now I think we've talked ourselves in circles," Ethan chuckled. "You wanted lower costs, not cutting costs to make room for the price of your craziness."

"Nothing can contain my crazy," I grumbled. But my heart warmed at the realization that he was still thinking about how to help me get what I wanted – a life doing stunt work – regardless of whether he was comfortable with it. "What would you do, if you were me?" I asked softly, raising my eyes to his.

"I would... well, I'd definitely talk to the family. And, listen, this isn't set in stone, even though I wouldn't have mentioned a number I wasn't reasonably sure about. Let me talk to my appraisers, get one in here, and pull in some of my banking contacts. Sit with your brothers and your sisters. And your dad, of course. Ask them how committed they are to this gym being sustainable for the long haul vs. the importance of building a liquid cash pool. Mention the numbers. See what they think."

My stomach flipped. "I don't want them to think I can't make a decision on my own. This is, what? The second meeting I've called since they handed control over to me?" 25-year-old women were in a precarious spot, professionally. We couldn't make stupid mistakes, but we also couldn't ask for so much help that we appeared incapable. I knew from my business classes that women in business navigated this obstacle course every day. I remembered how exhausting it had been just thinking about it. Now I was living it.

"And it'll be the last one for a while, I think. After that we're just giving you a base level of insurance and drawing up a plan contingent on the improved building and business plan. And, Natalia, I'm not going to lie – it's going to take a while. Several weeks. A few months, maybe."

"So," I said, drawing out the word as the realization of what he said dawned over me, "you're saying that you and I are going to have to work together at least that long."

"Not, like, intensely. But yes, I'll remain on the case for that long. We'll need to check in regularly." His eyebrow flicked up so quickly I might have imagined it if I hadn't seen it a dozen times before. That was Ethan's mischievous look, and it always preceded him doing something deliciously wicked.

"So, more crazy dates?"

"If I must. At least, crazy dates to match my calm ones, until you realize that you don't have to be crazy to have fun with me."

I narrowed my eyes. He was insufferable about this, that was for sure. At least it was a cute kind of insufferable. "Still a deal?" he prompted.

Slowly, I stretched my hand over the desk. He took it in his, not like a prince would, not like I was something delicate. Palm-to-palm, our fingers folded firm over each other's, we gave the agreement a firm shake. "Still a deal," I agreed. Finally, I smiled.

. . .

Ethan had asked if I minded if he worked for a bit in the gym lounge area, then squeezed in a workout with Rodrigo. Apparently, Rodrigo had challenged him to learn how to box. The fact that he'd accepted had made me smile once I'd headed back to my office. Maybe the idea of dangerous stuff with me really was changing Ethan, even if only a little.

He'd showered and stuck his head in my office, and I hadn't been able to resist chatting with him about his day. That had turned into me noticing a pretty good cut above his eyebrow, which had turned into me dragging him upstairs to my place to patch him up. Now we were making out against the wall, first aid kit forgotten.

My phone buzzed against my hip, where I'd shoved it in the waistband of my pants. Not the most elegant solution, but I was not a purse sort of girl. I'd learned from my backpacking trips in South America that if you couldn't carry something on your person, you didn't really need it anyway – learning not to get bogged down had been the object of my four years away from home. I would have answered it, or at least looked at the screen to see who it was, but at that moment Ethan had started to do something to the inside of my forearm with his fingers, lightly tracing patterns there, moving toward my elbow slowly, that made my brain completely fuzzy. I looked up at him though heavy lids, and the soft look of adoration on his face made my heart stutter. Here was this guy, this *man*, who I'd found once, lost, and then found again. Who liked spending time with me, who wanted me, who adored me. *Me.*

Whose hand had moved from stroking my arm to reaching for my hip. Ethan pulled me in to him, and my whole world condensed to the point where his thumb had worked its way under the hem of my shirt and was now drawing a slow, intense circle around my hip bone. We'd been together less than twenty-four hours ago, and here I already wanted him again.

My thighs clenched together, and he tugged me closer, dipping his head to press his lips to my jaw in that way I loved so much.

And then my phone buzzed again.

"Do you want to get it?" Ethan said, voice low, at my neck. And then the reality of my life came flooding back. The Knockout. Dad. The House. So many factors that meant no, I couldn't just ignore a call.

"I don't want to," I sighed. "But I should."

"Probably a good idea," he chuckled as I fished the phone out of my waistband. "I have a meeting downtown in an hour. Would have been cutting it close."

"Presumptuous of you," I said with a grin. He just shot me a smile back, and I sucked in a recovering breath before touching the green button to answer the call.

"Natalia, sweetie," a rehearsed, syrupy voice came through the speaker before I had a chance to say a single word. "Thank God you answered, I thought my day was about to be positively ruined."

"C-Carol?" I asked, my brain finally catching up enough to identify the voice.

I'd signed with Carol about four months after arriving in LA.

"You're not thin, but you're not a body builder," she'd said. I remembered thinking that I had thought I was thin, up until that moment. That was LA for you. "And that hair," she'd gushed. "The movement is just to die for."

I'd been lucky enough to snag some roles as a stunt extra in one of those Godzilla films. A few dozen of us all jumped off a rising platform and landed on foam mats below. The platform would later be green-screened as the top of a building against the backdrop of a night sky, and we'd all be jumping to our deaths. At the time, it was an easy way to snag a few hundred bucks for a couple days' work. Most of my fellow extras had walked in with the same attitude. I'd walked away with an absolute love for stunt work. It was a rush, knowing I was helping to make something spectacular in my own small way. I'd loved the fast-paced, quickly changing nature of the job. It was good money that was also pretty safe.

The "safe" part changed pretty quickly, though, as I started feeling my way through the levels of stunt performing. I moved from jumping off stuff and running away from invisible monsters to working with simple combat skills on battle fields. The stunt directors picked up pretty quickly that I had a boxing and martial arts background, and within a couple months my name had started to float around as someone who could pick up fight choreography quickly and look good doing it.

The stunt actor community in LA was, by and large, supportive, and there was a small network of us that would exchange lessons on specific skills. I taught boxing to someone in exchange for him doing bo staff work with me. Another girl taught me basic fencing in exchange for what I could teacher her about hand-to-hand combat basics.

It was fun, sure, and for a few months, I was enjoying life, I had enough money to eat, and even enough to put some away.

Carol had helped me take all that disjointed, rudimentary work, and start to flesh out a career for myself. Together, we'd mapped out the things I'd need to do to reach the different levels of certification in the Joint Industry Stunt Committee's register, which would allow me to work for years to come as a much better-paid professional.

She'd booked me on a couple steady jobs and set me up on three times as many auditions when I'd gotten the call about Mamá. Everything had come to a halt then, obviously.

But now, she was calling me again. What had been a pipe dream, something theoretical, when I'd made this dating bet with Ethan, was now flooding back to my memory and reminding me of all the things I'd wanted for myself, of the person I'd been, before The Knockout took over my life. Just hearing Carol's voice had me pining or the LA stunt life again.

Hearing her description of the job in question only made me agonize that much harder. Before I'd left LA, I'd only started to train for motorcycle and other moving stunts – basically, putting all the skills I'd already learned in use while in motion. It was the height of exhilaration – the wind whipping around you, cameras right there in your face to capture every twitch of your shoulder, every beat of your heart apparent in the pulse at your jugular. In those moments, I may have been a stand-in for some famous movie actress, but that was just fine – I knew that when the movie hit the big screen, it would be my breaths, my heartbeats, my drops of sweat running over skin, that would make the audience go nuts. It was like this huge secret I got to keep from the rest of the world, and it was delicious.

"I've got an amazing opportunity for you, honey. Four and a half weeks from now. So it would be a series of stunts, this first one is really just motion, but then a couple months down the road we're working on moving on to automobile work, and I know this is branching out a bit for you, honey, but it would be with the door closed. I told them you didn't have the exact training for that, but I did show them your head shot and your stunt reel, honey, I hope you don't mind... and they said it would be a waste to send one of my LA girls out to the East Coast when none of them would be as perfect as you anyway, so it's kind of a miracle that you're back home in Philly now, if you think about it, and because you're such a dead ringer match for Natalia – can you believe that's the actual actresses' name too, sweetheart, I mean it's just too perfect –"

I sighed and dug a thumb into my right temple. Carol's non-stop run-on sentences had always made my head spin, but at least sitting in her little office in the Wholesale District had allowed me to see her mouth as it moved, and to take notes. To ask her, in person, to repeat herself. This phone call format was not going to work out for me going forward. If this ever happened again, that is.

God. *Was* this going to happen again? Was it possible that I'd be able to keep up with the stunt thing while working for The Knockout, in Philly?

I knew as soon as I thought it that the answer was no. There was no way I'd ever be able to work toward my stunt certification if I was stuck here in Philly instead of immersed in the stunt world. I'd have to at least live in New York. It was so close to Philly, but not close enough to manage the gym while living there and pulling stunt work, too.

Carol's chatter interrupted my spiral of hopeless thoughts.

"They'd be willing to get you on set a couple days early to do some training with you, and to get you fitted out in some extra safety gear too, of course, we love you so much, we'd never want you to get hurt."

And just like that I was jolted back to reality.

Me. Hurt. My promise to Ethan.

"So, anyway, when this dropped in my lap, at first I almost turned them down, can you believe it honey? But then I remembered you'd gone home and I *had* to call you. And you know how impossible it is to lock down a gig like this, so…"

"How long do I have to let you know?" I asked, chewing on my lip.

Carol let out a long whoop on the other end of the line. If we weren't on the phone, I swore I might have been able to hear her all the way in California.

"I didn't say yes," I said. God, this made my stomach twist. This decision. It was the first time in my entire life there hadn't been a clear "yes" or "no" lighting up in front of me. Yes, of course, I wanted this. Could I leave the gym for as long as it took to film these scenes? Maybe. Probably. Could I go back on my promise to Ethan, to not do any crazy dangerous things until the gym had been settled? Until our dates were done? Until our relationship had been settled?

"I'll let you know," I emphasized.

"Okay, babe. You let me know. The absolute latest I need to hear is four weeks from now, okay?"

"I promise." I hung up the phone with a deep breath and a sigh. Being an adult really sucked sometimes. Especially when you'd never signed up for it.

"Who was it?" Ethan mumbled against my collarbone.

My stomach flipped at the feeling, and my face flushed with the shame of keeping this from him, at least for now. I knew I couldn't bring him into this decision. He was far from reasonable when it came to me and stunt work. That didn't mean it was any easier to keep secrets from this man who already was entwined in every other aspect of my life.

My mind raced through what I'd actually said out loud to Carol. The lie came easier than I expected it to. "Salesman," I gasped out as his teeth worried against the skin of my shoulder. "Wanting to sell us new punching bags."

"See?" Ethan growled, sending shivers down my spine. "It could've waited."

My stomach flipped again, and I pushed out a laugh. It sounded breathless, even though it was really just nervous. As Ethan pushed my shirt off my shoulders and pulled my body close to his, I let all thoughts of Carol and stunt work and New York City fade to the background.

"...And that's why I think every aspect of this suggested renovation is completely necessary," I whispered to the empty room, testing the phrase to see how confident I could make it sound.

I'd set up chairs for all five of my brothers – even Alejandro – and their partners in the break room, which I'd been taking pains to tidy up and make look more like a professional work-space than the neglected lounge it had been since I was a child. If you wanted people to take you seriously, I remembered my instructors saying from one of my business classes, you had to look serious. That included the spaces in which you hosted meetings.

Yes, I knew my brothers were family. Ethan reminded me of that in the days of this week that I'd spent hammering out the details with him of his suggested renovations and improvements, calling and re-calling contractors to get adjustments and exact quotes, and, yes, stressing about how the actual meeting with me and my brothers would look. Feel.

Plus, there was the whole conversation with Carol hanging over my head. Ever since I'd spoken to her a few days ago, it had felt like my old self – the self I really wanted to be, deep down – and my new self – the businesswoman transforming her family's gym from the inside out – were both warring for my focus at one of the most stressful times of my life.

I surveyed the room while setting out the papers I'd prepared for my siblings to review. My cheeks flushed red when I saw the old couch in the corner, remembering the particular tinny squeak of its springs when Ethan had taken me from behind there just a few days ago.

Yeah, he'd made cleaning up the break room one of "his" dates. We'd been dusty, sweaty and gross, and smelled faintly of cleaning solution, but mine had been skateboarding lessons - by just showing up at a skate park. I knew from growing up in the city that the kids would be only too happy to lend us a board and a few minutes of tips just for fun. I'd expected the shock and terror Ethan had expressed at our lack of helmets, pads, and even our own boards, but I didn't imagine it being as hilarious as it was. We'd left with only a few scrapes and very sore quads.

Not too sore to tumble into bed afterwards, mind you.

I pulled in a deep, slow breath as my eyes flicked over to the clock. Ten more minutes now. I hadn't wanted to be so obvious as to put on actual business clothes, but I had taken extra care with my makeup - neutral, carefully painted colors - and with my hair, which I'd smoothed with leave-in conditioner and diffused dry to make my waves more polished and less wind-blown. I'd traded my sneakers for ballet flats and slid a jacket over my button-up. I breathed out. We were ready.

Almost like I'd called to him with my thoughts, Ethan appeared in the door, bearing a couple brown paper sacks. "What's this?" I asked, striding toward him, unable to suppress the smile on my face. He shrugged.

"I talked to Joey at Joey and Hawk's a bit about what you're doing here. Opened up a floodgate of stories from when she and Hawk redid the restaurant years ago, which took up about an hour of my life I'll never get back. Upside? She sent us free snacks for tonight."

I wrinkled my nose. "Sorry. But they smell incredible, so I'd say it was worth it. What's in there?"

"The usual incredibleness. Little spinach quiches, bacon wrapped around... something. Dates, maybe? And homemade salsa with chips."

"Mmmm," I said, not bothering to mention that my family knew how to make salsa, and it was always, always better than anything you could find at a restaurant. I pushed up on my tiptoes and touched my lips, whisper-light, to his.

He pulled back and looked at me curiously, smashing his lips together. "What's this? Lipstick?"

The entire time I'd known Ethan, I hadn't put on more than a swipe of mascara or a little Chapstick. My face wasn't flawless by any means, but my warm skin tone and dark hair made it easy to go without makeup. My eyelashes were thick and dark, and my face didn't even get blotchy in the sun. I'd learned as a preteen that makeup was a waste of time and just plain silly if I was going to spend so much time in the gym. There was no point in making my face into a work of art if all that face paint was going to melt off in the ring.

I shrugged with one shoulder. "I want to look nice for this," I said. Honestly, I couldn't explain it even to myself. Just hoped that if I looked the part of Serious Business Woman Who Knows What She's Doing, my family would believe it. Wouldn't get a whiff of my plan to get The Knockout set on a good path and then, basically, to abandon it.

Alejandro came in first, looking simultaneously at his watch and phone. He gave me a flash of a smile before he smashed his thumb down on his phone and started barking at someone into his earpiece. He shifted from one foot to the other in the back of the room while the rest of my brothers, Amalia, Sarah, and Daniel trickled in. Arturo scanned the table of food that Ethan had set up, his eyes flicking back and forth, with a look of slight confusion on his face. I could almost see him working out the answer to a question he didn't bother to ask.

Ethan had tucked himself into a far corner of the room where he was tapping away on his computer, quiet and unassuming, like he was nothing more than part of the furniture in here. Arturo's eyes flicked to him, then settled on me. "Everything okay, Nati?"

"Perfect!" I said, wincing at the too-perky sound of my own voice. "I, uh..."

"Brought food," he finished, his suspicion evident in his tone. Then, decisively, he grabbed a tortilla chip and scooped up a generous helping of salsa with it, shoveling the whole big bite into his mouth. Mamá used to joke that Arturo was like a snake -

able and willing to unhinge his jaw just to fit more food in. These little memories about her usually caught me off guard, but tonight, I could almost hear her scolding my brother for wolfing down food, and it made me feel warm inside. Almost like she was right here with us.

"Homemade," Arturo nodded with satisfaction and complete confidence in his own assessment. Then he looked down and scooped a dollop of salsa off his uniform shirt and put that in his mouth, too. I rolled my eyes.

"Glad you like it," I replied without bothering to correct him. Sneaking a glance at Ethan, I caught his smug grin. I'd have to ask him where Hawk got that recipe. If Arturo was happy with it, the salsa must have been almost as perfect as Papá's.

Papá, who I hadn't seen in two weeks. He came in with Sarah, listening to Mariana prattle on about the differences between Facebook, Snapchat, and Instagram and which of her fifth-grade friends were allowed to have profiles on each. Sarah gave me a light hug and, noticing my curious look over at the unlikely pair, explained, "All he said was that he doesn't understand all this instachat and facegram business everyone seems so obsessed with, and she was off." Sarah tilted her head, considering them as Papá sat down wearily in one of the folding chairs I'd set up. "Actually, he seems pretty calm. Much less restless than he's been lately."

"That's good," I said, smiling absently. I tried to calm the shaking in my hands as Amalia, the last to arrive, took her place. All of my brothers held plates full of food - of course they did - and I made a mental note to than Ethan for thinking of bringing snacks. Of course, people were more amenable to changes of plan when they weren't hungry.

"I won't beat around the bush," I said. "I called you here because, while Ethan was doing the insurance assessment, we discovered that The Knockout will need a lot of work if we want to keep it open for the foreseeable future."

The group was silent for a beat, then two. Alejandro was the first to speak up, massaging his temples and muttering, "Of course it does. How much will it be?" And then the rest of my brothers all started talking at once. I tried to pick through the various shouts of "Did you get another opinion?" and "How much of that was the windows? Because I know a guy..." and "How long has this stuff been an issue?" and answer their questions calmly. The butterflies that had been multiplying in my stomach since I started talking whipped into a frenzy. Still, I held it together, and calmly explained the various assessors' recommendations for everything from the foundation to the security system.

It was in the beat of silence that followed when my father spoke. "It's so much money, querida."

"It is, but remember that we can leverage it against the value of the building. This real estate is gold, Papá. It's worth far more than you thought it was. Its value is at least twice what you told me."

He was pressing his lips tight and shaking his head slowly, though, which made my stomach twist in a knot. "This work - basement painting, beam replacement, new insulation and drywall - we can do all that ourselves. Right? There's no reason to pay contractors when we have seven strong men to lend a hand, right?"

His question to my brothers fell on silence. I pursed my lips. It figured that Papá would sooner count himself as a manual laborer before he considered that I could do twice as much as he could. Alejandro was suddenly looking very intensely at his phone, and Sarah was concentrating on feeding cheerios to Camila, who bounced on her knee. Christian and Daniel laced their fingers together and exchanged worried glances.

Shit. Shit, shit, shit. The recommendations I'd worked so hard on were going to get shot down, and I'd be back at square one. Be that much further away from getting back to the life I really wanted.

"Well," I said, wanting to be as careful as possible with my words out of respect for Papá, "It's really more of updating, instead of repair..."

"Meaning lighter work. *Mija,* you are strong. You can help me with drywall and the other things."

"Yes, Papá, I can help with framing and drywall. But I cannot lift the building up and repair cracks in the foundation. Or install all-new windows. Or climb on the roof and strip it down to tacks for a new one." Blankness overtook his features for a second. "It's too much work, Papá," I said, gentling my voice. "Plus, you..." I trailed off, not wanting to state the obvious. Thankfully, my siblings knew it.

"Amalia, tell them," my dad said, gesturing to all of us in the circle. Rodrigo squeezed Amalia's hand, and Sarah and hand. They both looked worried. Mariana glanced up from her phone, looking concerned as well.

"Ernesto," Amalia began, her voice gentle. "I know what the doctor said, but that doesn't necessarily mean..."

"Tell them! It's good news! We made a good decision and now it is paying off, no? I step down, I feel better, I can help Natalia a little."

Amalia let out a long breath, then smiled, like whatever happiness she had about this was a halfhearted afterthought. She looked up, not exactly meeting any of our eyes. "We saw Dr. Bastianon this morning. She said that things are looking..."

"Great!" Papá interrupted.

"Better," Amalia corrected. "Things are looking better."

"Tell them, Mali. My heart rate, my cholesterol. That *asqueroso* oatmeal you've been making me eat and the slow walks with Pepi have been helping." I smiled. Pepito was Papá's little old pug dog, who couldn't walk much faster than a turtle. "All that rest has been helping, no? And now I can get back to work. Just a little bit of work, some drywall and nails, to make my old man soul happy." Papá leaned back in his seat, slapping his palms to his knees like he'd solved everything by taking a couple weeks off.

Just like that, all of my brothers erupted into protest, flinging their hands around, sitting forward, Daniel even getting up out of his seat for a second, telling Papá that it was too soon, that there was no way he was getting back to work. Amalia just sent me a tired look, her lips pressed in a hard line, and I felt guilty all over again that Papá's care was falling most squarely on her.

Amalia must have noticed the expression on my face, because she stood up and crossed over to me where I leaned against the wall, watching my brothers have it out with Papá. "His labs did look better, Natalia," she said softly. "The EKG showed a little improvement, even. He just has to keep going to his follow up appointments. He promised he would. I think he was encouraged."

I ran a palm over my face, only thinking about my mascara after the fact.

"What if he really is doing better, though?" Alejandro said in a lull in the noise. He was still sitting there, quiet, his face open and hopeful.

"Okay, everyone just stop," I said, raising my voice on the last word. Everyone else fell dead silent. A fire lit in my chest and I suddenly wanted it all to be laid out there – that my brothers had passed The Knockout off to me because none of them cared about it to take charge of it themselves. That once I was in control, and proposing all these changes involving a lot of money, they regretted that decision. That now, they were thinking I really couldn't do the job after all. That maybe, deep down, they'd been expecting me to fail.

I glanced over at Ethan, who sat there, watching me steadily. His eyes shone. He was waiting for me to step up. And, I realized at that moment, it was exactly what I had to do.

"*Oigan, chicos,*" I said, in my kickboxing instructor voice, clapping my hands together once. They all fell dead silent, and I swear I saw Alejandro and Rodrigo sit a little higher up in their seats. All ten pairs of eyes around the circle were wide. "You entrusted The Knockout to me. We signed papers. There were lawyers involved. I *own* The Knockout now, do I not?"

Alejandro shifted in his seat. His fingers played with the edges of his cell, like he wanted to look at it, but was too afraid to look away.

"Perhaps," I said, trying to hide the shaking I felt in my voice, "We should all look through these pages again. I'm happy to start from the beginning, bearing in mind that the final decision is mine. I did not call you here to get your approval on the very educated business decisions I have made. I'm looking for support, and for constructive input."

I snuck a look at Ethan, who was looking at me like the damn sun was shining out of my face. Just like that, the shakiness started to dissipate.

Alejandro pursed his lips, and gave two curt nods. I knew he was playing out the scenarios in his head, and my other four brothers knew the same. After a few moments, he sighed, looked up at me, and said, "First of all, I think at least two more estimates for the foundation repairs will help you better plot out the rest of the budget."

"Okay," I said, grabbing a pen. "Now we're getting somewhere."

. . .

Thirty minutes later, I'd marked up my proposal with dozens of comments and things to consider from my brothers. We would do a couple DIY projects, and we'd source some materials ourselves to save on those costs. They had some great suggestions. Papá had been mostly silent, communicating in grunts and nods. It wasn't ideal, but it was something I could work with.

I promised everyone final decisions included in an updated proposal within a week, and they began to file out, giving me hugs and back pats and filling the plates Ethan had left out with the rest of the Joey and Hawk's goodies for the road. As I was giving Daniel a squeeze, I noticed that Alejandro was hovering in the back of the room, quietly talking to Ethan, who'd stood up. The conversation was quiet, and Ethan's expression was intense. Then again, Alejandro was always intense.

As soon as I caught sight of them talking, they shook hands and Alejandro turned and walked toward me. He pulled me into strong hug and squeezed me for a second. "You sounded like Mamá for a minute there, you know that?"

I laughed into his suit jacket. "Come on, Ale." My heart wrenched, and to hide the surge of emotion, I shoved him a little, breaking whatever physical intensity there was between us.

"You're doing good, Nati," he said into my hair, and then, without another glance, he was out the door.

Ethan still hadn't moved from his spot in the corner. He watched me, not saying a word.

Seeing him there, waiting, listening, the stress of having to put on the front of looking like I knew what I was doing in front of my brothers lifted off my shoulders. I was exhausted – more than I would be if I taught three classes back to back. Like a wet noodle, I slithered into a chair. Ethan crossed the room to me and sat in the chair next to me, then scooted it along the floor until his thigh ran flush against mine.

"Well?" he said after a few quiet moments.

"Well," I replied, "Let's get to work."

Ethan stretched his arm out toward me and spread his fingers wide. Without a thought, I slid my palm against his, and I heard the faintest sigh pass his lips.

"What did my brother say to you?" I asked, feeling the beginnings of drowsiness settling into my bones.

"Nothing," he murmured, leaning over to press a kiss to my head. "He was just asking me about my job with the firm."

"Mmm," I replied, knowing that that couldn't been the extent of what Alejandro had said to him. I also knew that I was so exhausted now that belaboring the point wouldn't help anyone. I decided to let this one go, for now. I let my head fall on Ethan's shoulder, and we sat there in the break room, listening to the buzz of the florescent bulb, until our feet fell asleep and we worked up the energy to leave.

CHAPTER 20

ETHAN

NATALIA'S FAMILY seemed really grateful to me that night for my help with Natalia's proposal, especially Alejandro and Mr. Ortiz. But really, Natalia was the powerhouse behind the changes that transformed The Knockout from an old traditional gym to something essentially the same yet also completely new. The two rings remained standing, so that the middle-aged men hoping to prove their strength and stamina in their regular weekly fights could still do so. The traditional locker room remained as well. But there was an abundance of extra space at The Knockout, especially once the contractors had done their magic in the basement. Slowly, there popped up a women's locker room, a yoga studio, and a small spin room with a dozen stationary bikes and black lights. Quietly, at Sarah's suggestion, Natalia put drywall up at three-quarter's height and lined the room with colorful flooring to serve as a babysitting space.

The gym regulars didn't say much about any of it, only casting wary glances as Christian and Daniel hauled in play pens and bouncers, which they'd purchased and delivered themselves out of the back of their SUV. A week after Natalia announced the babysitting rates, Jose, one of her dad's best friends, brought his four-year-old grandson to the babysitting room's check-in desk before his workout.

We popped a bottle of champagne that night.

Natalia and I spent a lot of time together over the next few weeks.By day, she was in the gym and I was in my cubicle, working on one of a dozen or so other insurance accounts Mr. Kennedy. Once or twice a week I made it over to The Knockout for a workout, even dragging Mark with me. I'd even convinced Toby, the sound girl for the Bro Show, to come to kickboxing class once, and Natalia instantly adored her. Some shit about growing up as girls learning to deadly sports – Toby's mom had her in Krav Maga - Israeli martial arts - since she was young.

Mark looked happier than ever when the four of us were together like this. My heart had been in the right place, pushing him and Toby together as part of The Bro Show, but I was worried now that it was going to turn out all wrong. I knew two things about what I was watching unfold between him and Toby – he was in love with her already, and she was in danger of getting there herself. The only bad part about it was that she didn't want to settle down. At all. No attachments, no roots. No taking care of anyone but herself.

Which was fine, but it was the absolute opposite of Mark's goal. Oops.

As the days, and our time together, stretched longer and longer, she even convinced me to go running with her. She never said it, but it became really clear really quickly that this was when Natalia did her thinking. We always set off together, but rarely talked unless she started a conversation. On some runs, we'd talk for twenty minutes about what we wanted to eat for dinner that week – on others, we'd spend 30 seconds in total agreement about what movie we most wanted to see next in the theater, and run the rest of the course in silence.

I didn't care either way. Just like in the bedroom, Natalia

and I were perfectly matched on the running trail. Our strides fit together, and we both started getting tired at around the same point. We worked together in tandem nearly flawlessly.

[Urrrrgh. Insert car date here?]

Rarely, Natalia would blindside me with something. It was early May, the day before her dad's birthday dinner. "Do you think I wounded him? Like, do you think he felt like less of a man, or something?"

She stopped at a bench, propped her heel up on the back, and stretched, even though we were nowhere near the end of our course. I jogged in place, trying to stave off the chill the wind was painting over my sweaty, bare arms. Normally I would have been happy to ogle her legs. Even though she wore long running tights, their shape was still clearly on display. Besides, I knew what was underneath them.

But I didn't ogle anything today. Natalia looked like I'd never seen her – fundamentally sad. Her complexion sallow, her lips curving down, her eyebrows pulled together – like her heart was in the process of breaking into a hundred pieces. The sight made mine feel like it was about to do the same.

"Who do you mean? Your dad?"

Just like that, Natalia's face crumpled. The tears that must have been gathering behind her eyes made their way to her lower lashes, streaming down her face as she nodded.

"Aw, Tali," I said, stopping my jog and walking to her side. She'd dropped her leg, and now looked at me with big, wet eyes. It was clear she wasn't going to run anymore, but she also seemed frozen in place. I knew what I needed to do for Natalia. I pulled my phone out and called an Uber, then pulled her into the circle of my arms.

Rubbing her back, I asked gently, "What do you mean? What made you ask that?"

"It's just... he hasn't been by in a couple of weeks, you

know? To The Knockout. He seemed okay with all the changes at that first meeting, but not, like, excited, you know? Then he stopped by couple of times to hold up drywall and swing a hammer, but still. I don't know."

"Okay, but is your dad *ever* excited?"

"I've seen him excited about soccer games," she conceded. "But still. This is what he called me home to do, you know? And then he wasn't at Sebastian's birthday thing early last week. I've called a couple times in the past few days and he doesn't seem like he wants to talk. And now it's his birthday and I can't avoid it anymore, you know? I can't avoid looking into his eyes and just knowing I've disappointed him."

I pressed my lips to the top of her head and sighed, holding her closer. Our car came and I held her in the back, rubbing her arm occasionally. We were a fifteen-minute jog from The Knockout, but the ride only took three minutes. I tipped the driver generously and made it clear how grateful I was to her as I guided Natalia up the stairs.

"Okay, the party's in two hours, right?"

"Yeah," Natalia said as she plunked herself down in one of the dining room chairs, undoing her laces with short, jerking motions. Apparently, she'd crossed over from sad to tired with a healthy dose of frustrated. At what, I still had to find out. "I just... I don't know. I don't want to go."

I pulled up a chair next to hers and held out my hand for the shoe she'd just taken off. She handed it to me, then started working on the next one. This was one thing I'd learned about Natalia – she would talk when she was ready. In the meantime, she would give me hints as to how she was feeling. The second shoe came off, I took that one too, and set it on the floor next to my chair. Then Natalia stood up and did something I'd never seen her do before – she started to pace.

It wasn't pent-up energy that needed to be punched out. It

wasn't the little shuffle I'd seen her do plenty of times now that signaled she wished the person talking to her would hurry up and stop wasting her time. No, this wasn't it at all. Her eyes looked at the ground one step ahead of her, empty and a little wider than usual. One clear thought came to my mind: This is what Natalia Ortiz looked like when she felt trapped.

After a minute or so, she stopped and stared at me, that same off-kilter look in her eyes. She blew out a long breath, and her shoulders slumped forward. "I've gotta get ready," she said, helplessly.

"Want me to come with you?"

She looked at me like she hadn't understood the question. Suddenly, a weird energy buzzed from my chest down my arms. My stomach pitched. I'd been in the same space as Natalia and her family several times, of course, and worked out with Rodrigo and Arturo a fair bit as well. I'd never attended a family function with her, though. Not as a business acquaintance or even a friend. Certainly not as anything more than friends. I realized that I was nervous – something I'd never felt with Natalia. Maybe, the moment before our first kiss... but everything up until this moment had felt so right, so certain. Now, it was like this one little question had pitched my entire outlook on our relationship into uncertain waters.

"No," Natalia finally replied. "I mean... you don't have to do that. It's, um... it's a family thing, anyway." Her eyes flicked to mine, and knowing that she was nervous too loosened something around my heart.

"Come on," I said, squeezing her arm. "How bad could it be? Your dad doesn't carry around a shotgun, does he?"

She looked up at me, her eyes wary. "Ethan, they don't even know that we're... whatever we are."

I bit my tongue. Hell, I didn't even know what we were. A time-limited sex-fest peppered with dates that we were only going on to settle a friendly score wasn't a relationship. At least, it wasn't one that Natalia had asked to acknowledge. I'd only asked her about the party because it was my knee-jerk reaction in support of her. Now I realized I was basically asking her to tell her whole family we were an item.

I didn't say any of that, though. I just waited. Whatever decision she made, I wanted it to be hers. I was watching my buddy Mark go through the utter angst of wanting a girl to want to be in a defined, serious relationship with him. It was like watching him be dragged through Philly by a bus. It might end up okay in the end, but only after a lot of hard work after the fact.

I didn't want to hitch myself to that bus, no matter how fun and sexy she was.

I also didn't like seeing Natalia like this – in this space between sadness and dread and guilt. Didn't want to know she was enduring it without me for support.

So I took a deep breath, and I lied.

"It doesn't matter what we are, Tali. I want to support you. We work together. Plus, we're friends, aren't we?"

"You work with me," she said, squeezing my hand where it sat on her lap.

"Whatever," I said. "I'll say I was hungry and you dragged me over."

"That's not something I would do."

"It is if I told you I was headed to Taco Bell and you couldn't stand to let me eat shit instead of Amalia's cooking."

A soft smile curved her lips, and my heart soared. "There she is," I said quietly, cupping her face. Her big brown eyes framed by lush, heartbreaker lashes, blinked at me. I'd seen them filled with lust or laughter, but never seen anything quite like this sparkle.

I didn't want to think about it, because of the possibility that it wasn't what I wanted it to be – attachment.

"What time are we leaving?" I asked.

"I was planning to leave at 6:00. That's when it starts, but ever since my stupid brother and his boyfriend moved to Haverford, getting there for dinner is a traffic nightmare. I'd rather try to hit the tail end of traffic instead of the middle."

I glanced at my phone. It was four thirty – just enough time for me to get home, shower, dress like I would have been at work, and come back. I stood up, disentangling myself from her before she had a chance to respond. "Okay," I said simply, "I'll see you then."

Her mouth dropped open like she was going to say something, then closed like she'd thought better of it. I was no fool. I was clearing out of here before she had a chance to change her mind.

At home, I sped through my shower, making sure to lather my hair with the shampoo Natalia had said she loved the smell of. I realized mid-scrub that I probably shouldn't be thinking about that particular shower sex memory if I wanted my dick to be calm enough to spend an evening not touching her. It was too good not to think about, though. I'd been pounding into her while she clawed at my back and bit at my ear. And that wasn't even the best sex we'd had. Maybe not even in the top ten.

Ah, memories.

I started to get dressed in my typical work clothes - neatly pressed pants, button down, and tie - but looking in the mirror, realized what overkill it was. For reasons that still weren't completely clear to me, Natalia was dreading this dinner. None of her other family members would look like they'd just stepped out of a conference room, since Alejandro most likely wouldn't be there. I wanted to blend in, not strike fear and discomfort and thoughts of insurance policies into the hearts of the other family members.

At exactly five minutes to six o'clock, I stood in front of Natalia's house in a sweater and dark jeans - respectable, but unremarkable. At least, I hoped.

But all thoughts of my own appearance flew out of my head when Natalia hauled open the heavy door that led to The Knockout. She was wearing a sweatshirt, but that was where any similarity to her typical appearance stopped. I didn't even know she owned a pair of jeans, but here she stood in front of me, with her perfect legs encased in tight, dark denim. My mind went instantly to an image of peeling and tugging the denim off of them, inch by inch.

Down, boy.

Instead of training sneakers, she wore boots with a few inches of heel, making her almost my height. Her calves curved deliciously thanks to the platform under her heel. And her sweatshirt. Before I started seeing Natalia, I would have sworn to you that it was impossible for a woman to look drop dead gorgeous in a sweatshirt. Like with so much else in life, Natalia proved me dead wrong. This one was a mottled red color, the kind that made it look vintage even though there wasn't a rip or tear on it. It had a wide, high bottom that I just knew would ride up and expose her waist, a swooping neckline that showed her collarbones, and just enough fuzzy drape to its appearance to make me desperate to shove my arms up inside it so I could experience the softness of the fabric and the skin of her torso, which I already knew to be silky and warmer than you'd expect. Almost like she ran a degree hotter than everyone else.

It would have made sense.

And her hair. Dear God, her hair. I'd seen it down outside the bedroom few times before, but most of the time she had it in a high bun. Tonight, she'd let it down. Thick and shiny, it flowed over her shoulders and down her back, almost reaching her waist. She'd curled it, but it didn't look stiff with hairspray at all. I was overwhelmed with the desire to run my fingers through it, top to bottom. Then, I wanted to start over again, but grab a handful right at the roots and kiss her until she couldn't remember where she was.

Even though she had some black goop coating her lashes and lining her lids, her skin had a slightly unnatural glitter to it, and her lips looked glossy and sticky, she was stunning. It took every ounce of willpower I could muster to reach for her hand and say, "Let's get going."

Her eyes flicked to where my car waited at the curb. "Together? Like... in the same car?"

I shrugged with one shoulder, like her question didn't make my chest hurt just a little. Her eyes were unreadable. "Makes sense. Better for the environment, and, you know. If there is traffic, I'd rather have company." She squeezed my hand and followed me down the front steps of the gym.

As she ducked into her seat and I made my way to the driver's side, I tried not to think about every time I'd dated a woman and not particularly cared about whether she wanted to ride together. Was it really possible that every other person I'd dated had caused zero anxiety when I considered whether she wanted me to join her for a party, what I should wear for that party, and whether we should drive to that party together?"

It wasn't possible, it was a fact, one that worked its way into my mind and sat there, heavy, as Natalia pointed me through every twist and turn and light of the route to Christian and Daniel's house.

"It's kind of ridiculous," she said, turning to me and looking sheepish as we would our way down a backroad in Haverford. "Just turn here."

The driveway was lined with forest and made of gravel. It was the kind you wouldn't be able to drive up or down if the winter weather got particularly icy. "Oh, it's one of those houses," I said.

She scoffed. "I grew up in the city. The outskirts, and in a neighborhood, but still. There's nowhere I feel more at home. I guess that Christian felt exactly the opposite. When he first met Daniel, he gushed about his house just as much as he gushed about the actual dates with him. We still tease him about which one he fell in love with first."

My amusement turned into awe as we came to the end of the drive and saw a house that looked like it belonged in a modern architecture magazine. The roof was flat, dark wood, and the outer front wall was 2/3 glass with another wooden panel making up the bottom. There was a traditional stone walkway leading up to the heavy wooden door, and as we got out of the car and walked it, I realized there was an actual moat surrounding the place. Okay, it wasn't a moat, but it was a stream fed by trickling water coming from somewhere and, as far as I could tell, housing actual fish. I'd have to ask. Or maybe I wouldn't.

Natalia and I weren't holding hands. We weren't even walking close enough together to touch fingers. But that didn't matter, because three seconds after Natalia made her signature hard, business-like rap on the door, Amalia swung it open, her flawless white teeth showing in wide grin. "You made it!" she trilled, and I couldn't help but think it was directed at the both of us. She snagged our hands in hers and pulled us over the threshold. Music blared from some hidden, flawless-sounding speaker, and the biggest TV I'd ever seen hanging on a wall played some video of scenery from around the world.

Natalia's entire family was there – that much, I'd expected. On top of that, though, there was a *party*. I counted two adults I didn't know for every adult I did, at least. Some guy played a guitar softly while a lady sat next to him, singing. A dozen kids under ten years old ran around, the older ones playing a game of keep-away that bordered on teasing the smaller ones, but still had them entertained. Their squeals of delight at trying to snatch the small Nerf football away from the big kids filled the air. Another adult I didn't recognize stood at the counter helping Daniel mix drinks, while another passed them around.

"What is happening?" I asked to Natalia when Amalia finally left us alone, having guided us into the wide, open living room and taking Natalia's bag.

"What do you mean?" Her brow furrowed as she waved to Christian, who applauded and smiled our way.

"Took long enough to get here, Nati! The *sorullos* are getting cold."

Natalia bent down to where a plate of what looked like tiny, stickless corn dogs sat on the coffee table and shoved one whole into her mouth. "Whatever, *chotas*," she called, which sent Rodrigo and the three guys surrounding him into a fit of laughter.

With that, Natalia plunked herself down on the couch. Seconds later, Amalia shouted from some unseen corner into the kitchen, "*Ay*, what is your problem? You don't want Natalia and Ethan to have a good time?"

The room went quiet for a split second, and then Rodrigo said, "The boss has spoken!" Within a minute, margaritas appeared on the table in front of us. Natalia shook her head and sighed, but took hers anyway.

She took a long pull from her drink and then leaned back on the couch, humming and letting her eyes drift closed. As always, she was stunning, and it occurred to me that it was because she was in her element. Not the same as at the gym, but despite the fancy house and the bustling crowd, the conflicting sounds of the TV and the chatter and the guitar and singing, Natalia very clearly felt at home here. At peace.

Which was insane, because by most people's standards, this would be the party of the year.

"What is happening?" I repeated.

"Papá's birthday?" she said, her eyes closed, her entire body conveying much more relaxation than I would have expected given her nervousness over the whole thing. Maybe all she'd needed was a little liquid courage. When I stopped to think of it, I'd almost never seen Natalia drink. This may have actually been the first time. Or maybe she'd had a glass of wine at one of our dinners.

"Natalia, this is, like, bigger than any party any of my friends' families threw my entire childhood. Bigger than a party at Joey and Hawk's, honestly. Is this... normal?"

She sat up and eyed me curiously. "Yeah. It's Papá's birthday. This is what we do for everyone's birthday."

"Who are these people?"

"Friends? My brothers have lots of friends. Especially Christian and Daniel, but I think they just love to have people over. Obviously."

"But this is pretty normal?" I asked, processing.

"Well, yeah. All these people will stay for a while and then about halfway through the football game they'll start to leave. We'll have cake and then the rest of them will leave. And then the family will stay until Christian and Daniel kick us out. It's sort of the tradition. They'd be offended if we didn't."

My brain worked to process all this, and now I was shaking my head back and forth too. But my disbelief was accompanied by this warm pressure in my chest, like a hug from the inside.

The guy with a guitar in the corner started playing a catchy song, and out of the corner of my eye I saw Sebastian take Sarah's hand and pull her to standing. She still balanced Camila on one hip, and the little family danced together with fluid, practiced steps while Mariana looked on, teasing them while filming them with her cell phone camera. A few other couples joined them, and Natalia dragged her eyes open to watch them. I tugged on Natalia's hand.

"Want to go watch them?"

Arturo shuffled by with some blond-haired woman wearing a tight pencil skirt and tank top.

She laughed. "They're only dancing because they're halfway drunk."

"Well, if they're halfway, you're a quarter," I teased her, wondering if she'd object if I planted a kiss on her neck right here. I so rarely saw her like this, relaxed, outside of bed. When we'd gone on "her" dates she was always keyed up, trying to impress me, maybe, or to prove something. When we were in bed, we were alone. This was like seeing an iteration of comfortable Natalia that I never imagined seeing. I liked it. No. I loved it.

"Papá wants you," Rodrigo said as he plunked down next to Natalia. She let her head fall back on the couch and made a grunting sound.

"Why the piggy noises?" he asked. Natalia, eyes still closed, punched him on the arm. He hissed and rubbed it. "You're crazy. Seriously, Papá heard you were here and is grumbling that you didn't say hi yet."

Natalia sat up again and looked at him carefully, like she was trying to discern some truth from his words just by looking at him. "He is?"

"He is. You know you're his favorite, Nati."

"You are? His favorite?" I asked.

"It's stupid. Of course I am. I'm the only daughter. I'm the jewel in his crown. The apple of his eye. I just... I don't know," she said, turning to her brother. "He hasn't been the same and I think it's my fault."

"And with all that, you really think he's mad at you? Because of the changes to the gym?"

She pressed her lips in a line and nodded.

"Well," I said. "Those changes are happening no matter what. You're here. I'm here with you. No better time to go see him, wish him happy birthday, and find out."

Natalia gave me a long look, took a lingering sip from her margarita and nodded once. We stood, and though she didn't hold out her hand for mine, I could feel the pull between us – like she needed me next to her in order to move. I followed her through the living room, maneuvering around the small clusters of people talking, laughing, and dancing.

A dozen people sat in a semicircle of couches, ottomans, and chairs in the next room, including Christian and Alejandro. Kickoff for the Eagles game wasn't for another hour, but you wouldn't know it from watching these guys. They were engaging with the pre-game commentary as though the players were making breakaway runs down the field and perfectly completing passes.

Natalia's dad sat in the corner of the leather sectional, nestled back deep with a blanket on his lap, like he'd been tucked in there by someone. But he smiled and chatted with the men around him about the game, responding with trash talk when one of his sons would tease him about a player he had apparently bet on. He chuckled softly as the pre-game clips started to play, relaxing back into the cushion. He seemed... small, somehow, but that was probably just because I was standing, looking down at him. Not to mention the last time I'd really interacted with him, he'd been in an actual business meeting.

This was a different kind of get-together with Natalia's family. This is what I had wanted.

I caught Natalia's eye and moved my head a fraction of an inch toward the small empty space next to her dad. I couldn't hear her shuddering breath inward, but I could imagine it, just by watching the small tremble in her lips. It occurred to me that I didn't know Natalia well enough to know if she had a legitimate reason to be worried about talking to her dad about the business again.

Just another reason why I'd wanted to come. Family mattered to everyone, but Natalia was different from most people. Even when she was halfway across the country, her family and what they'd think of her affected every one of her actions.

After all, that was the reason she'd come back to Philly in the first place.

And, I realized as I watched her talking softly with her dad, watched her give him her hand and thread her fingers through his and rest her head on his shoulder as he kissed the top of it... it was one of the reasons I loved her.

Suddenly, it felt like the entire world had been reduced to me, and Natalia, and this house, and this party, and this moment. Her taking her rightful place in the family's livelihood, and me supporting her. The two of us showing up together and, later, going home together.

Natalia laughed at something her dad said and my heart felt like it would burst from happiness. Hell yes, I loved her. I wanted her, I respected the hell out of her, and half the time, I wanted to talk some sense into her. But, so much more than all those things, or maybe because of them, I loved her.

If I was lucky, she'd tell me she felt the same way. There were so many "ifs," so many things to worry about, but the enormity of the realization kind of knocked all of them out of their usual orbit around my brain. I was so awash in my feelings, they were so powerful and all-encompassing – that I struggled to focus on the game on TV. I made small talk with Natalia's brothers for another quarter. As much as I loved being with her family, I wanted to be alone with Natalia so much more.

Finally, out of the corner of my eye, I watched Natalia carry on an increasingly animated conversation with her dad. She sat up and they both began to talk with their hands, something that made me grin. At one point she even pulled out her phone and started tapping at it, showing her dad something on the screen every few seconds. During a time out, Natalia pulled him into a hug, and I noticed again how small he looked, how his body sagged against hers. She held him, instead of him holding her.

She stood up the, walking toward me, and her radiant grin inspired one of my own.

"Wanna get out of here?" she asked. She didn't hold out her hand to me, but I knew what she was asking. By the looks of the people in the room, I wasn't the only one who knew, either. Her brothers watched me carefully. Alejandro's look might have even been called approving, if still deliberating.

Hell, that was good enough for me. I walked out of that party on a cloud. I was practically catching air under my feet when she threaded her fingers with mine in full view of the front porch, where several people were hanging out. It was almost like any stress she'd had over what people would think of her bringing me to the party was gone.

It was almost like we were a team.

And, seeing as how I'd just decided that I loved her, that felt like the best possible outcome of this whole day.

CHAPTER 21

NATALIA

PAPÁ WAS OKAY. He really was okay.

He hadn't been angry at all. Just busy, he told me as he brought up change after change I'd implemented in The Knockout over the past several weeks. Granted, he said, he'd never imagined The Knockout becoming the kind of gym with a sauna and a daycare and a space that was clearly going to turn into a juice bar, for God's sake, but he was happy with the rising enrollment numbers. Toby had taken some flyers to her engineering TA sections, and we had a steady trickle coming in to see the renovations we'd done, take a class schedule, and eventually sign up for a membership. I played him a clip of a hip-hop dance class a friend of Amalia's had come in to demo, and though he made racist remarks about the music - "How do you even understand what they're saying?" - when I pointed out the attendance, and that in time, each attendee would pay at least eight dollars to be there, he grinned. "I guess the music is fine," he conceded, nodding at my phone. "What else do you have there, querida?"

Several minutes later, and I could tell he was getting tired of talking about the gym, which honestly, was a good thing. If he was upset about it, he wouldn't have been able to stop ranting.

Ethan walked silently by my side to the car, then opened the door for me. I normally hated that, rushed to get to the door before he could, but tonight, there was too much buzzing through my head to even plan that far ahead. The door softly closed and a few moments later, he was in the driver's seat.

"Okay?" he asked.

It was only then, supported by the solid car seat, in the contained, safe space of the car under only Ethan's eyes, that I realized I was shaking.

I held out my hands in front of me, fingers spread, and watched them tremble.

"Better than okay?" he amended.

"I think so," I said softly. "I mean, yes. He's okay with the gym, all the changes. I know it might seem silly to you, but to him, this was a big deal. Having his youngest kid take over what he and Mamá had built. And the youngest kid being... me," I finished, self-censoring.

"You mean, a woman?" he asked softly, as he blessedly turned the key in the ignition. I didn't mind having this conversation with him, was grateful he was here to have it, actually, but I didn't want him looking at me while we did.

He pulled out of his parking spot and I sighed at the rumble of the car beneath me. "You know that's what I mean," I said.

"Yeah," Ethan replied, softly. "Baby steps, I guess. It's only been a few weeks."

"It feels like forever," I groaned, finally letting my body settle into the ache that all the tension of going to the party in the first place had left for it.

"Does it?" he asked softly. "Seems like it's flown by to me."

His meaning washed over me like the rapidly darkening night. "I don't mean the time with you," I said. "If anything, you've made it as bearable as it could have been. I'm glad I ran into you."

"I can't tell you how glad I am," he said in an impossibly soft voice. It was this sort of tenderness that Ethan was capable of accessing, and expressing, on the turn of a dime. In the beginning, it had made me feel uncomfortable. Feelings expressed by men were certainly not something I'd grown up with, and the stunt double, adventure, cliff-jumping types of guys I was used to dating weren't scared of anything nearly as much as they were discussing emotions. I'd always dated those guys because that's what I'd liked. No muss, no fuss, no messiness.

But now my whole life was a mess. Suddenly, hearing a guy talk about his feelings for me, explicitly or implicitly, like Ethan was doing right now, felt more like a rudder keeping a boat steady than the waves making it rock.

I'd always been my own rudder when things got a little rocky, but that was because for the most part, I knew what I was doing, what path I was following through life, however winding it was. Now I was busy bailing water out of my boat. I needed another rudder. And Ethan had volunteered.

"You hungry?" he asked. I hadn't even thought about food the whole time we were at Christian and Daniel's, despite the incredible appetizers Daniel had cooked up. The margarita I'd downed had gone past making my head light and my thoughts fuzzy, and the traces of the tequila left in my system now just highlighted the empty pit in my stomach.

"I am," I said carefully.

"I have stuff to make mac and cheese at home. Not the box kind. The ooey gooey homemade kind, that you cut into squares to eat the next day." I had no idea what he was talking about, but I didn't say so. Comfort food in our house had always been empanadas, and *arroz con pollo*. The way Ethan talked about this mac and cheese, though, just sounded so full of love.

"Do I get to sit and watch you cook?" I asked, shooting one of those little smiles I knew he loved his way.

"That's actually the only way I'll cook," Ethan said.

Twenty minutes later, I was perched on a bar stool next to Ethan's kitchen island, wearing his sweats, which covered my feet completely so that I didn't even need socks. I still wore my tank, and I'd shrugged my bra off just in the name of regaining a little bit of my sanity. Sometimes I thought that if I had more body fat, the pinch of the straps and clasp against my skin wouldn't be quite so bad.

Ethan wore a pair of identical sweats, and a soft t-shirt that clung to his back muscles as he moved around his small kitchen, boiling noodles and stirring up a cream sauce on the stove.

The back of his shirts listed the members of the Penn-Tones, an a capella group he'd sung baritone in during his sophomore and junior years of college. Fittingly, he was swaying his hips at the stove and singing along, one of those songs about spending a lazy morning in bed with someone.

"Did you love it? Singing?" I asked. My voice came out louder than I'd expected it to.

"Huh?" he asked. He turned around, holding a dripping pasta fork. Steam rose from the pot behind him and his face was the perfect blend of sleepy and attentive. My chest tightened.

"Did you love singing? Or, like, do you love the radio show?"

"I like both, yeah," he said. "Why?"

"Well, you're good at it, right? Why didn't you try to... do it? For a living?"

Ethan pursed his lips, then turned back briefly to stir the pasta. "I like a lot of stuff, as you know. The conservatory and Joey and Hawk's and walking dogs that I don't have to bring home later and spending time with you."

"So, you could have done any of those things for a career. Well, besides spending time with me."

"If you were more famous, I could have been your manager," he said, pointing the pasta fork at me in mock accusation. "Then I could make money by spending time with you."

I laughed. "True. Might still happen," I mused, more to myself than anything. What if, one day, I was a well-known, well-respected stunt double? I'd have to travel a lot. Would Ethan support me? I never imagined myself needing or even wanting a manager, someone who would help me cope with life in the movie business. But thinking of Ethan in that role gave me that same brave, safe feeling I'd had in the car right after we left the party.

"I didn't do any of those things for a job," Ethan said as he scraped the sauce from the pan on the stove to a baking dish, "Because I knew I could make enough money as an actuary to keep doing all those other things in my free time, if I wanted. I'm good at the work, and I don't hate it. And now, look at my life." He lifted his arms and I couldn't help but notice how dry my mouth went watching his arms move. "I have a nice place. I have the Bro Show. And, as long as you're in Philly, I have you."

My heart jumped and a big, stupid smile took over my face. "Yeah. You do. But I'm not doing stunts here." It wasn't a lie. My conversation with Carol still loomed in the front of my mind, and in my heart, I still desperately wanted to do the stunt work. I didn't think I'd ever stop wanting that. No matter how happy I was in the calm life, I'd always be waiting for the next time my blood would roar in my ears from pure exhilaration, from the sense that I was living life on the very edge, if only for a moment.

"You're not doing stunts here," he agreed with a soft smile. I was sure he didn't mean it to seem self-satisfied or patronizing. "Which is much better for your insurance."

I just sighed. And here we were again. Ethan loved that I wasn't doing the stunt work. Heck, he was almost gloating over it. Natalia from six weeks ago would have spouted off these low-key frustrations in the loudest, most dramatic way possible. But as I watched Ethan move through the kitchen, stirring pasta, wiping the counter as he went, shaking his butt the slightest bit with the music he'd put on in the background – some electronic dance type I never would have put on otherwise – a soft warmth wrapped around my heart like a blanket. Yes, it sucked not doing stunts. No, I hadn't really asked for any of this, even if I'd agreed to it. Not Ethan, not the gym, not growing up and considering a dozen other peoples' wants and needs before my own.

And yet, in a very different way than I had been that one time I jumped out of an airplane, I was happy. Living a calm life offered a lingering contentment that I never felt after doing stunt work. I wondered if this life and the one I'd imagined for myself a month ago could ever co-exist. Thinking of the possibility made my heart skip a beat.

My phone buzzed against my thigh from the pocket of Ethan's sweatpants. I jumped a little, then half-pulled it out, checking the screen. Carol's name flashed across the display. My breath caught in my throat.

The last few weeks had been so intense that I'd almost completely forgotten about Carol's call. Almost. In the very few quiet moments, I'd considered taking her up on her offer. It always made my heart and head hurt. I wanted it so badly, but every other sign pointed to "no." Things were going so well at the gym, and with Ethan. Combined, those things gave me enough excitement to not want to run away all the time. Tonight, between getting some time with Papá and feeling right at home watching Ethan dance around his kitchen cooking comfort food, was the most unexpected happiness I'd experienced in as long as I could remember.

If I was so happy here, why was I even keeping the possibility of taking Carol up on her offer? There was no good reason except my own insecurity, the worry that I might never get another stunt work chance again. In that moment, I knew that if I really wanted to be present to feel every one of the gym's successes, and every happiness that being with Ethan brought me, I had to talk to Carol. Now. "Be right back," I said to Ethan, flashing my phone at him as I ducked out of the apartment.

There in the hallway, I told Carol I wouldn't be taking the job.

She spent a few seconds cajoling me to reconsider, but I could tell just by listening to her that she knew I'd made my choice. "Well, they needed you for a *series* of stunts, honey. You could probably still get some work on that set. If anything changes in the next month or so, give me a call. I told them nobody on the East Coast could hold a candle to you for this job, and I still believe that. They would take you on in a heartbeat, if I told them to. And I would. I'm counting down the days 'til you get back to LA, honey."

She sounded so sad, I almost told her that I couldn't wait to get back there myself. It would have been true, a couple of weeks ago. Now, I wasn't so sure. Regardless of what I felt, I loved that she wanted to keep me on her radar, so I thanked her and said I'd call her the second my situation changed.

Ethan's warm smile when I got back into the kitchen confirmed that I'd made the right decision. Every time I saw him, I felt a little happier. Why would I throw that away for a couple days of work? "Nice butt shakin'," I commented as I reached over to the counter for a baby carrot and popped it in my mouth. He looked at me with fire in his eyes.

"Why didn't you ask me to dance?" Ethan asked.

"Huh?" I mumbled under a mouthful of roughage.

"At your dad's party. Why didn't we dance, like your brother and his wife?" He spoke softly, like he was afraid to startle me with the question.

For a second, confusion kept me from saying anything. Then I realized I hadn't taken Ethan to my favorite Latin club yet. Probably because it didn't exactly fit either of our ideas of 'Dangerous Dates,' like we'd originally discussed. Still, maybe I should consider it. It was dangerous in a whole different way, after all. "Because when I dance to Latin music with you, it's going to be too inappropriate for Papá and my brothers to watch."

His eyes flared, and with a few practiced movements, he drained the pasta, stirred it into the sauce, and popped the dish into the oven. Then he approached me, slowly. I swore his eyes darkened just a little with each step. "Say that again," he said in a voice several notes deeper than usual.

"When we dance to salsa, Ethan Anderson," I said, pitching my voice lower to match his, "It is going to be so dirty that I don't want anyone even remotely related to me to see it."

He grabbed my hand and gave it a little tug, pulling me to my feet. I faced him, and we stood there, suddenly panting, only enough space between us to feel the snapping tension that stretched there.

"Show me," he said in a low, demanding growl.

Never breaking eye contact with him, I took his other hand and moved it to my hip, then an inch lower, so his fingers spread across the top of my ass and his thumb rubbed over the jut of my pelvic bone, which just peeked out of the top of his sweats. I wondered if this was sexy, me wearing his clothes. When I stepped in so that our bodies were flush, touching from chest to thighs, I didn't have to wonder any more. He was rock hard, just from this. And we hadn't even kissed yet today.

I'd never felt this much desire for a guy who'd been in my life for this long, I realized, as I moved my hand to the back of his thigh and tugged his leg forward. He let out a quiet groan. I pushed up on my tiptoes and let my breath out, hot against his ear, hoping to make him think of something else hot, wet, and ready for him. "How long is the food going to take?" I asked quietly, holding my body still and solid against his.

Ethan didn't answer, just let out a deep rumbling growl and tightened his grip on my hip, digging his thumb in hard enough to leave a bruise. I gasped, then let my slightly open lips close around his earlobe, pressing down gently. I knew exactly what I was doing, and when he growled again, then slid his hands under my ass and hoisted me up in the air, I knew I'd succeeded in putting him over the edge.

I beamed as I planted a messy kiss on his lips as Ethan strode with purpose toward the bedroom. A laugh of pure joy bubbled out of my throat when he tossed me on the bed, and in one smooth movement, tugged his sweatpants off me, then tossed them to the floor. His eyes raked down over me - I'd shucked my panties off along with the tight jeans I'd worn to the party, and hadn't bothered to fish them out again - and he whispered a curse.

"You too," I said softly, licking my lips.

The room was just dark enough for us to see each other's outlines, illuminated by the light from the hallway. Even so, I felt like I saw every inch of him in exquisite detailed relief. What I couldn't see, I'd already memorized. Hunger for him rolled through me, and I let out a breath of relief as he crawled over me on the bed.

There was that mix of feelings again. Held. Safe. Invincible.

I drew my knees up to cradle him between my hips and let out a long moan when I felt his cock drag gently through my folds. "That's it," I gasped, like I'd been starved for days and suddenly a feast had been laid out before me. Like I needed this to survive.

"No, it's not," he murmured, kissing me long and soft while pushing a hand under my tank, cupping my breast and flicking his thumb over the nipple, before tugging it over my head. The opposite strap tangled in my hair, and I huffed as I tried to extract it. Ethan rolled completely onto one elbow, disentangling it with nimble fingers, smiling down at me fondly.

"You too," I whispered. I teased my fingers at the bottom hem of his shirt, knowing he was ticklish there. His abs contracted in a hard, surprised laugh, and his cock bobbed against my thigh, making my throat go dry.

"You're going to pay for that," he said after tugging the shirt off and tossing it to the floor.

"Oh yeah?" I gasped as he rolled fully on top of me again, lodging the head of his dick right up against my clit.

"Mmmhm," he said, kissing me long, slow, and soft. My body heated to a thousand degrees and I was suddenly desperate to have him. "As soon as I get a condom," he murmured in my ear, returning the gentle bite to my earlobe that had gotten him so riled up in the first place.

When he pushed off me to walk to his dresser, where he kept his condom stash, cool air swept over me, blanketing me in emptiness. I knew why he was getting up, but for the first time, I couldn't let him go. Not at this moment.

"We don't need one," I said. It was true. I'd had IUDs for the past seven years, ever since it had become clear that, with my erratic and spontaneous schedule, filling prescriptions for pills and actually remembering to take them was the same as playing with fire. Except at the end, I wouldn't get burned – I'd be chained to a house with a baby. The IUD meant I was covered, no matter what. I mostly used condoms when I didn't know the guy very well or when I sensed that he was starting to get too attached.

This was the first time I'd felt like maybe I was the one getting attached.

"Natalia, I don't think either of us is ready for a baby, or –"

"IUD," I gasped as the head of his cock nudged at my entrance again. "Promise, we're fine. *Please*, Ethan."

He huffed out a hot breath into my neck, let his forehead fall against my shoulder like a man defeated, then grabbed at my hip just like he had when we stood in his kitchen. In one smooth, sure motion, he thrust inside me, filling me up and sending shocking jolts of sensation down my thighs. I knew that some girls didn't like it when their cervix was bumped, and I hadn't either, the first time I'd experienced it. That guy had been big enough to slam into it, but for some reason still seemed to think he had something to prove, and rammed into me every time like a jackhammer.

Ethan was big too, but instead of pounding away at me relentlessly, he moved in and back out with long, sure, powerful strokes. He lifted his chest from mine just enough to change the angle, and I cried out when he grazed my G-spot. He swallowed the noise with a soft, deep kiss, the perfect contrast to the strong pace he was setting with his hips.

"God, Tali. You're perfection. This is... oh, fuck." Something inside Ethan seemed to shift, and his strokes slowed but intensified. He stayed inside longer and barely pulled out before thrusting back in again. Our hips were glued together, lazily rocking in a dance that only we knew the real depth of. "I don't know how I ever –" Ethan groaned as he bottomed out again. He pulled out, almost like he couldn't stop himself, and I whimpered with the sudden emptiness. He plunged in again, and I cried out as every cell in my body felt lit on fire. He gasped, and finally managed, "It's never been like this."

Hot electricity traveled from the base of my spine and shot down through ever nerve, every pore, every cell. Every piece of me moved in perfect harmony with every piece of him, and the tightening pleasure was more intense with every passing moment, with every gasp we shared, with every rustle of the sheets caused by the perfect steady movement of our bodies in tandem.

He was right. Or, at least, I agreed. It had never been like this for me either, and I told him so, gasping as he sped up a little more, pulled out an extra millimeter before slamming back in just a touch harder. He was close now, I knew from the subtle change in the pitch of his groans, in the way his hands grabbed at me slightly more frantically. And I was close too, savoring that feeling of being so full you're about to burst, wanting to be filled to the brim with pleasure for as long as possible before it all spilled over and left me spent.

"Ethan, you're... oh, fuck!" I shouted as the most delicious orgasm ever raced to its peak.

He slowed just a touch, even though I could already feel his cock hardening even more, could feel my own slickness increase around it, knew that this was going to be one for the record books. If there was a dictionary for my life, this moment would be described in the entry for "incredible sex." Or maybe "incomparable" or "unforgettable" or...

"No, don't stop," I gasped, digging my fingers into his ass and pulling him impossibly closer to me.

"Wasn't stopping," he groaned, his breath eddying against my collarbone. "Savoring. Tali, honey, are you -?"

"So close. Fuck!" I shouted before gulping for air again. "Ethan..." His name left my lips like a plea and a song of worship all wrapped up together. It seemed to inspire him. He planted one hand beside my head, worked the other down between my legs, and glided his thumb over my clit in rhythm with his smooth, long thrust. A few seconds later, stars swam through my vision, heralded by a throaty scream that accompanied my back arching toward the ceiling.

Seconds later, as my muscles clenched around him, Ethan came, spilling inside me with a hoarse shout, then kissing every inch of my face before lowering himself, panting, to my side. His arm and leg still draped over mine, and he ghosted kisses on my shoulder and across my collarbone before I turned into him, situating my knee between his, tucking my forehead against his chest, savoring the warm, slightly sweaty air that seemed to wrap us in a bubble that protected us from everything else in the world.

Our breaths fell into a common rhythm, and after a few more moments I lifted my head to look into Ethan's eyes. They studied me, content and adoring, like I was everything he ever wanted, everything he'd ever need.

And at that exact moment, my heart, expanding and flooding me with warmth, told me that I felt the same way. I loved him. That didn't mean I found the courage to say the words.

"You're amazing," I sighed, before kissing his mouth, savoring the taste, wanting to memorize the feel of his lips, soft and sure, against mine. Finally, I released them, and leaned my forehead against his chest again. It only took a breath for a small sliver of fear to creep in.

I'd never told anyone besides my family that I loved them before. I'd never *wanted* to, so I'd never even considered it. In fact, if a man got so attached to me that I sensed he was about to say it, I'd always broken it off. I didn't need to be tied down anywhere anyway, and especially not because of a guy who I didn't feel that way about.

But a second later, he traced the outer shell of my ear with his lips, and whispered, *"We're* amazing." Then his arms wrapped around me and pulled me in so tight that I felt the air rush out of my lungs. I laughed and pressed kisses to his neck, his chest, his throat, and then his lips again. I wasn't sure I'd ever experienced pure, perfect happiness, until that very moment. Ethan loved me, and I loved him. Neither of us had said it, but it didn't matter. We both knew.

We kissed for a long time in his bed, letting our warm hands wander over each other's bodies. Giddy laughter between kisses turned to sighing when lips and tongues and teeth hit the right spots, which turned to whimpers and then groans. Eventually, Ethan rolled me on top of him, anchoring my hips over his. When he pushed inside me again, I gasped at his perfect fit, the perfect way he held me, the perfect feeling of being loved and cherished and desired so desperately that he couldn't imagine wanting anyone the way he wanted me. When he flipped me onto my back and brought me to the edge of completion with those solid, delicious thrusts, he kissed my throat and whispered praise and adoration into my skin. I came with a low groan and panted praise in his ear, telling him to let go, to come inside me, that there wasn't anything I wanted more in the entire world.

When he did, we both lay there, stunned. The sheer power of us together, tonight, was different than anything I'd ever experienced – anything I'd ever imagined.

There wasn't much in the world I felt certain of – never had been. But that night, two things became crystal clear – I loved Ethan, and I didn't want to let him go. Not for anything.

We stayed that way, clinging to each other, until we fell asleep.

CHAPTER 22

ETHAN

I WOKE UP, slightly sticky and smelling a little like sweat. But that didn't matter one bit, because the most perfect woman in the entire world was in my arms. She'd shifted in her sleep, so that her back faced to me and her ass nestled against my front, doing nothing to calm the incredible morning wood that was growing between us at a shocking rate. Natalia was dead asleep, though; I knew that when she woke up, she generally did so ready for action and that 'action' usually consisted of kickboxing. I was sure there would be plenty of mornings where we'd have sleepy, slow, delicious morning sex, but with her body weighing my arm down heavy as a boulder and her hair, which covered her face, puffing up in the air with each of her soft snores, I decided that all signs pointed to "not today."

Plus, I was really damn hungry.

I'd known when I popped the mac and cheese into the oven last night that I was going to take Natalia to bed about two seconds afterward. The chances of me getting up to take a damn noodle casserole out of the oven in the middle of that were less than zero, so I'd turned off the oven and figured it would cook enough in there, while the temperature slowly dropped so it'd be edible after we were done. *If* we ever got done.

Turned out, we hadn't, which was the ideal outcome. Wasn't the best for the mac and cheese, though. I ambled into the kitchen and took the cold, oily pan of noodles out and dumped it into the trash. It didn't matter. We had plenty of chances ahead of us for eating mac and cheese.

I rifled through my fridge and took out ingredients for a simple cheese omelet, then hummed quietly as I mixed up some eggs, making sure to remove a few yolks so that they were as pale as Natalia liked. My mind wandered while I manipulated and flipped the solidifying circle, then dropped cheese on it and stepped to the side to slice up some apples to go on the side.

The sound of footsteps pulled me out of my daydream. "I hope there's nothing green in there," Natalia said, her voice raspy. My pillowcases weren't satin like Natalia's, which meant her hair fared far worse after a night spent in my bed. She hated it – I loved it. Loved that there was a tuft of slightly frizzy hair puffing out of the back side of her head, loved that I could already see a couple tangles she'd need my help pulling out. Loved that I was the only person who got to see her like this, for as long as I could manage to keep her in my life.

I was going to take that more seriously than any challenge I'd undertaken in my entire life.

"You love green things," I teased. I knew what her response would be.

"You know I do. And you also know how I feel about putting them together with cheese," she grumbled. I laughed as I pulled her into my arms. She was soft and warm and pliant when she first woke up, her head lolling helplessly against my chest, her breath stale and familiar. I loved every single part of it.

"Just cheese," I chuckled. "I promise. And four eggs, two yolks."

"Just like I like it," she hummed appreciatively. My heart swelled.

I poured her a cup of coffee from the press and slid it over the surface of the kitchen island and she took the signal, settling herself down on what had quickly become her stool. She took a long, slow sip, blinked her eyes open, and took a deep appreciative breath when I plated the halves of the omelet, then carried them and the apple slices to the island.

"You're not going to sit?" she asked as she made a grabbing motion in the air.

"Right. Forks," I said. "See? No. I'm not going to sit, and that's why. The second I put my butt on a chair, you're going to need something else."

"I'm not a child," she said, before looking around the table forlornly again.

I laughed. "Salt, right?"

"And hot sauce?" she asked sheepishly.

I grabbed it out of the cabinet and slid it to her, imagining what it would taste like on my tongue when I took her back to bed after breakfast. "Plus," I said, "My arms look better when I lean, as opposed to sit."

Natalia chewed a bite of apple and rolled her eyes at me, but couldn't hide her small smile. She dumped a ton of hot sauce on her eggs, then moaned and slumped a little bit. "You don't make eggs for me often enough," she said.

"What do you think? Should we change that?" I was already halfway done with mine. It was like last night had set this constantly burning fire inside me that made me starved, both literally and metaphorically. I was already planning how I could keep her with me for the duration of the day.

She shoved a bite of omelet into her mouth and nodded slowly. When she swallowed, she said, "Yeah. I think so."

We ate together quietly for a couple more minutes as my heart grew ten sizes. That projection of the future I'd had waking up with her my arms just got more and more detailed. And we hadn't even talked about anything past the dates we'd promised each other which had, admittedly, gotten greater in number than I'd expected.

It had put me in a good enough mood that I was willing to ask the question that had scared me so much, until now. "So, when's our next scary date?"

Natalia's eyebrows climbed up, and her look of surprise was quickly taken over by a grin of delight. "Oh, I'm so glad you asked that."

Uh oh. That meant she already had one planned. Probably was going to spring it on me at the last minute, so I wouldn't have a chance to argue. For the first time ever, I didn't feel worried. Not one bit. I trusted the feelings churning between us and the sparkle of excitement in her eyes more than I was willing to give in to my trepidation.

"Your eggs are getting cold. Eat them so you have enough energy to jump out of a plane."

It was a miracle I managed to chew and swallow. "To do what?"

"For once in your life, don't overthink it. Just trust me."

I felt like someone had hit pause on the world around me. It was a miracle I managed to stammer and blink. "We're going skydiving," I said, trying to appear calm as I gathered our empty dishes and rinsed them in the sink.

Natalia dipped her head in a confident nod. "I'm going to keep you safe, baby. And you're going to love it."

CHAPTER 23

NATALIA

I DIDN'T GIVE Ethan a chance to refuse. I'd booked this trip weeks ago, when we'd first made our dating deal. It was with a friend of a girlfriend of mine from LA. She'd promised that Tom would explain things slowly and thoroughly for Ethan, and that he'd been in the business for years. If anything could make Ethan feel safe about skydiving, a trip out with Tom could.

After we finished our eggs, I dragged him into his bedroom to get dressed, pulling some workout clothes, including a long-sleeved jacket, out of his drawers and tossing them at him. "They'll have safety gear there?" he asked, and I just nodded.

"Hurry up, slowpoke. We have to stop at my place for my clothes."

He didn't talk much on the drive out to the flight field where we were going to meet Tom, which was just as well. I spent the time cranking up some salsa music on my car stereo and singing along. Ethan had never said it, but I could tell he loved it when I spoke Spanish. He may have been stressed about our impending date but he couldn't resist watching my lips hungrily as I mouthed the lyrics, singing them softly under my breath.

When we arrived at the small stretch of concrete and I

turned off the ignition, Ethan's whole body went stiff. I followed his line of sight to the small white prop plane waiting for us just a few hundred feet away.

"Small planes are much more dangerous than large ones," Ethan said as I pulled the handle to open my door.

I stopped and turned to him. "But..." I prompted. I knew him well.

He shut his eyes tight and conceded, "But driving in a car is still more dangerous."

"Especially down the Schuylkill Expressway," I finished, squeezing his hand. "And we've done that lots."

"Right," he said, blowing out a long breath. He opened his eyes then, and turned to me. "You've done all the research, haven't you? So that you could talk me into this?"

I nodded. "There's a 0.0007% chance of dying from a sky-dive, compared to a 0.0167% chance of dying in a car accident."

"Based on every 10,000 miles driven," he said. "I think I drive less than that. I try to, anyway."

Right. Because of his mom's accident, Ethan hated driving on winding roads or in bad weather more than he would admit even to me, I thought. But I pushed on. "No, you don't. Or you won't this year," I amended. "We'll be going to lots of dinners at Christian and Daniel's."

Ethan took a long, slow breath. "We will?"

"Yeah," I said softly, putting as much emotion in my expression as I could. "You're safe with me," I promised. I meant more than the skydiving, today. Maybe it was silly, since I was far from certain about my own future. Something had changed, though. I didn't know what I wanted to be doing a year from now, but I knew I wanted Ethan to be part of my life.

Half an hour later, we'd signed the release forms and suited up. Ethan gripped my hand tightly. "Just focus on me, okay?" I said. He nodded, and even though I really loved watching the

Pennsylvania mountains come into relief when we soared above them, I liked being Ethan's safe place to look more.

Ethan's harness was hooked into Tom's, and I was connected to Tom's girlfriend, Laura. Tom said something next to Ethan's ear, and he nodded in reply, then let go of my hand.

"Are we gonna jump first?" Laura asked.

I glanced at Ethan. His jaw was locked, like it was when he was determined to do something. I reached out for his hand, and when he grabbed it, I leaned forward to smack a kiss on his lips. "Come after me, okay?" I yelled against the roaring wind.

He nodded, then said, "I promise." There was more to that promise than just skydiving. I knew it, felt it in my bones.

Laura and I turned and tipped out the open door sideways. I loved this moment of freefall, every damn time. I knew I looked ridiculous, with my face flapping in the wind, and my mouth stretched into an uncontrollable grin. I didn't care.

This feeling, of being on top of the world and completely vulnerable, was everything I'd always chased. Nothing matched getting the high of danger and adventure. Nothing, that is, until Ethan was right by my side for the whole experience.

While Laura and I were in freefall, I managed to catch the moment Tom and Ethan leaned out of the plane and let themselves fall. Ethan was white as a sheet, his eyes wide, but his jaw still had that same determined set. I knew he didn't want to skydive. I could only interpret this as his devotion to me. My stomach flipped when his eyes met mine, and his cheeks did the same silly flap in the powerful wind as mine did. I was a little lighter, so he reached freefall at my altitude for a few seconds. I didn't realize it until that moment, but this was everything I wanted from skydiving with Ethan. All this time, I'd been thinking there was nothing that compared to soaring high over the rest of the world, completely untethered. As Ethan and I joined hands, I knew that this was the new feeling to beat –

experiencing all that with him. Knowing that he was willing to confront his fear so he could share it with me.

As we started to drop farther, we had to unclasp our hands. For the first time ever, instead of enjoying my time in the air, I was anxious to get back down to the ground so I could throw my arms around Ethan. He and Tom landed about fifty feet from us, and as soon as Laura unhooked my harness from hers, I took off running toward him. Tom unhooked himself from Ethan and then helped him to his feet just before I reached him and threw my arms around his neck. He chuckled breathlessly before his legs went out under him, and his ass hit the ground again. I followed him down, laughing, until I was laying on top of him, right there in the middle of the grassy, sun-lit field. I fumbled at the straps of both of our helmets and tossed them to the side before laying a long, hard kiss on his lips. I couldn't bring myself to pull away. His shaking fingers threaded through my hair as he mumbled against my mouth, "Sorry. Still kind of shaky."

I laughed, feeling more intense, pure happiness than I'd ever felt in my life. I rested my head in the crook of his neck. This time, I didn't turn the words over and over in my head, didn't worry about their implications. I didn't consider the safest course of action, didn't fret over the conflicting circumstances of each of our lives, didn't worry whether he felt the same way. Just said them. "I love you," I said, loud and clear and unmistakable.

Ethan halted – I could feel his chest stop for a moment, pausing against mine. Then he gripped my shoulders with his only slightly shaky hands, and tugged so that I lifted my head too look into his eyes. "I love you too," he said in a gravely, stunned exhale. "So much."

We lay there in the field, still hooked into skydiving harnesses, laughing and kissing breathlessly until Tom and Laura approached us. "Hate to break up the party," Laura said with a smile in her voice, "but we've got another pair of divers in an hour."

"Next time you go sky diving," Tom said, "You can propose. If you're gonna make out like that in a meadow, might as well have a good reason."

My stomach flipped over. Proposals? Marriage? I had never thought of that as part of my future. But as I helped Ethan to his feet and he slipped his hand in mine, a flash of what it would feel like to look down at him like this while he slipped a ring on my finger took over my thoughts. For the first time ever, the thought of spending my life with someone didn't make me feel trapped. Thinking about a life with Ethan was like watching my world open up in front of me. He'd shown me he was willing to do what scared him most, as long as I was with him. What would a life full of sharing my adventures with someone feel like, as opposed to tackling them all on my own?

I felt steady as ever on the drive back home. We didn't talk very much, just held hands and smiled at each other like fools every few seconds. "I know you were shaky afterward," I said, "and this may be a stupid question, but what did you think?"

"Of the sky diving?"

"Yeah," I said with a laugh.

"I just told myself I was going to focus on you, and then we'd only fall for a couple minutes. I'm not afraid of planes..."

"Did my statistics help?" I interrupted.

"Yes, smartass. They did," Ethan said with a squeeze to my hand. I beamed. "Anyway," he continued, "Going up in the air wasn't bad. I thought the going down part would be terrifying, but honestly, it never felt scary. The air underneath me on the freefall felt almost solid, you know? And then after that, the parachute was there." He shrugged. "So, I guess it was no big deal."

I was struck absolutely speechless. I pulled off the highway and the clicking of the turn signal was the only sound in the car for a few seconds.

"Tali?" Ethan asked. "You okay?"

There was a small lump in my throat. "I never thought that I would be taken by surprise by you, Ethan," I said. "But you've done it. I'm shocked. And glad."

We turned twice, and then we were in front of The Knockout. Once we were out of the car, I pulled Ethan into my arms, holding him tight to me. For some reason, I wanted to hold him fast, as long and hard as I could.

Eventually, Ethan led me upstairs. I followed him into the shower, where we stood, embracing and indulging in long, leisurely kisses, until the hot water ran out. Then we fell into bed, where we crawled under the covers and pulled the sheets over our heads, laughing softly. I rolled on top of Ethan and guided him inside me like I had done it a million times before and would do it a million times again. Our bodies moved in tandem like waves lapping on a shore, and we came together with declarations of love softly moaned into each other's skin.

Minutes after, in the quiet dark, after our breaths had slowed, Ethan whispered into my hair, "I didn't mind skydiving that much, you know."

"I don't mind boring movie nights that much, either," I admitted. With a measure of sleepy, contented surprised, I realized I meant every word.

Ethan didn't reply, but the way he held me tight to him told me all I needed to know. He may not be winning the bet, but I'd told him everything he needed to hear today. In that moment, it felt like the quiet, happy compromise of it all would last forever.

CHAPTER 24

NATALIA

ETHAN HAD COME to oversee the installation of the new wood-look floor in one of The Knockout's back rooms. With some persuasion from a few of our female members and a lot of market research, we'd decided to include a yoga studio space in the gym. Sarah had volunteered to do some scouting for yoga instructors who would rent the space for regularly scheduled classes.

I had to admit, part of the reason I agreed to the renovation so quickly was that it would keep Ethan around for at least another few weeks. He couldn't write a comprehensive insurance policy until our changes to the gym were done.

We stood together on the brand-new floor, admiring the look of it. "So," he asked, "when are you taking me out to that salsa club?

"Tonight," I said decidedly with a smack to his lips. He beamed at me. The flicker of desire in his eyes only made me more excited for him to see me in the dress I planned to wear to the club.

Maybe it was because I'd grown up with five brothers, or because my mother never gave much thought to fashion. More likely, it was my career choice that kept me in sweats, that had my closet stocked with rows of sneakers and only two pairs of passable dancing heels. One little black dress, and one red, were the only two non-pants articles of clothing I'd taken with me on my travels.

My little black dress was a treasure of contemporary technology - it was clingy, soft, forgiving of the washer and the dryer, as well as being sweat-slicking like my best workout tops. The neckline plunged low, but not as low as the 'V' at the back, topped only by a single tie at the nape of my neck. And the skirt...well, let's just say that it put the hard work I'd done on my quads fully on display.

I told Ethan to go home and put on something nice, and to pick me up at seven. We'd been spending almost all our down time together – being with him was addictive, and I never found myself wanting to fight it. But something about tonight felt different. I wanted to look extra gorgeous for him when I felt his body grinding against mine in the heat and noise of the club.

I swiped some mascara and long-wear red lipstick onto my face and swept my hair half-up. I knew I'd be covered in a sheen of sweat within fifteen minutes of dancing at Ponce Pequena, and nobody liked trying to unstick hairs from their face. I slid my feet into my strappy black heels, which were actually designed for dancing and other footwork. I'd picked them up on an LA set when I'd been one of the stunt doubles for a ballroom fight scene.

As I was finishing up the quick check of my apartment to make sure lights were off and heat was turned down, I heard Ethan's knock. I hustled over to the door, loving the unusually feminine feel of my breasts jiggling in a standard bra, as opposed to being held firmly in place by my typical sports bra, and my hair swishing against my mostly-bare back.

I pulled the door open and was treated to the sight of

Ethan's face going from his calm-and-cool pre-date smile to completely shocked in less than a second. "Wow," he said. "You look..."

My lips twisted into a smirk. "Watch where you tread here, my friend."

"You look ready for a night out." He reached out, smooth as anything, grabbed at my waist, and tugged me to him. He lowered his lips to my ear and murmured, "I'm not used to seeing you in a dress. That's all."

My breath hitched at the way he ground the words out, as if seeing my curves through my clothes was very much different than seeing them without my clothes.

"Stop that," I said, trying to make my breaths even, "or we'll never get out of here. And I heard the band is going to be incredible tonight."

"As long as you promise we can come back here," Ethan said as he pulled back, his eyes sparking. "After I see those curves in action." He kissed me once more, soft and slow. The gesture had a patience to it that I rarely experienced with him. It spoke of something abiding and true.

"I love you," I breathed, responding to the sweetness of his kiss with words.

"Is that why we're going on a relatively calm date now?"

My brows furrowed at him. "I don't understand."

He leaned in to kiss right beneath my jaw, which he knew made me weak in the knees. His question had set me on edge, though. "I just mean that if we're going to be together for a good long while, like people in love plan to be... maybe you're thinking of laying off the life-threatening hobbies just a little bit? So I can sleep at night?"

"Are you saying that you only love me if I agree to stop skydiving?" I stepped back and planted my hands firmly on my hips. If it weren't for my skimpy salsa dress, I would look like my mother standing in the kitchen, reacting to one of my brothers saying they wouldn't be attending Sunday dinner.

"Natalia," Ethan said, his expression instantly softening. "No. That's not – I'm sorry, okay?"

"No, not okay. What did you mean when you said that?"

"I didn't mean anything. I spoke without thinking. It's just – I've been on cloud nine since you told me you loved me, and I guess my thinking just got away from me. I want a future with you, Natalia."

A lump formed in my throat. "And you only want it if I agree to calm down, stay home?"

"No. That's not what I meant. If it sounded like that, it was wrong. I swear." Ethan got down on one knee, and the sight made my heart kick against my ribs. Half a second later, though, he got down on the other one, and raised his clasped hands up in front of his face, the very picture of a begging man. "Please. Forget I ever said anything. I love you, I love your dangerous hobbies, and I'm sure I will love salsa dancing. Just... please promise you'll be as careful as you can."

I didn't know exactly what he meant by that, but hopeless affection for this man rushed through me. I didn't agree with what he'd said, but I still reached my hand down, motioning for him to take it. "Get up, Ethan," I sighed, making sure he saw my smile.

Looking giddy, he pulled himself up, then glided his hands over my arms, thumbs brushing my biceps. "Have I ever told you how sexy it is that you're so strong?"

"You can stop with the groveling, *mi amor*," I muttered.

"Good," he grinned. "Because I don't want us to be late for our date tonight."

"You actually sound excited for one of my dates," I said as I stepped into the hallway and locked the door behind me. "Maybe I didn't try hard enough to shock you."

"Don't get me wrong," he chuckled. "I am like one percent excited for the dancing and ninety nine percent excited to see you doing the dancing. Besides, I thought this was one of my dates."

"Going to a salsa-dancing nightclub is your idea of a safe, calm date?"

"Well, it's not skydiving. Besides, I asked you to take me, didn't I?"

"I guess you did," I said with a soft smile. "Okay," I said as I followed him down the dingy concrete stairs to his car. "I guess this date belongs to both of us, then."

"I like the sound of that," he said as he opened the car door for me. I wondered if this date was only time we'd ever be able to find middle ground on something we truly enjoyed. I wanted to believe it wasn't, but Ethan's comment from earlier haunted me. Could it really be possible for us to find a space of compromise between our two lives?

We'd gone on so many dates by now that our routine was like breathing. In the weeks we'd been together, we'd been to farmer's markets, horseback riding, rock climbing, and cooking classes. Whichever one of us had planned the location would punch it into the GPS, and we'd let the robotic voice direct us. The surprise of the location was part of the fun. Though the salsa dancing date was no surprise, the location of Ponce Pequena would be.

About twelve minutes later, we'd arrived halfway across the city, in a section of a North Philly not known for much of anything – *unless* you were into salsa dancing. Not the kind of salsa with glow sticks and flashy lights and half assed 'classes' for newcomers, either - this is where those of us who had grown up surrounded by the music and the moves could come to blow off some steam. I loved it so much here that I'd made it a point to never date anyone I'd met at one of these places, or to even go home with one of them. I wanted to keep this place separate. All to myself.

Until Ethan.

Maybe that was what tonight was about. I wanted to show him the real heat and chaos and recklessness of an authentic salsa club, because, in some way, it was a metaphor for my life. Nothing more, nothing less.

The club was simply the very large concrete basement that stretched underneath a couple of unassuming office buildings in North Philly with worn-out signs. If you went around the side of those buildings to the alley, there was a heavy metal door that you could tug on just the right way to wrench open, which opened to a narrow concrete stairwell with flickering lights. I didn't miss the uneasy look on Ethan's face as he took the whole process in, and I let myself smirk a little at his Philly innocence. This city was nowhere close to the craziness of Manhattan, but for any smaller town, an underground salsa club probably seemed exotic and a little dangerous. Which, I figured, would make this fit into our date parameters. Technically.

With a slight pang, I realized I didn't know exactly where Ethan had grown up. Didn't know that much about his childhood, or life before UPenn, at all. But I shook the thought off. I could ask him about those things later. Tonight was for amazing music and dancing.

"When they ask you the question at the door, say L.A. style," I said to him with a grin.

"Okay...." Ethan trailed off as we approached the second door.

A tiny woman with a long, shiny ponytail, fingerless gloves, and a tight-fitting leather jacket opened the door. She tilted her chin up at me, taking me in. "Natalia. It's been a long time, chica."

"I know, Solana. I'm here for just a few weeks, and I wanted to show this place to my..." My eyes flicked to Ethan's. "To my boyfriend."

Solana raised an eyebrow. "This young man came here to dance, did he?"

"Y- yes. Yeah, absolutely," Ethan choked out. Everyone was terrified by Solana the first time they met her, despite her being barely over five feet tall. There was a hardness to her pretty face and an elegance to the way her she held her hands that suggested she could lay out someone twice her size and barely ruffle her perfectly shiny hair.

"*Si, verdad? Bueno, Cubano o Rueda, chico?*"

"Uh... I prefer L.A. style," Ethan adorably squeaked. I couldn't help but let out a little laugh.

With that, Solana's chin tilted up and a wide smile stretched her lips. "Ok, *bienvenidos* then! Enjoy Ponce Pequeña, you two."

I laughed and dragged Ethan inside the low-ceilinged room by one hand. "What does the name mean?" he asked, speaking into my ear so I could hear.

"Ponce Pequeña," I said. "Little Ponce. After the town in Puerto Rico the owner comes from."

He nodded, taking everything in. His eyes roved everywhere, taking in the tight space, the Tiffany-style light fixtures that dotted the space with light here and there, leaving some places highlighted in absurd color and others almost too dark to see your partner. The scent of cigarette smoke wafted in and out - it was allowed here, at the bar and on the edges of the dance floor, unofficially. In the middle of the vast, poorly - lit space was a mishmash of amps, microphones, speakers, and a drum set on fold-out riser platforms that could very well have been made and purchased before I was born. Situated between all those things were several musicians, one standing ready at the *timbales*, a couple trombone players, and another holding a cowbell at her side while adjusting the angle of the microphone.

"Ay, Natalia!" The woman with the cowbell stepped down and embraced me, pulling me close. "It's been too long," she said, rocking me back and forth slightly, like she was savoring the hug. I couldn't lie - I did, too. Esperanza was one of my mother's oldest friends. She'd always lived in this area of Philly, which meant I'd only seen her for holidays, graduations, and the occasional Sunday dinner but they'd still been close. I knew seeing her here would be a weird mix of happy and devastating.

"Since the funeral," I said when I pulled back and gave her shoulders a squeeze. "This is Ethan," I said, stepping back a little so that he could move to my side.

"You came to show him a real salsa club, huh?"

"What makes you think I'm not a pro at all this?" Ethan asked with a teasing smile.

"Because, my dear, this is the only *real* salsa club in the city, and I am here almost every week, and I've never seen you in my life." Her eyes flashed, and she reached up to pinch Ethan's cheek with the hand not holding the cowbell. My heart panged, watching her. Totally something Mamá would have done.

It hit me like a punch to the gut, then. Mamá would have loved Ethan.

Thankfully Esperanza excused herself to get ready for the next set before the tears stinging my eyes could fall.

I took the opportunity to pull Ethan, who peered at me with his typical brow-wrinkle of concern for a second, to the side to teach him the basic moves. "So, it's on an eight count, yeah? Forward one, back two and three, rest four. Then start with the other foot and do the same thing backward. One hand in mine, the other on my back," I continued, ducking into the circle of Ethan's arms, "And then I just do the opposite of whatever you're doing."

"Okay. And that's it?" He was a little too confident about this for my liking. I wanted to keep him on his toes.

"Well, there are twirls and traveling and some fancy twists," I said. I could see panic rising in his eyes and grinned. "I'll lead. We'll do whatever you're ready for. The point is for everyone to have fun, not only for the best dancers to be allowed to dance. Good music, good people, yeah?"

Ethan nodded. "Gotta say, this is nothing like the clubs I've been to."

I nodded, squeezing his hand. "And this is going to be about ten times more fun. You'll see."

A trumpet blasted the opening notes of *Ese No Soy Yo*, and I stepped in close to Ethan. My whole body thrilled when he pulled me tight to him, and I could practically feel everything from the hard planes of his stomach to the flex of his bicep to the vague hardening of this below-the-belt equipment. My heels put me at about equal height with him, so I only had to lean forward, tipping onto the balls of my feet, to brush his ear with my lips. "Just feel me. Okay?"

Ethan huffed out the same laugh he always did when he was happily overwhelmed, and I tucked my head into his shoulder, grinning against the skin of his neck. For a few dozen bars of the song, which was one of the slower pieces of this band's set, we just rocked through the 4-count back-and forth steps, until I felt that our legs were nearly as close in their movements as our middles were. I added in a twirl, spinning in the circle of his arms and making sure my ass brushed his crotch halfway through. When I faced him again, there was a fire in his eyes that meant happiness and thirst all at the same time.

I always felt sexy when I danced this way, but dancing with Ethan to this music, in this place, with these moves that were as natural to me as breathing, to thrusting my hips forward or my chest out when we were in bed together... this was something electric. Something that enveloped my body and mind, something that connected me inextricably to my partner. Sure, we stepped on each other's feet plenty, and I received more than one elbow to my side. My ankle tweaked once or twice when I tripped over his misplaced foot, and I was pretty sure one of my big toenails had been chipped and would now look gross for weeks.

But then Ethan got more and more comfortable with each spin or double-step and he started to pull me tight to him at the end of each one. His hands moved sure and strong to grip at my waist, to cup my ass cheek and haul my thigh up over his hip. After only four songs, I would have sworn, standing there in that low-lit concrete room, that something between us had changed. It was like our bodies had communicated without our minds getting in on the action, and now that the connection had been made, it would be nearly impossible to sever it.

The music stopped, and I looked up to realize that Ethan and I had not, in fact, been the only two people in the room. The dance floor had gone from dotted with dancers to nearly full – it was like they had come out of the walls, or something. More likely, they were mixing especially strong margaritas, and the only thing that could pull all these mostly middle-aged people from the excellent bar was the even more excellent music.

"That's it for this set, we'll be back in ten," Esperanza's low alto announced from the mike. "Antonio's making his famous Cuba Libres, I hear, and nothing would make him happier than to put too much Don Q in one for you. He gets less generous as his supply drops, though, so get over there sooner rather than later."

"What is a Cuba Libre?" Ethan asked. "Honestly, I'm kind of embarrassed that I have no clue. With all the partying I did in college, you'd think I'd know."

"Not even you can know everything," I said reaching up to tug at Ethan's tie. "I know it's hard to believe, Mr. UPenn, but there are some things you can't learn by living at school for four years. No matter how like a fish you are."

I could have sworn I felt him stiffen just a little at that, and a flash of heat went through me at the thought I had hurt him somehow. But he just dropped a soft kiss on my lips and said, "I can't think of anyone better to teach me the things I don't know. Which you have to admit are very, very few."

I tipped my head back and laughed, relief more than amusement coursing through me. "How about if we have a Cuba Libre – a rum and coke, by the way - then dance some more, then you can show me some things I might not know yet? In the bedroom?"

He tugged me close to him again, like he was ready to step back into the dance, even though the music had gone silent minutes ago. "Your plans might be crazy sometimes, Natalia, but they are always, always fun." Then he kissed me hard and said, "Take me to the bar."

I laughed again, then pulled him through the crowd toward the three folding tables set up in front of a wall of rolling coolers that constituted the bar. I knew that lots of patrons here had tried to convince Antonio that he needed to upgrade, even if it was one of those cheap DIY projects where you re-fashion a couple of leftover shipping palettes into a bar. But he would just scowl and wave each and every one of them off, then launch into a long speech about how this was cheap and portable, and did we want him to lose profits just so he could have some fancy bar that he couldn't even take anywhere with him?

Plus, if you complimented his business savvy and frugality, he tended to add more spike to your drink.

Drinks in hand, we settled into a spot against the wall, with our shoulders pressed against the pitted concrete bricks. I smelled like sweat and the wispy hairs that had broken free of my updo stuck to my forehead. I twisted my hair and hefted the thick mass over my shoulder, then fanned my chest with my free hand.

"You were spinning like a tornado out there," Ethan said, letting his eyes sweep down to where I was trying to wave the sweat away with that gaze I knew only as *hungry*. I grinned.

"You weren't so bad yourself. And you got just as sweaty as I did, so..."

"I don't know, I kind of think that makes me more pathetic." Ethan's lopsided smile made my breath catch. "You were hardly even panting. By the end of that set, I didn't know if I could handle another song."

"Well, you'll get better."

"Call me crazy, but those words sound like they're coming from someone who's planning on bringing me back here," Ethan said. He watched for my response, patient and unguarded. My heart seized. Wanting to show Ethan this place came from my heart. Planning to bring him back here was a promise about my future that I still couldn't give. Philadelphia wasn't my home – it hadn't been since I was a kid, and since then, I hadn't wanted it to be. Yes, I had a job here – no, it wasn't my dream.

Ethan cleared his throat. "So, my little cyclone, I still don't think this is dangerous enough to be one of your dates."

"It's dangerous because... I don't know." All I knew when I imagined this date with Ethan was that it was something he'd never do, something he'd hate. Something to prove to him that the stuff I loved could never be the stuff he loved. But maybe that wasn't the case. Maybe he loved the rush of dancing salsa in a place like this as much as I did. "Because... collision risks? High heels?"

"I'm not wearing heels," he smirked, "And I really don't plan on it anytime soon."

I arched an eyebrow at him.

"Ever. I don't ever plan on wearing heels in my lifetime."

"I'll give you that," I said, brushing my lips along the rim of my drink. "But you can't deny that you're definitely a victim of the collision risks."

With that, Ethan gave an exaggerated wince. "True enough. Between those heels stepping on my toes and your bony elbows digging into my side, not sure my body is going to agree to go running for a few days. But I hope you don't mind taking me home anyway, even if I am damaged goods." He slid his big hand around my bottom, giving just enough pressure with his palm to tug me toward him. I went willingly. The familiarity of his gentle teasing, the intoxicating swirling heat of the small club, the bite of the rum I'd just tipped down my throat, and the hypnotic beat of the music all combined to make my head swim in the most pleasant of ways.

"'Don't mind' is a severe understatement," I murmured as I brushed my lips against his. "'Can't wait' would be more accurate."

"Natalia Ortiz," Ethan said, the hint of amusement coloring his voice, "You weren't kidding about Antonio's mixology. You're drunk."

"No," I said, pulling back just the slightest bit before his hand moved up to my waist and pulled me tight to him. I practically purred at the feeling of our bodies pressed flush together. "Okay, a little tipsy. But nowhere near too drunk to let you take me home and have your way with me."

He seemed to hesitate for a brief moment, and then nodded. "It's not like this is our first time."

"Or our tenth time. You know that it's okay with me if you fuck me," I said, leaning into him as we crossed the floor.

"Keep talking like that and you're going to get it in the car again. Don't say I didn't warn you."

Blood rushed to the space between my legs, which clenched involuntarily at the memory of that night. It hadn't been the best sex we'd had, or even the only car sex I'd ever had. But something about doing it in the car with Ethan that night had been... sweet. A memory that made my heart swell. I wondered if I'd ever have to savor it without Ethan.

We'd just stepped out into the cool night when Ethan stopped in his tracks. "Ah, your phone's buzzing."

My eyebrows drew in as I watched him dig into his pocket and wiggle my phone out of the tight space. "Nobody calls me," I said, reaching for it and seeing a Philly number I didn't recognize on the screen. "It's probably just a telemarketer," I said, trying to explain away the unknown reason for my stomach suddenly twisting itself into knots.

Ethan peered at the screen, as if he somehow had caller ID in his brain and could better guess at the owner of the number than I could. "At ten thirty on a Wednesday?" he asked.

"You're right, I should –" I went to accept the call, and noticed my fingers inexplicably shaking. *Probably a wrong number.*

"Yes?" I answered, holding the phone tight to my ear so that I didn't drop it with my unsteady hands. What if it was Carol calling with another offer, from a different number? As content as I'd been with Ethan, I didn't want to dismiss any future offers out of hand.

"Yes, hello, I'm trying to reach a Miss Natalia Ortiz?"

My heart lurched. The voice was not familiar, and carried a tinny, distracted quality.

"Miss Ortiz?"

"Yes. Y-Yes, it's me."

Her voice was muffled and garbled against the background of the salsa band's trumpets and drums, which had seemed so bright and cheerful just minutes ago. I located the exit and marched toward it, dimly registering that Ethan was at my side, matching my pace step for step.

"Miss Ortiz, I'm calling from Mercy Philadelphia Hospital. Your father has been stabilized and is in no immediate danger, but we do need you to get down here as soon as possible."

I choked back a sob. "Is he - will he be? - oh, God." My thoughts broke on a wail.

Ethan's hand, firm on the small of my back, had guided me to where our car was parked, nearly a block away. I must have been moving fast.

He opened the passenger side door and helped me inside, holding my seatbelt out to me and waiting 'til my trembling hand took it. Seconds later, he was in his seat and taking the buckle from my frozen hand, clasping it into place before doing up his own.

"Where is he, Tali?" Ethan asked, his voice calm and steady.

"Mercy Philadelphia," I said. My voice broke. "They said he's stable. For now. Just -"

"We're going to get there as soon as we can without getting a speeding ticket. Got it."

Horrible images flashed through my mind of Papá pale and cold, lying silent in a hospital bed - Papá lying on a table, waiting for surgery - Papá groaning in pain, with nobody able to help him. My breathing quickened and my chest felt tight. My vision swam, the lights of the city blurring together before it like a neon watercolor.

"Hey," Ethan said, grabbing my hand. "I'm here. We're going to do this. Together. Okay?"

Somehow his words let me take in a long, deliberate breath through my nose. "Okay," I managed before needing to close my lips again. I was too afraid I'd throw up.

When we pulled up to the doors of the Emergency Room, Ethan undid my seatbelt for me, then leaned over me and popped open the door handle. Even my face felt like it was shaking. I looked at him with wide eyes.

"Go on in, I'll meet you."

"But what if you can't get in? Because you're not - because we're not -" My voice broke again. "And what if I can't get reception, and you don't know how -"

Ethan's eyes didn't leave mine, he just gave a quick nod and popped his own handle, shutting the door behind him. I watched as he bounded to the entrance, speaking to a guy just inside the tall glass door with a semi-official polo shirt on.

Then he was pulling my door open, offering me a hand. "They're going to call valet out."

"Ethan, I'm sorry, I just -"

"Don't. That was stupid, of course you want me to come with you. I'm not leaving your side 'til you say so, okay?"

Briefly, relief flooded my chest, and I felt the tiniest bit steadier. Ethan knew what I was worried about – that we weren't married, so he wouldn't be given access to Papá's room unless he walked up with me now. Tears leaked from my eyes, like they couldn't keep themselves in a second later and my body had absolutely no interest in fighting them. I nodded, ignoring the salty streams slipping over my cheeks.

Ethan expertly navigated us through the emergency room and all the way up to the floor where my dad had already been taken, only stopping to ask for directions a couple times. Once there, I heard him say my father's full name - Ernesto Julian

Ortiz - and then, softly, "Yes, we're family. This is his daughter."
He squeezed my hand and I stepped up to the desk beside him.

"I'm sure my brothers and sisters in law are already here," I
explained. "His should be the room packed full of loud annoying
guys that look like me," I said in a lame attempt at humor. The
nurse answered me with a tight smile and keyed Papá's name
into the system. "Okay, you're Natalia, is that right? You're his
first emergency contact, hon. You're the first one here."

My eyes swam with tears now, flooding too quickly for them
to flow out and make room for new ones. Ethan kept that same
steady hand on the small of my back as we followed a nurse,
who was moving way too quickly down the silent hallway, to a
door, and then to the foot of a hospital bed.

Papá was pale, and still, with a tube stuck in his arm and in
his nose. His body left a couple of feet of empty space at the end
of the bed, and I found some small part of my brain frantically
wondering if he was actually this short, if it was actually him.
But once I swiped at my eyes, settled into a chair, and clasped
his still, cold hand in both of mine, it was clear to me. This was
unmistakably Papá.

There were the laugh lines I'd seen working overtime at
every stupid joke my brothers and I had ever told him. There
was the strange one-inch patch of silver hair that had changed
years before the rest of his jet-black head had even shown signs
of peppering, right behind his left ear. There was his wedding
ring, years of wear making the unique braided design on it
standing out in relief.

"Papá," I breathed. His head shifted to the side, but his eyes
didn't open. Tears streamed down my face.

"Do you want me to call your brothers?" Ethan asked.

"Oh, *Dios*. Yes. Thank you," I said, patting my bra and then
my pockets, wondering where on Earth I'd shoved my phone
after I'd gotten the second worst call of my life.

"I've got it. But shit, it's almost dead. I'll just run downstairs for a charger, they've got to have one in the gift shop –"

But that sent a flash of panic through me. "Please. Just stay until the doctor comes in."

Ethan nodded, then squeezed my knee and reached over to pull another chair from the wall.

Thankfully, there were only a few awful minutes filled with my sniffling and the slow, steady beep of the machines hooked up to Papá before a doctor came in. She crossed to the other side of his bed and pulled a chair from the corner, then sat down in it to face us from across Papá's thighs.

"Hi there, you two. I'm Doctor Kippins, and I'm overseeing your father's care tonight."

"Thank you," I said, my heart twisting. "I'm Natalia, and this is Ethan."

"Okay," Doctor Kippins said gently. "I'm glad your husband was with you, Natalia. It's very important for you to have someone to take care of you in a situation like this." She gave me a warm, cautious smile.

"Oh, I'm –" Ethan stuttered. But I just squeezed his hand hard and interrupted.

"I'm glad, too." I had a feeling Ethan wouldn't be allowed back here at this late an hour if he wasn't directly related to my dad or to me, and I couldn't let him go now. He was the only reason I'd made it to the hospital so quickly, the only reason I still had some semblance of clear thought. I couldn't afford to risk him getting kicked out now.

"Okay," started Dr. Kippins, "Your dad had a heart attack."

"He had an almost-heart attack a few months back," I said, weariness seeping into every word. He'd just told us that things were turning around. What in the world had happened between then and now?

"That's right," Dr. Kippins said. "His doctor put him on some medication, some things to lower his blood pressure and make sure his blood could run smoothly through his veins. He - Dr. Campbell at the practice on Sansom, it looks like - also prescribed him a nutritional plan and exercise regimen, as well as instructing him to get enough sleep and abstain from rigorous activity. Now... I assume that you are his primary caregiver?"

"His care - no, ma'am, I'm sorry, but my dad doesn't really have a caregiver. He's been doing okay on his own at home."

Dr. Kippins mashed her lips together and frowned, nodding as she glanced at my dad. "Whatever he's told you about how well he's doing on his own is clearly... not the best representation of how he was actually doing, I'm afraid. He lives alone?"

Tears welled up in my eyes again. "Yeah. My mom passed away a few months ago and ever since then it's just been him in the house. But... he's been going to his appointments, getting blood drawn, everything. We just got an update from his doctor, saying he was doing well. Is that - can you not - I mean, is that not in his files?"

Dr. Kippins frowned at her tablet, scrolling through screens with practiced speed. "It's possible that the system is experiencing some issues, though it's rare.... but I do see that he signed this release for his doctor to share any and all appointment info with our hospital system. Nothing's showing up here."

"What are you saying?" I asked, aware of my own voice rising in pitch. "That he - I mean, do you think he wasn't - could he have been lying to us? About what his doctor said?" I hiccupped out the sentence fragments, barely able to grasp the concept myself. "I know he's been filling his prescriptions - at least, I've seen him with bags from the pharmacy. Oh, man," I moaned, running my palm across my forehead, "What if he hasn't been taking his medication? Can you see that on there?"

"Okay, Ms. Ortiz." The doctor's voice lowered and softened noticeably - a trick to get me to lower mine, I knew. "We can't know for sure until we can speak to your dad, or at least call his doctor in the morning. Computers aren't perfect, just like people."

"Okay. Right," I said, forcing myself to suck in a breath.

"I can see that the prescriptions were filled by his pharmacy on a 90-day supply three months ago. Unfortunately, I can't see whether or when he was taking that medication."

I blew out that big breath. "Okay, maybe - are there ways to make sure of that? I mean, going forward?"

"One step at a time, okay?" Dr. Kippins leaned forward and placed her hand gently over mine, where it covered Papá's. Her nails were curved and perfectly kept. That comforted me, for some reason. Like if this doctor had her shit together enough to make sure her nails were well kept, maybe she really did know what she was doing. I nodded. "We're going to monitor him. For now, we've placed him on some anti-clotting medication, as well as run a heart catheter into his arteries to remove the blockage that caused the heart attack."

"Wait, you did what?"

"It's a fairly common procedure for this kind of heart attack. There's a large artery that runs directly from the groin to the heart, and our team simply went in at that entry point to scrub out the arteries a little. Then we placed a stent, which is just a little piece of plastic, in there to prevent any more blockage from accumulating quickly. But it won't do all the work. He really is going to have to follow doctor's orders if he wants to keep himself out of the hospital."

Guilt twisted my stomach. "I should have been taking better care of him," I murmured, and at that, Ethan moved his hand from covering mine to lacing his fingers together with mine. He squeezed it.

"Natalia," he said softly. I heard everything in the way he

said my name. Sympathy, understanding of what I was thinking and feeling, a gentle reprimand for thinking this was my fault.

"The good news," Dr. Kippins continued, "is that he was not alone when this happened. He was with his friends, playing cards, and they called 911. The EMTs got to him quickly and our ER wasn't very busy this evening. All told, his brain was barely deprived of oxygen. We expect him to wake up soon, and not to suffer any lasting damage. Except maybe to whatever mindset that led him to think that he didn't have to follow doctor's orders." She gave me another gentle smile, and a gentle parting squeeze on my hand, as she stood up. "I'm going to be on call here for the next nine hours or so, if you have any questions about your dad's condition or his treatment plan. The nurses will be in and out to re-run his EKG and check his vitals, but it shouldn't wake him up. I expect him to open his eyes around breakfast time. The sleep will do him good, allow his brain and body a bit of time to seriously recover. I'd recommend that you two get some sleep, if you can. He'll be fine if you go home, but if you don't want to do that, this couch folds out into a very narrow version of a full bed. The nurses can bring you some blankets."

I nodded, swallowing down the lump in my throat. "Thank you, Dr. Kippins."

She stood at the door now, poised to leave. "Miss Ortiz? I can tell that you love him very much. He's going to be okay. And we can only go forward. Looking backward on his care won't help us too much at this point. And guilt certainly doesn't. Okay?"

Tears were dripping from my eyes again like rain sliding off a tin rooftop. I just nodded, swiping under my eyes with my sleeve. "Thank you," I repeated. When she was gone, I collapsed back in my chair, rubbing my palm against my forehead. My brain felt full of static, and the shaking that had run through all my limbs from the moment the hospital had called was now a bone-deep exhaustion.

"You going to be okay here while I find a charger for you?" Ethan asked gently.

I looked over at him and a quick flash of warmth spread from my chest down through my stomach. He was just here, beside me, ready to help - like a strong, steady constant in my life, sure as anything. I was certain I looked disgusting - puffy eyes, snot collecting at the corners of my nostrils - and ridiculous here in this little black dress and dancing heels. I was suddenly aware of just how much of my skin was showing, and on cue, goose bumps pebbled my arms, chest, and thighs. I shivered.

"I'm sure they have something more comfortable for you to wear, too. Until I can get Amalia to bring you something."

"Why are you so good to me?" I asked, sniffling.

Ethan chuckled as if I'd asked something rhetorical, or ridiculous. He stood and kissed the top of my head, and right before he stepped out the door, said, "Because I love you. Obviously."

His words filled the close space of the hospital room, punctuated by the steady beep of the heart monitor. He loved me. He'd said it so many times since the first time, but this was the first time he was really showing up to prove it.

I'd said it, too. I'd dated plenty of guys, but never, ever gotten to the "I love you" stage. It had never bothered me, either. I had enough excitement to fill my life - I didn't need to hear that someone loved me to feel passionate about something or someone. Love was what happened on telenovelas, what prompted jewelry and flower delivery commercials, what pulp romance novels on grocery store shelves were about. Sitting through a hospital visit? If you had asked me for a definition of what it meant for someone to be in love with me four months ago, "holding my hand after my dad had a heart attack and buying me sweats as I sat in the hospital" wouldn't have been part of it.

Yet, here we were. And it felt... large. All-encompassing. Unmatchable. Terrifying.

Like some part of me wanted to push against it, just to see how much it could withstand.

Ethan returned twenty-five minutes later with a phone charger, a pullover sweatshirt with the hospital's logo on the front, and the thickest, softest sweats I'd ever seen, branded gaudily with PHILADELPHIA. They were a full size too big, and I managed a laugh as I cinched the drawstring waist to its tightest setting. "I think you overestimated the size of my booty," I teased gently as I tugged the sweatshirt over my head, and Ethan blushed.

"I just wanted to get back here to you. I don't know, 'medium' sounds like 'one size fits all'. Or at least, it did down there." He stifled a yawn. "Geez, I should have gotten some coffee."

"Mmm, these are so soft," I practically moaned.

"To be fair, even if I overestimated the size of your booty, it's because I fully admire it. For its size, and... other things."

I gave a small shake of my head, then curled back up in the chair right beside Papá. "I'll take it. I'm just glad I'm finally getting warm. Thank you."

Suddenly, my eyelids were so heavy I could barely even fathom lifting them.

"Okay, cyclone. You might as well sleep while your dad sleeps, right? Let's get you onto this couch. I'll sit there, call the family, and wake you if anything happens, okay? If all your brothers are going to be in this room in the next several hours, you're going to need to be alert."

"But what if -"

"If he wakes up, I'll wake you up. Promise." Then he was

there, helping me up, tugging my hair out of the back of my sweatshirt, and bringing me some of the thick socks from the hospital room's cabinet. We didn't even bother to pull the couch out into its sleeper configuration - I slumped right back on to its pleather cushion and sighed at the feeling of Ethan draping a blanket over me. With a kiss to my forehead, and feeling safe and secure, I was dead to the world.

CHAPTER 25

ETHAN

IT WAS ABSOLUTE HELL, watching Natalia go through the past few hours. I loved her, even more than I had allowed myself to admit until tonight. Seeing her go through so much pain and feeling it like a knife straight to my heart - well, that really forced me to realize it. Watching her cry in disbelief, watching her body shake as her brain struggled to process every piece of awful information coming at her, being beside her as she saw her father lying so still, so pale, attached to wires and tubes, really hammered it home. Love meant more than just hot nights at a salsa club, spontaneous sex in the car, and following someone as they literally jumped out of an airplane.

Love meant sitting with someone at the worst times, shouldering their pain, trying to be everything and anything they needed.

Love meant begging the hospital staff to open up the gift shop and spending way too much on sweats so that the woman you loved didn't have to worry about her father dying and be freezing cold while she did it.

Love meant calling her brothers, who didn't even know you were together, and explaining to them why you were the one who drove their sister to their father's hospital room in the middle of the night.

Love meant sitting there, guzzling green tea from the vending machine hoping to get a mega hit of caffeine, after you'd tucked that woman in, and waiting for the return calls to trickle in.

The first to return my call was Sebastian. He just swore under his breath as I listened to him stumbling around apartment, then heard him wake Mariana and ask her to sit with Camila while he came into the hospital, since his wife was working an overnight shift at another hospital. Next was Amalia, who sobbed into the phone with wet, gulping breaths to rival Natalia's panicked short ones in intensity. She vowed I would see her in fifteen minutes, and asked that I speak to the nurses at the front desk about letting her come up to the room. I promised her I would, even if I didn't know if it would do any good.

As dawn broke over the city, which we had a gorgeous view of through the hospital room window - maybe the only good thing to come out of this whole night - I heard from Natalia's other two brothers. They'd be in as soon as they could, they said, but assumed Natalia had things under control. I said she did, but that she had asked for them. Alejandro was the only one who took an extra second of convincing to come in from New York, but soon, I was rubbing Natalia's shoulder, gently telling her to wake up, since her family would be here soon.

She groaned as she fought to drag her eyes open, and I gently brushed her long, tangled hair from her forehead, wishing I'd had the skill to pull her hair down from its half-up style and pull the whole wavy mass off her face in a top knot. Natalia hated messiness, especially when it came to her body, and having out of control hair would only make this situation more unbearable for her.

"Hey, Love," I said, gripping her arm with gentle pressure, then leaning in to brush a light kiss on her cheek. She was a disaster - swollen eyes, stale breath, smudged mascara - but when she looked at me and I saw relief in her eyes, I thought that I'd never seen anything more beautiful. "Sebastian should be here in a few minutes. I'm going to go find some toothpaste and a hair brush, okay?"

"And some coffee, maybe?" Natalia croaked.

"On it," I said.

By the time I arrived back with the supplies, Sebastian, Rodrigo, and Amalia were there. Amalia sat in the chair where Natalia had been perched last night, in the exact same pose - hands clasped around Mr. Ortiz's, eyes anxiously flicking from his face to the monitor and back again. Instead of the tears that had streaked Natalia's cheeks, she was rocking gently back and forth, her expression desperate, her face pale. She sat on the couch, eyes closed, her lips moving almost imperceptibly as she clutched a string of beads with a metal cross dangling between her hands.

"Mamá's rosary," Sebastian explained when he saw me watching her. "Natalia hadn't wanted to take it out of Philly when she went back to LA. Was worried she'd lose it on the plane or something. When I heard your message, though, it was the first thing I threw in my bag."

My chest tightened, and I strode to the corner, where Sebastian leaned against the wall, and clasped his hand in mine. When he leaned in and put an arm around me, clapping my back in a half-bear hug, I had to fight to keep my tears back.

I would have given anything for this many people around me, hell, for *one* person sitting next to me in support when Mom died. Would have given the world for her monitor to still be beeping like Mr. Ortiz's was.

"That was a great idea," I said. "That, uh -" I cleared my

throat against the lump that had formed there, "that means a lot to Tali, I'm sure."

"She's always loved that thing. Maybe... I don't know. Maybe I thought bringing my mom's rosary would make it feel like she was here, too." His voice broke at the end.

I clasped his shoulder, and gave him a nod. "If it feels that way to you, man, then she is. I lost my mom, too. This shit is rough."

He pressed his lips together and nodded his thanks. "Hey, they have any coffee down there?" Sebastian asked. "I'm running on empty."

I held up the cup I'd found for Natalia. "Sure do. Want me to head back down there?"

"Nah, I think I need to walk."

I nodded my understanding, and once he'd left, I sat next to Amalia.

"Who was with him?" she asked, her voice cold and silent. She was talking to me, but wouldn't break eye contact with Mr. Ortiz.

"His buddies," I said. "They were playing cards, having a beer."

Her jaw clenched. "He promised me he'd given up drinking. That he was going to bed every night after Jeopardy. Now I come to find out he's been out with these guys all these nights every week... dammit, Ethan."

"I know," I said quietly. "I know. Natalia felt bad, too."

"But I was the one who was taking care of him," Amalia ground out. "He - God, my own dad died of this shit. Heart disease. And I didn't take care of him like I should have, so I thought -" She blew out a long, labored breath, and then touched her forehead to where her hands gripped Mr. Ortiz's.

There wasn't anything to say that would help. I knew that. I didn't know what Amalia needed to hear, so I knew it was best to say nothing. To just be there. Still, watching the process of fear and tentative, impending mourning was very different from going through it myself. The silence was heavy. Natalia's occasional punctuating whispers and the beep of the machines were the only thing breaking up the stretch of nothingness that filled the room.

At exactly 7:00 in the morning, as the sun was sending brilliant hues careening off the Philly skyscrapers, Sebastian made it back, four coffees in hand, followed closely by Dr. Kippins.

By now, Natalia had finished with the Rosary, and gave me a soft smile when I sat beside her and rubbed her back. We still hadn't talked about what her family thought our relationship was, about whether and when to tell them about us, but right now, it seemed like the least important thing on the planet.

Dr. Kippins took up the same seat as she had done last night, holding the same chart, and had the same talk with Amalia that she had with Natalia and I last night. Instead of getting progressively sadder, and displaying obvious feelings of guilt, though, Amalia sat up straighter with every sentence, her eyes getting narrower, her hands withdrawing from Mr. Ortiz's and eventually squeezing so tight that her knuckles were white.

Natalia saw, and pulled up a chair beside Amalia, just like I'd done for her last night. She didn't dare touch her sister-in-law, though - Amalia looked like a grenade whose pin had been pulled, ready to go off with the slightest extra bit of pressure.

"Why didn't they call me?" Amalia asked.

"Pardon?" asked Dr. Kippins.

"Why. Didn't the hospital. Call me? I'm the one who takes care of him. Checks in after all his appointments. Makes sure he's filling his prescriptions. Checks the bottles to see if he's taking them. Goes with him to the market."

"So, *you* are the primary caregiver?"

"I... I mean, not officially, but..." Amalia blew out a breath.

"Look. It's just my husband and me. I don't have any kids... yet. I'm sort of in between jobs. And I went through all this with my dad a few years back, so... I've been the one checking in with them."

"I'm so sorry, Mrs...."

"Ortiz," Amalia confirmed. "I'm married to his son." She jerked her head over to the wall, where Rodrigo stood, whispering something to Sebastian. Her jaw stayed tight, her words barely finding the space to make it out.

"Well, *Miss* Ortiz – his daughter - she is the one who's listed on his forms. I didn't know he had any other children."

"Five," Amalia interjected. "Five sons. God, why isn't that on there?"

"Well, you're here now. Maybe you can help me understand some of the information we've been missing..."

A few moments later, Amalia had revealed that she'd been taking Mr. Ortiz to the hospital for every appointment, dropping him off, waiting for him in a nearby cafe or running an errand, and then picking him up when it was over.

"He's a very private man," she'd explained. "He didn't even want to move in with us when - when his wife – well, anyway. He certainly didn't want me to hear the doctor talking about his health."

"And have you actually spoken to any of the doctors after his appointments?"

Amalia's brow furrowed in confusion. "One, a few weeks back. He asked me to come up to meet him, said the doctor had good news for me. Other than that...no."

"What I'm getting at, Mrs. Ortiz, is that the hospital system shows no record of Mr. Ortiz actually seeing any of the doctors he was scheduled to see after the cardiac event he suffered a few months back. So, we're trying to get to the bottom of that. Did you accompany him to *any* appointments? Or speak to any of the doctors or nurses afterwards?"

"No, I - he told me after the appointments that he needed to keep taking meds, restricting activity... a few weeks ago, he said he'd gone and the report from the doctor was good, that he could get back into some exercise..." Her hand flew over her mouth. "Do you think -?"

"I'm wondering if he was skipping appointments, yes," Doctor Kippins explained. "Now, about the medication... his labs indicate that he may not have been as diligent about that as he should of them. What arrangement did you two have for him remembering to take those?"

Natalia and I watched as Amalia's face grew increasingly horrified, and her voice shakier with every second, as she explained to the doctor how she'd gone into the house weekly and methodically set out Mr. Ortiz's pills in a 28-sectioned container, that had an alarm attached, and checked in with him every couple of days to make sure he'd stayed on schedule.

"But you didn't actually look at the organizer?" Doctor Kippins confirmed. "No judgment," she rushed to explain, "but it will help me get a clearer picture of what's going on here. That's all."

"Oh, God," Amalia repeated. "I can't believe - I just thought he'd be taking them. Taking care of himself, especially after -"

At that moment, a deep grumble came from Mr. Ortiz's chest, then a light cough. Dr. Kippins pressed the nurse button, then placed her hand on Mr. Ortiz's and stood to raise the bed a bit. Slowly, his eyes opened, and the corners crinkled with a soft smile when he saw his daughter and daughter-in-law.

"Girls," he said. "*Lo siento,*" he managed before starting to cough again. Amalia burst into tears, throwing herself onto Mr. Ortiz's lap and weeping. Natalia sat, calmer than I would have expected, and watched for several long minutes. The nurses came in and took vitals, adjusted his nose cannula, and conferred with the doctor.

"Listen, Ms. Ortiz, Mrs. Ortiz -" Doctor Kippins started as she turned to leave. "Regardless of what happened in the last few months, it's in our best interests to focus on how we can help your dad going forward. See what you can find out from him about how he's been managing his care. I'm going to have the next attending doctor on shift speak with you on her rounds, in a few hours. Can both of you stay that long?"

Both women nodded.

"Great. Remember, focus on going forward, okay?" And then she was gone.

Amalia settled back down in her seat as the doctor left and I went to grab my coat. Natalia had pulled it over herself while she slept on the couch, and now it smelled like her perfume.

"Where are you going?" Natalia asked, following me to the couch. She looked so different, here in the pale fluorescent light of the hospital room. Empty. Lost.

"I just thought I'd give you some time alone with your family. You know?"

"Oh." Her eyes turned down, and I noticed her lips tremble just a bit. "Sure, and you probably have stuff you need to take care of, so...."

"No, Tali, really, it's -"

"So I'll try to call you when we fix all this up, keep you posted, if you -"

"Hey," I interrupted, gently tipping her chin up with my fingers. "I have nothing more important to do than whatever you want or need me to do, right this minute. For the rest of the day, and until your dad leaves the hospital. Later, even. We're in this together."

She could have taken that opportunity to make a comment about how, yes, I worked for her dad and the gym. She could have refused. But my heart soared when, instead of either of those things, she looked me steadily in the eye and whispered, "Thank you."

"So, you want me to stay?" I asked, keeping my coat slung over my arm.

"Just until we figure out this doctor shit," she said. "If you could. I have a feeling this is not going to go well. At all. And you always... make things better. Calmer."

I settled in on the couch while Natalia went back to the seat beside Amalia's. I couldn't ignore the happy swell of my heart at her words.

CHAPTER 26

NATALIA

"WHAT ABOUT THE DOCTOR, PAPÁ?" Amalia was asking, her brows knit together, her tone imploring. "You've been going to all those appointments, haven't you? The computer must be wrong, *sí?*"

I knew the answer already, deep in my gut. I hadn't prayed the rosary in a long time. Too long. Since Mamá died and I was trying to pray for my soul to quiet, for my path to sort itself out before me. Then I'd gone to LA, left her beads behind, hadn't bought my own. Today, in the hospital, I'd stumbled over the prayers, but I'd been grateful for the habit of it all, the rhythm, the way I didn't have to think about the words but I was still able to say them, the way they opened up the floodgates for peace to trickle in, for me to feel a little more grounded.

"Ah," Papá replied, his face the picture of contrition. "You know I was feeling pretty good a week or two after the hospital, Mali. And all these appointments they had set up for me... it seemed like a lot of appointments."

"Yes, they were to help you, Papá. Make sure your care was going well, that you were on track."

"Listen, *querida. El doctor.* You go, tell them what feels bad.

They send you to another guy. Then that guy sends you to another guy, no? And that's how they get you. You go here, you go there, and in the end, you pay seven doctors and you still don't know what you have."

"Papá," Amalia replied, clearly trying to keep her voice steady. She wasn't succeeding. In fact, in that moment, she reminded me of my mother, who hated yelling but managed to let us know when she was enraged anyway. It turned out that a low, almost-too-quiet-to-hear voice terrified us more than any screaming fit from any of our friends' moms ever could. Amalia's rage gave her voice the same quiet trembling that Mami had always employed to let us know that we were in a world of trouble, and we were about to hear all about it. "We knew what you had. You had an almost-heart attack. You had the beginnings of heart disease, and you had chest pain, and then next thing that happens after that if you don't take care of yourself, if you don't relax and eat right and take your medicine and go to the doctor –" she ground out that last word through tight teeth – "is that you have an *actual* heart attack. *Ataque al corazon.* Which has now happened. Which was beyond serious. Which very nearly *killed you.*" Finally, her voice broke, and her tears started up again. I put my arm around her, gripping her upper arm lightly, and was surprised with the shock of feedback when she stiffened instead of leaning into my hug, as I would have expected her to do.

"What I'm trying to understand," she continued, "is why you let me take you to the doctor's office, and then didn't actually go inside."

Papá met her eyes sheepishly, but only for an instant.

"Why I filled all your prescriptions, sorted them out for each hour of each day, double checked them, and, apparently, you didn't bother to take them."

Papá shrugged weakly. "They made me feel funny. Upset my stomach. And I felt tired when I took them."

"So, let me get this straight," Amalia said, somehow sounding even angrier than she had at the beginning of this conversation. "You had me do all these things for you, manage all your care, and then you lied to me about actually accepting that help? And then – *then* – you didn't even bother to list me as your emergency contact for when this all inevitably happened again? For when you would definitely have a heart attack because you weren't even bothering to try not to?"

Ah, here it was. Now her voice was getting louder. And she was pausing between sentences to suck her snot back into her nose.

"I did take it easy, Mali. I made some tea. Whenever I was feeling run down, Mamá would make me some tea, and that would fix me right up."

The silence after he mentioned Mamá was deafening.

"If Mamá was here," I interjected, my voice soft, but steady, low, but devoid of sympathy, "she would have taken you to the doctor." Silence fell again. Inside, I was shaking with rage, but outside, I was determined to stay even-keeled. "She would have taken you to the doctor, and sorted out your medication, just like Mali did. So why am *I* your emergency contact?"

"Because you are my only daughter. And that's why you came home, *mija*. To help with these things. When you said you were coming home, and then I filled out the papers at the doctor, I thought –"

"You thought I was coming home to replace Mamá."

My lips, my entire face, went numb as the truth washed over me. Shock, for myself and how little I understood what my life had become. Anger, for Mali, who had dedicated her life to Papá, who apparently didn't even want to accept any of her help.

"You said you were coming home to help."

"With the *gym*, Papá! With The Knockout. That's what I can do. That's what we agreed on."

"*Sí*, and you're here, and you're taking care of the gym, and I'm in the gym every day."

"You can't just expect these things of me, Papá! I am not a replacement for Mamá! I can't do what she would have done. And you shouldn't be in the gym at all, especially if you're not taking your medicine!"

Amalia brushed her hand down my arm, but I jerked it away.

"No!" I shouted, at everyone and no one. "None of this is okay. I can't – I have to – I *need* to be my own person. Don't you understand that?'

Papá just looked at me, confused. "I... Nati, when did my nurse say she was coming back? I need another pillow or something." He grimaced as he shifted in the bed. I could see that he was in pain, but in this moment, with the anger and resentment flashing through my body, setting my spine on fire, I couldn't bring myself to care.

"I've got it, Papá. Here, we'll go get your nurse." Amalia's voice, soothing as ever, accompanied her hand firm on my shoulder. Ethan sat in the corner, watching with his brow furrowed, probably frozen. I was grateful for it. I wouldn't know what to do if he got involved in all this, at this moment. She steered me out the door by my elbow, and once we got out to the hallway, I spun to look at her. I could feel the anger behind my eyes, making them burn, spreading upward in the beginning of a fierce headache.

"Natalia, I am saying this with absolute love for both you and your father. I am just as angry as you are, but we can't stress him out any more right now. You need to walk this off."

The red hot rage flared. "Great. One more person telling me what to do. You're right, that's *exactly* what I need right now."

She deflected my sarcasm with a blink. "It's not because I want you to go. But before you start screaming at a sixty-seven-year-old man who just had a second heart attack, maybe you should take a walk."

"The first one was just an almost," I grumbled. Amalia gave me a look.

"Like I said," Amalia continued, "I think we could all benefit from taking a step back right now. Everyone is tired. Everyone is stressed. You are still wearing most of last night's hairspray. Let's regroup. Go home. Rest. Get a shower."

Ethan made his way out of Papá's room. "He just dozed off, so... yeah," he said. "Just heard Amalia say 'shower' and I think that's the best idea I've heard in a while. Let's get you home."

He said it so naturally, like the decision was already made, like he'd be the one taking me home from now on, like his steering my comings and goings were a matter of course. He said it so sweetly, with a protective hand brushing the small of my back with that slight pressure pushing me toward the exit, that I almost felt bad freezing in place. He didn't know what was going on in my head. Didn't really know where I should go, what I should be doing with myself. How could he, when I barely did myself?

Numb, I started walking down the hall toward the elevators, taking stiff steps just a little too quick for Ethan to keep contact with me. I stared at the numbers above the buttons, trying to ignore how they were fuzzy around the edges. *Don't think. Don't feel. Just do. Just get home. Then you can regroup.*

Ethan fidgeted beside me in the elevator. In a back corner of my mind, I knew this couldn't be easy for him. He'd been so supportive, from driving me here to buying me sweatpants and a phone charger, to being the one to basically forcing me to go home for some much needed rest now.

But I knew, deep down, I could not let him take me home right now. I needed to pull myself together, and I couldn't do that with him around. Mostly because, the more confusing things got, the more I realized that he was the most complicated piece of this puzzle. How to get out of this mess and keep Ethan at the same time seemed like an impossible riddle. Having him standing beside me while I tried to puzzle it out would only make everything that much harder. Suddenly, there we were, standing in the hospital lobby, the late morning staff trickling in and the day's appointments just starting to clog the various waiting areas. Ethan stuck a thumb over his shoulder. "Oh, the garages are that way. I think we're on –"

Ethan was interrupted by my phone, buzzing in his butt pocket. "Shit," he said, reaching back to pull it out. "Do you think everything's ok up there? He seemed – Oh. It's not Amalia. It's... Carol?"

I practically lunged for the phone, snatching it from his fingers, not missing the confused look that twisted his features.

"Hey, Carol," I said, injecting every ounce of strength into my voice I possibly could.

"I have good news for you, honey!" Carol chirped on the other end of the line.

The hand holding the phone shook. I blew out a long breath and watched as Ethan's eyes grew progressively wider in the silent space before I answered.

"Tell me the good news," I urged impatiently. God help me, I wanted to know. Wanted her to give me a reason to run away. My heart galloped in my chest.

"The girl they hired for the first stunt was awful. The girl that did the next episode was worse. I know you said you didn't want to do it, and I promised wasn't going to call you, sweetie, but they practically begged for you, so I told them I'd try you again."

I narrowed my eyes, even though Carol couldn't see my glare through the phone. "You re-sent my reel, didn't you?"

"That's neither here nor there. They want you for this show. It's a motorcycle job – it'd be amazing for you. You'd be amazing for it. There's a crew worker's strike looming in New York, you know, and they're not sure how much longer they'll have their effects guys, and technically, you can get there faster than anyone in LA, and you know, Natalia stunting for Natalia, and you look just like her too, it's just too perfect to – "

"Yes," I said, strong and decisive, like the gavel banging at the end of a court judgment. In the end, she'd barely had to babble at all. "Yes, I'll be there. When do they need me?"

Carol let out a high pitched scream. I winced pulled the phone away from my ear, dimly realizing that Ethan had started pacing, three steps one way, three steps another. "Call time is seven o'clock tomorrow morning!" she screeched. "I'll text you the details now! Natalia, baby, we are back! Love you to bits! Ciao!"

My hand was still shaking. It was only physical evidence of what I knew to be absolutely true – committing to this job terri-fied me, which was exactly why I had to do it.

"You're taking a stunt job, aren't you," Ethan said. "Are you –" He stopped abruptly, rested his hands on his hips and blew out a breath. When he spoke again, it was like someone had turned the volume down to just above a hiss. "Are you kidding me right now?" He didn't wait for me to answer. "What kind of stunt is it?"

"Motorcycle," I said simply. "It'll be fine."

Ethan scoffed. "Fine. Yeah. You're gonna – are you even trained for that?"

"Listen, Ethan. I am freaking out right now, okay? About all this hospital shit, and about... everything. I need – I need something to make me feel – alive." I looked down at my feet, realizing how lame that sounded, but not being able to bring myself to care.

"Your dad needs you, Natalia. Your family needs you, and I need you. Safe, and sound, and here."

"No, they don't. You don't. Amalia has all this under control. She is the grownup here. Dammit, Ethan, she just dismissed me from the hospital room! Just because my father left me in charge doesn't mean I should be making any decisions about his health."

"The gym needs you, too."

I shook my head, mashing my lips together, hoping that would help keep my responses more even. "Sebastian and Rodrigo can handle it for the next two days. They'll probably like having something else to do besides hover around Papá's bed."

Ethan was very clearly dumbfounded, and I wished I could have found something to say that would have wiped the shock off his face. But I didn't. We both knew what Ethan was leaving left unsaid. We both knew that him saying it would change everything.

"I'm going to head home," I muttered. "I'll call you, okay?"

"Natalia, don't go. I need you here, not doing crazy stunts. I need you to be safe. Please, just – I don't think I can do this if you're really going to leave and put your life in danger at a moment's notice."

And there it was.

"Don't do this," I said, my eyes filling with tears.

He swallowed hard, a contrast to his strong, stubborn jaw. He wasn't going to budge. "Why not? Haven't things been going well, Natalia? Haven't we been having fun? I thought we were happy here, together. Jumping out of airplanes once in awhile. I thought we were good."

"Well, maybe *we* shouldn't be making big decisions about *my* life."

Ethan's jaw clenched, working back and forth almost imperceptibly. "Not even if we love each other?"

"Maybe... maybe it's not enough." The only way he heard that awful sentence come out of my mouth was if he was hanging on every word.

"Jesus, Natalia!" His voice broke, and I didn't dare look at his face.

A tear slipped from my eye. He was hurting. I was the one causing the pain. I could see and hear all the evidence. And I was still walking away from him.

One more time, the voice inside me said. *Kiss him one more time before you leave for New York. Even if it ruins the whole damn relationship.*

Gingerly, I took two steps in to Ethan. I curled my hand around his shoulder, raised up on my tiptoes, and brushed a kiss to the corner of his mouth. He stiffened, and the small rejection rolled through me like a wave. He was making this almost impossible. Almost.

Still on tiptoes, I whispered, "I *love* you," before lowering myself and taking a step back.

Ethan just scoffed in reply. Yes, it stung. But what did I expect? Still, the decision about the job was so clear. Like I was standing in the eye of the storm, and it was the only thing that wasn't spinning like crazy, uncontrollable, pinning me in place. I didn't know if I could salvage this situation later, but I knew, as surely as I knew that I loved my family and I loved Ethan, that I had to take the job.

What else could I do?

"I'll call you when I'm on my way back from the city, okay?" I said, willing some strength and clarity into my voice.

"You know what? Don't," Ethan managed through gritted teeth. "I'm sure if you manage to get yourself killed, one of your brothers will call me. After all, I'm just the guy helping you with the gym. Just the guy who keeps you entertained while you're here doing what you need to do, until you inevitably run off again. Just the guy who would kill to have a family like yours, and you can't even be bothered to appreciate it when you very nearly lose it."

A choking heat spread up through my throat, like Ethan's words had the power to suffocate me.

My hurt bound together with my mother's indignation from deep within me, protesting that anyone would say such terrible things to me. "Don't say another word. Don't you dare."

But Ethan had found his fire, it seemed. Exactly at the time that he could use it to hurt me most. His lips pulled up in the beginnings of a snarl, and my heart stuttered as my body recoiled. "You don't need to call me to tell you you're still alive," he growled, "since you don't actually give a shit what I think about all of it."

"Ethan, that's not fair. I –"

"You what? You care about me?" The way his lip curled up in a sneer when he said that made my heart twist in on itself. "Because that's not fucking true, Natalia. Obviously not. This is the one thing – the *one thing* – I can't bear for you to do. And you're doing it anyway. Do you understand how excruciating this is for me? I lost one person in a car crash. Now you're going to purposely do insanely dangerous things on a moving vehicle? For what? For the thrill, while you're killing me?"

A terrible silence hung in the air for a long beat. Then he said, "I can't go through that again, Natalia. I can't." His voice broke on the last word, and then a single tear rolled down his cheek. He wiped it away angrily, then crossed his arms over his broad chest, a monolith cemented firm in the middle of the hospital lobby.

There were a million things I could have said. "Get your head out of your ass." "I love you." "Don't do this to us." "I'm sorry." But none of them would have helped. So I took a step backward, then another. "I'll call you," I finally said, forcing every word in hopes that he understood how determined I was. Then, with one more heart-wrenching look into his stunned, red-rimmed eyes, I walked out of the hospital into a cab.

This was going to be absolute hell, but I knew I had to walk through it.

CHAPTER 27

ETHAN

MY CO-HOST for the Bro Show, Mark Mahler, just happened to text me when I had almost arrived back home. I didn't know how I actually managed to operate my car and make all the necessary turns to get back to my place. My brain was filled with fuzz, and it took effort to breathe in and out.

I'd been thinking that, in this fishbowl of life, Natalia and I were little guppies swimming side by side for a while. Turned out that I was a guppy. She was the water. Take her away, and my whole world would change really fast.

The text tone repeated insistently, so I as soon as I was at a red light, I pulled out my phone.

Mark: Beers tonight?

My eyebrows went up. In the recesses of my mind, I knew that the time I spent hanging out with Mark had gotten more and more sparse. Not that I'd really cared, on the couple occasions I'd noticed; I had Natalia, and there was no love lost between Mark and me. Guys weren't like that.

Still, I had to admit that hanging out with Mark sounded like exactly what I needed right now. Mark wouldn't try to reason with me. Mark would listen to everything and only comment if I asked him to. We weren't the best of friends, but we were close enough to know that.

Me: Beers now?

I squinted as I looked up at the sky on my way into my building, realizing I had no idea what time it actually was. Minutes could slow down to feel like hours or hours could compact into what seemed like seconds in a hospital. Natalia had slept, and I'd dozed, waiting for her dad to make any kind of change. I'd eaten here and there. At some point, the sun had come up.

Like he read my mind, Mark responded.

Mark: It's three thirty in the afternoon.

Me: Yeah, and by the time you get here it'll be almost four which is almost five.

Mark: Is something wrong?

Me: Yeah. Or maybe it's for the best. But I could use some company.

The three little dots that told me he was responding appeared and reappeared a couple times over the next

Mark: Ok, just changed plans with Toby. I'll see you soon.

Hell if tears didn't well up in my eyes at that. Since I'd graduated and all my college friends had dispersed to jobs across the country, Mark had been my only good friend in Philly. We didn't hang out quite enough and I hassled him a little too much, but shit like this made me feel like at least someone in this town had my back.

He arrived at my door in under half an hour, with a dorky secret knock that wasn't secret because literally everyone knocked that way when they were trying to be funny. I would have made fun of it under normal circumstances. Under normal circumstances, I would have changed my clothes from the salsa club the night before. I knew I stunk.

It was amazing how everything you'd ever used the time and energy to care about your entire life could be negated by just one broken heart.

I hauled myself off my couch and yanked the door open, hating myself for not having given Mark a key. I hadn't given anyone a key, I realized. If I died alone in this house, something that was looking more and more likely by the day, nobody would find me until my body started to smell. There was no one close enough to me to notice or care. Not even a cat.

God, even when he was a pathetic single guy, Mark had a cat.

"How is Hawthorne, anyway?" I asked him, and he looked at me quizzically as he crossed to my kitchen island and set down two six packs of beer and a bottle of vodka. I chuckled to myself at my joke.

"I think you had most of that conversation in your head without me, buddy," Mark said, looking at me with concern etched across his brow.

Dammit, he was right.

"She dumped you, huh?" Mark asked, clapping me on the shoulder with one hand and tugging my drawer open for a bottle opener with the other.

"No. I dumped her." It sounded so dumb, so unreal to me, that I groaned and covered my eyes with my hand.

"No. I don't believe that."

I nodded, taking a long pull off the beer he'd brought me. I resisted the urge to stick my tongue out – it was warm, cheap, and tasted like piss.

He still noticed that I thought it was gross. "It was all I had. Maybe that means you won't drink the whole pack and you'll be able to tell me what the actual hell happened to make you break up with the only girl I've ever see you truly crazy for."

"That can't be true," I scoffed, drinking again. Might as well drink fast so I didn't have to taste as much of the shit. "You knew me when I dated..." but I couldn't think of a single woman I'd dated that I'd even felt close to the same way about as I had Natalia. Every time I got close to an "I love you" or a "come meet my parents" with someone I was seeing, things cooled off and then, within a few weeks or even a couple months, died.

As badly as I wanted someone to love forever, a family to surround myself with, none had ever seemed right. Until her.

"Fuck me, Mahler," I cursed while staring down into my lap. "*Fuck.*"

"No thanks, bro. That's Natalia's job."

I shot him a poisonous glare, and only felt a little guilty about it.

"You fucked up, huh?" he asked, nodding like he knew anything about it.

"No, she —"

"You're saying she made you break up with her? What, she held a gun to your head?"

"No, she held a gun to hers."

His brows pulled together, and a truly lost expression took over his face. "You lost me."

I sighed and took another pull from the beer bottle, trying to gather my thoughts in that one long swig. "Remember the last time she left the city? What she was going to do?"

"Oh..." Mark said with a slow nod. "That's right. She was doing that bull-running thing. Obviously, she survived." He watched me with an eyebrow raised, waiting for me to connect the dots.

"Came home with a six-inch scar next to her navel. She liked it. Loved, it actually. Wanted to do more... I don't know. Adrenaline-inducing shit."

"So?"

"So she did. Base jumping, sky diving, gun slinging. The whole nine yards. And then she went the extra mile. She started doing this stunt actress thing." I closed my eyes tight and covered them with a closed palm, leaning forward to set my beer on the coffee table. It was suddenly too heavy for me to hold. "Jumping off buildings, stunt driving. Stuff like that. Dangerous shit, man. And I thought I convinced her she didn't need to do it anymore, but today, she accepted another job. A really scary one."

"Oh. Man. She was a stunt driver, wasn't she? That's what she left town to do this time, isn't it?"

Suddenly, I couldn't get any words out. It took everything in me to swallow the lump in my throat back down so it didn't turn into tears. Every time – every damn time I imagined her driving that motorcycle too fast, cutting the wheel too severely to the side, putting herself at the mercy of a two thousand pound cage of steel, plastic and rubber, my brain shorted out. So I just nodded.

"Ethan, I'm sorry."

"Thanks," I half-choked.

"So," he continued gingerly. "Just to get the story straight for myself. You gave her an ultimatum, said you can't be together if she was going to put herself at risk with the death-trap job. And she chose the crazy car driving over a life with you."

"Pretty much," I said. I cleared my throat, mentally banishing the sobs lying in the wings. "It's a motorcycle, not a car." God, I missed her. Soul deep, already. It was like she'd turned her back on me and not only left a hole in my life, but in the entire damn city. She probably hadn't even gone yet. She was probably still in Philly, close enough for me to get to her, even though I didn't have the choice to go to her. Not really. Not anymore.

"So, then, I gather you were dumb enough to stick with your stupid threat?"

My eyes snapped open. I would have sat up rigidly straight if I wasn't so bone tired. "What the fuck, dude?"

"I'm just saying. I know 'pathetic in love' when I see it. That's where I am. I have no clue where things are going between me and Toby, absolutely no idea whether there's even a way for them to work out. But hell if I don't love her. She doesn't want what I want... what I think I want. I'm going to ride it out, though. However long it lasts."

"Except for you, there's not really a high chance in it ending with her traumatic death," I muttered, half-hating my friend and half appreciating the hell out of him just for being here.

"If I didn't understand where your emotions were coming from, I would ask if you were sure you weren't the one acting on a drama movie set."

If looks could kill, the one I shot him would have been instant murder. If it hadn't been clouded with tears. "Not funny."

"Seriously, though. You are so afraid of losing her that you push her out of your life because you anticipate her early traumatic death? How the fuck does that make any sense?"

"C'mon, man. You know my mom –"

"– I know she lived an utterly and completely safe life until a freak accident killed her. I know Natalia has been doing things that you seem to think spell instant doom and guess what? She's not dead yet. The universe doesn't work on an actuarial table, Ethan."

"I know," I said quietly. "I just... she didn't care enough about me to keep herself safe."

"Nobody's ever safe," Mark said. "Horrible accidents happen all the time to people who live perfectly boring lives.

There are no guarantees. You can't try to write a contract with the universe, Ethan."

That was when it finally happened. Every worry, every guilt, every horrible nightmare I'd had reliving the moment I heard Mom died, purged itself in a deluge of big, fat, silent tears. Mark saw, and let me cry. When I sniffled, then sobbed, he moved next to me on the couch and gripped my shoulder.

"Hey," he said. "Hey. It's okay. Call her."

"I can't now." I told him about her dad, about how Natalia was being pulled in so many different directions and had just thrown herself in another. "She probably just wanted to get away from it all. Including me," I said miserably.

"Then tomorrow. Let her cool off, then call her. Tell her you want her. Okay? Tell her you'll make it work. For now... drink it off."

I clicked the neck of my bottle against his. My heart ached for Natalia, but it also knew that going after her tonight would only make things worse. Mark was right – I was in love, but I was not an idiot. "To tomorrow," I slurred, only vaguely registering his answering chuckle.

"Yeah, man. There's always tomorrow."

CHAPTER 28

NATALIA

IF PAPÁ HADN'T BEEN SEDATED when I left the hospital, I would have never been able to leave Philly. Just the way that he looked into my eyes broke my heart. I couldn't look back into them and tell him I was about to break his.

Amalia understood when I told her I needed to go to New York for this job. For all the hard work I'd done re-establishing the gym, she had worked just as hard keeping herself apprised of all the ins and outs of operations. I promised her I'd check in remotely every morning and every evening. I wouldn't even be gone that long, I'd told her, parroting Carol's promise. It was just two scenes, and I'd be on my way back to Philly.

I should have known it wouldn't be that simple. Nothing ever was.

I checked into my hotel room, just a few blocks from the set where we'd be filming. Carol had told me I'd be riding a motor-cycle – something I'd done once or twice on my travels, once down a dirt road in the countryside, and another across cobble-stones, which rattled my jaw so severely I could still feel it vibrating hours later. I'd tried out a stunt cycle once, on the relative safety of a movie set, though I'd never ended up filming for that scene. I'd loved every second of every ride.

It was the promise of zooming somewhere on a roaring bike, my hair whipping through the air, that kept me distracted enough from the memory of Ethan's face, etched with pain, as I walked away from him. I'd known that I was breaking every bit of trust we'd built between us to smithereens. I knew that he would see my actions as proof that I hadn't meant what I'd said when I'd told him I loved him.

What I hadn't told him, what I couldn't tell him as I walked away from him, was that I was doing this precisely because I loved him. Loved him so much that I wanted a life with him, and that I wanted to see if I could keep my need for heart-pumping thrills and a devotion to him balanced. He'd answered that question for me even before I left the Philadelphia City limits. He'd broken my heart doing it.

I knew now that I'd be lucky to ever see Ethan again. It hurt like hell, but I deserved it.

My dreams of flying down the streets of Manhattan with an engine rumbling between my thighs were squashed when an exhausted-looking production assistant pointed me to a dingy-windowed warehouse, saying we'd be filming inside. Well, I reasoned as I tried to cheer myself up, I'd still be riding a motor-cycle. And I was getting paid. And I was going to be on televi-sion, for crying out loud. Maybe this was where the rest of my life really would begin. Maybe the gaping hole that had been torn in my heart by leaving Ethan alone and broken-looking in the hospital corridor would start to be filled in by a stunt work career that would begin today.

Carol called me after I'd already made it to hair and makeup. I was familiar with this part of the process – my makeup had to be caked on so heavily that, in the rare instance any part of my face couldn't be spliced out of a shot, I looked enough like the actress to allow the shot to be included. The makeup artist was in the process of gluing false eyelashes on as my phone chirped to life on my lap.

"So, darling, I have some news," Carol squawked into the phone before I even had a chance to greet her. "Good news and bad news. Bad news, they won't be able to do the helmet like we discussed."

"But, Carol, I –" As excited as I'd been about this job, at least some of Ethan's protests had sunk in to my sensibilities. I'd told Carol I wanted to wear safety gear.

"Good news, honey, you're not even outside. No other cars. So, much less danger, yeah?"

"But if –" I swallowed my jumbled arguments. There was no point. Carol didn't know, and didn't care, about all the dangers Ethan had worried to me about in those quiet moments we'd spent together over the last several weeks.

"You're going to be great. They told me there's a strong harness net, cushions galore, probably only need to do a couple takes. You couldn't hit your head if you tried. Okay?"

I blew out a long breath, probably filling Carol's ear with static. She wouldn't hear my answer anyway. Besides, even though I'd made promises to Ethan, he probably hated my guts now. What was the point in protesting the inevitable. This was what I wanted to be doing. I had chosen to be here, riding a motorcycle – indoors, somehow – without a helmet. "Net. And cushions," I reiterated into the phone, showing Carol I'd heard her.

"Call me when you're done, okay, doll face?"

"Sure thing," I said, willing as much confidence as I could into my voice before clicking off. The stunt coordinator stuck his head into the makeup room seconds later, getting the hair stylist's approval before whisking me off to meet my ride.

"Now, it's all pretty standard," the stunt coordinator, a

muscled bald man named Gary, told me. "We're just going to do the one today." I felt thankful for all my gym training as we practically jogged up three flights of concrete stairs inside the vast abandoned warehouse where we'd apparently be doing today's filming. We arrived at a concrete platform at the top of the last set of stairs we climbed, where a gorgeous gleaming Harley waited for me.

She was poised pointing down the stairs, and suddenly it hit me – I'd be riding the motorcycle down the stairs.

"The front wheel goes in this track here, honey." A steel track ran down the middle of the stairs, and was painted a solid matte green so it could be erased with CGI in post production. "We literally just need you to hold on to the handlebars. You'll go down the stairs, back up the track and over the ledge."

My eyes followed where he pointed, taking in the way the green track did indeed end where the ledge did. As promised, twenty feet beyond, a sturdy net waited to stop my path and drop me onto a thick green cushion below.

"And the bike? How will it ..."

"On a tether, honey," Gary chuckled, clapping my shoulder. "Carol said you were familiar with bike work. This bike won't even fall."

"Bikes, yes. It's just been awhile since I... you know. Have ridden them off cliffs. Or staircases." That was a gross exaggeration. I had never ridden a motorcycle off anything. Still, I ignored the dryness that had taken over my mouth and throat like slowly spreading scales. I was filming for a primetime television show with a major network. The budget was through the roof, and everything looked safe. Gary had everything under control.

I nodded, swallowing the dryness away and approaching the

absolute beauty of a bike with authority. "Okay," I said, straddling her and gripping the handles with my newly manicured
hands. Action heroines, after all, had to have flawlessly shiny
nails. This was show business.

I took a deep breath, settling my bottom on the seat. *You
should have a helmet, at least.* The thought rose to the front of
my mind, sounding annoyingly like Ethan's voice. Gary had just
explained to me why I didn't need a helmet, and yet here was
Ethan's stupid paranoia, somehow having hitchhiked with me to
New York. Even though I had explicitly not invited him.

Even though part of me would have given anything to know
that I could go back to the hotel and find him waiting for me. A
very strong, simple part of my brain wanted him in my life, even
though I didn't want my life to be simple at all.

I said a little prayer as I revved the motorcycle engine, re-
familiarizing myself with the feel of my heel dropping back and
the purring engine under my body.

"When I say action, just tip her forward and brace for the
movement, okay honey?" Gary called from his position beside
the camera. Unable to get any actual words, I gave a thumbs up,
then gripped both handles again, waiting for the call.

What happened next stretched on for long, torturous
minutes, or only a split second. It was impossible for me to tell
as I tipped down the stairs, then back up over the railing,
hurtling through the air with the bike between my legs for a
single, breathless moment before I felt the net brush my face.
The bike fell down and must have snapped back on its tether,
but my body kept hurtling forward against that rough, blessed
net. Instead of catching me and bouncing me on its promised
trajectory downward, though, it gave way. It only took me half a
breath to realize that I wouldn't, in fact, be bouncing on the
green cushion below. I would continue moving forward – right
toward the old, dusty warehouse window.

The last sound I remembered was a crazy, high-pitched scream filling my ears and drowning out all thoughts. Only later would I learn that the primal, otherworldly sound had torn forth from my own throat, right before my body hurtled through the glass.

CHAPTER 29

ETHAN

I WAS GETTING way too old for this.

Mark had stayed through the two six-packs of beer that he'd brought, then ordered a pizza and two more. We'd blown through those, too, as the sun sunk low behind the Philly skyline and Hawthorne yowled for food. It was then, stumbling through the kitchen cupboards for the bag of his kibble, that Mark had announced that Toby was coming to pick him up and that he would leave me alone in his misery. That was fine with me. For the past several hours, I'd been on the verge of crying. I wasn't too macho to admit that all I wanted to do was bury my face in the pillows on my bed that still smelled just like her and weep like a baby. That was exactly what I did for the handful of seconds before the alcohol and exhaustion sent me into a deep, fitful sleep.

I woke up the next morning and checked my phone first thing. Not a single damn call from her. Not even a text. Of course, my first reaction, to chug a gallon of water and punch it out at the gym, depressed me today. Natalia wouldn't be there, and the whole time I stood at The Knockout I'd be reminded of her. Plus, Amalia might ask questions – ones I didn't know how to answer. So instead, I jogged around the neighborhood, stopping often to adjust my headphones in case I got a call.

I knew Natalia was on a job in New York. I knew I could go after her, beg her not to do the stunt, whatever the hell it was. I also knew that would be the one surefire way to drive her even farther away from me.

I ran through the rain, until my legs were jelly and hunger gnawed at my stomach. When I stumbled back into my apartment, it wasn't a relief to be home. Memories of Natalia surrounded me. There she was, standing in my kitchen, her head thrown back in laughter. She was on my couch, too, insisting on resting her feet on my lap as we watched a movie. I'd pretended to be annoyed, but I never really was. I shook my head, checking my phone for the thousandth time that day. Nothing. Dammit.

The shower stream pounded down fiercely on my neck. There was no use trying to wipe the memories of Natalia in my shower from my mind. They were too good. Too intense. She'd written herself all over my life, and now an uncertain ending gaped before me.

I hated this. All of it. I scrubbed shampoo onto my scalp with a frustrated growl and set my mind, determinedly, to coming up with a plan for how I could fix all of this. As soon as Natalia got back into town, I would surprise her. There would have to be a nice dinner, for sure, but maybe I could really take a leap toward her. Or... with her.

That was it. I was a genius. I was going to book a skydiving session for the two of us. Propose, like Tom had joked about. I'd tell her that I felt braver than I ever had when I was with her, but that I didn't want to be without her any more. I could hardly keep up with my own thoughts, had no real plan for what my life would look like if I gave it over to Natalia's whims. I had no clue how I'd come to terms with her apparently insatiable desire for danger. Suddenly, none of that mattered. The only thing I could bring myself to care about now, after twenty-four hours without her, was how to get her back.

Researching engagement rings, though, made me nervous. What if she laughed in my face, turned me down? What if my behavior over the last day had made her never want to see me again? It only took a few minutes of scrolling through my phone looking for options before I reached for a beer to take the edge off. One beer became two, and two became six, as I grasped for a grand gesture that Natalia would appreciate that wouldn't make me feel like I was planning my own funeral.

It didn't take long before I passed out on the couch, tumbling headfirst into a series of weird dreams. My mom was driving behind me through the streets of Philadelphia in her car while I struggled along on foot, through the rain. She stuck her head out the window, screaming at me to take a risk before my own boring life killed me. I was overwhelmed with sadness, and exhaustion, before the rain finally let up and the sun came out. The car rolled to stop, and now, instead of my mom behind the wheel, it was Natalia. I grinned and started to walk toward her, but she just held my phone out the window of the car. Its ring screeched out incessantly as she said in that teasing, musical voice of hers, "Go on, Ethan. What's stopping you from picking up?"

I didn't know how to explain, how to describe what was happening. No matter how many steps I took forward, my body couldn't move. "Come on, Ethan," she said, her voice growing more desperate, weaker with every word. "I need you right now. You have to answer the phone. Wake. Up."

And then everything went black.

My eyelids were glued together, or at least weighted down by bricks, filled with their chalky dust. My head pounded, a situation that wasn't at all improved by the beam of early morning sunlight piercing its way through the curtains. I managed to roll on my back, groaning as my head followed a beat later like a sack full of concrete, before realizing that my phone was, in fact, ringing.

I rolled myself off the bead, groaning again – next time I should remember that getting onto my feet was the better choice. There wouldn't be a next time, though. A man of my age should never drink that much. Ever again. My tolerance was only going to decline further as I ventured into my thirties.

The caller ID didn't recognize the number on the screen, which also displayed a perilously low battery level. I was damned ashamed of myself. I never thought I'd be caught dead with less than five percent battery. My phone wheezed out another ring tone, and I mercifully answered it despite not knowing who the hell could be on the other end, this early in the morning.

"Yeah?" I rasped out.

"Oh thank God, Ethan," a tinny yet familiar voice came through the speaker. "I've been trying you for almost fifteen minutes now. I was about to send someone over to... wherever you are."

Finally, I recognized the faintest trace of an accent, pushed into her perfect English by the frequency with which she spoke Spanish. "Amalia? What's up? Is Mr. Ortiz okay?"

"It's not him, Ethan. It's Natalia. You've gotta get on a train. Now."

―――

Three hours later, I approached Amalia on a street in New York City. She pulled me into a quick hug before pulling back to talk to me "I know you two were arguing, and you were really angry with her. Last night... she told me you didn't love her anymore. I don't know what went down between the two of you, but I think she would want you to know."

The trip to the hospital in New York City had been the longest of my life. Still, no amount of time could have prepared me for the sight that waited for me once I got inside.

Natalia lay in a hospital bed, still as death. My eyes burned with tears in the split second that I realized the faint beeping of her bedside monitor and the pink flush of her skin meant that she was not, in fact, dead.

Alejandro paced on the other side of the room, muttering rapid-fire questions into his phone. Of course he'd gotten here first. Through a fog, I realized he'd never actually come to Philly from New York to see his dad. We'd told him that Mr. Ortiz would be okay, that he could stay put in New York. Thank God. Amalia settled on the couch tucked into the tiny bay window of the hospital room. Her eyes met mine, then flicked to the space behind me. I blinked twice, my eyes heavy, before I registered that she'd left the seat at Natalia's bedside open for me.

Amalia's eyes were filled with tears, but she was all business. "Alejandro secured her a private room. He's on the phone with his lawyers now. We told the staff you're her fiancé, by the way, so you'll be allowed to stay past visiting hours."

My face was numb, and my lips struggled to form words. "Thank you," I managed to choke out, turning my gaze to Natalia. "Is she – how did – I mean – what...?"

"She was injured in a motorcycle driving stunt. She's been through three surgeries already, to repair her small intestine, give her a small skin graft, and put pins in her leg. She has a traumatic brain injury, and between that and the surgeries the doctors determined it was best to put her into a coma." A small sob punctuated the end of Amalia's sentence.

"What does that mean? What the hell happened?"

"I watched the footage," Alejandro said, finally turning to me and shoving his phone in his pocket. "There was a track directing the bike, and a cable tethering it so it couldn't fall on her once she jumped the platform. They worried so much about the bike and whether it would hurt her, that they didn't double check the safety net in front of the window," he said, looking slightly ill. "There was an old plate-glass window a couple dozen feet from the net," he continued. "She went right through, and hit the scaffolding outside on her way down. Thank God for that, or she would have hit the concrete and been dead."

"Oh my God," I moaned, locking my hands behind my head and bending forward, trying to will away the nausea that churned inside me at the thought. "No." The top of my head nudged against Natalia's still thigh, and its warmth was encouraging. *Not dead. She's still alive. She's breathing.*

"She did the stunt flawlessly. Rode that bike like she'd been doing it her whole life. Even the fall was gorgeous. I wonder if they'll still use that footage for the show."

"Jesus," I muttered.

"She had zero protective gear on," Alejandro continued. "Just a neoprene suit. No helmet. She tucked herself into a ball quickly enough to avoid a lung puncture, but some big shards hit her in the abdomen, so there was some internal damage."

Oh God. I couldn't breathe. Could not make myself picture Natalia's body being tossed around atop a thousand-pound death cycle just waiting to ignite itself. And now here she was. Hooked up to monitors, looking like she was sleeping. Mercifully, something was different from my memory of seeing my mom there, dead on the ER table.

"There's no breathing tube," I said in a whispered rush. Somehow, that made it okay for me to scoot the chair in closer, reach my hand out to brush a strand of hair from her forehead. "Why isn't there a breathing tube?"

"It means that her brain is telling her body to breathe on its own." A deep bass voice sounded from the doorway, and I turned to see a doctor who looked as though he'd just graduated from high school step in the door. Immediately, I got to my feet, overwhelmed by the need to get every bit of information I could from him.

"I'm Dr. Rasal," he continued, reaching out a hand to grasp mine. It was only then that I realized my hand, hell, my whole arm, was trembling. I swallowed hard.

"She's breathing on her own, then," I said. "That's good."

Dr. Rasal nodded hesitantly. "It means is that that particular part of her brain was unharmed. While we don't know the extent of the injury, the MRI gave us reason to think that, given a little time, she should come out of the coma on her own. In terms of her verbal and motor function... time will tell."

I swallowed again, finally allowing my trembling legs to relax back into the seat. "Excuse me," I said, rubbing my palm across my forehead. "I wasn't with her when it happened."

"She will be okay," Dr. Rasal assured me, sounding convincingly sure of himself. "Before my shift ends, tell me what questions you have."

"Everything," I said, taking in Natalia's quiet, beleaguered face. "Every sling, pin, bandage and tube. Tell me what they're for, and how long it'll take for her to recover."

For the next twenty minutes, I listened intently as Doctor Rasal patiently explained everything. A complicated network of pins held Natalia's tibia, ankle, and foot together after it had shattered in her fall. There was a patch of skin about nine inches long that had been stripped away from Natalia's calf, filleted by the sharp glass as she crashed through that. Dr. Rasal explained that she'd needed surgery to reattach the muscle and she'd need another one to graft skin over the wound. "She will walk fairly normally, as long as she works hard in rehab," Dr. Rasal preemptively explained.

"Oh, she will," Amalia and I said in unison. We shared a small, fleeting smile, while Dr. Rasal moved on to her internal injuries. "Her liver had a lot of lacerations, and it was bleeding so much we had to remove a large portion of it. But she can live without that," he assured me quickly. "The most concerning thing was the damage to her small intestine. We removed some of that, and we'll need to monitor it closely to make sure none of the stitches come out. She'll have to take it easy for a while."

"You're talking awfully optimistically," I said on a sigh, running my fingers back through my hair. I was sure I was a mess, and I really didn't care.

"I am optimistic," Dr. Rasal laughed. It was a booming, boisterous sound that didn't match his skinny young façade. It was reassuring, but all the same, I glared. At that point, he seemed to remember his bedside manner. "If you'd seen the kind of things I've seen, and met the number of patients I've met, you'd understand what I'm trying to say. Her injuries aren't too bad, her surgeries went well, and from what you all are telling me, she's a fighter. I'd say we'll wean her off this medication keeping her unconscious within the next twelve hours, and see where we go from there. Ok? You won't even have to change the wedding date. I'd bet money on it."

My heart wrenched at that, and a kneejerk protest to Dr. Rasal's statement was half-formed before I remembered that Amalia had listed me as Natalia's fiancé. Just twelve hours ago, I would have happily given myself over to daydreaming about Natalia agreeing to be mine forever. Now, my wildest fantasies involved her waking up. Walking again. Knowing my name. So, instead of saying any of the dozen things I could say to the well-meaning doctor, I thanked him, holding his hand in a strong, grateful handshake before he moved on to his next patient.

Then, I settled into the chair at Natalia's bedside, gently holding her still, cool hand in mine. I prayed silently, desperately, she would wake up, that she'd speak again, walk again. Skydive again. It was the most fervent praying I'd ever done.

The next morning, God had my back.

CHAPTER 30

NATALIA

MY EYES FLEW open to a world I didn't recognize. A bright
light glared into the corner of my left eye, and pocked white
ceiling tiles filled the rest of my vision. My throat had been
rubbed raw with sand, and though I desperately wanted to move
my head to take in more of my surroundings, I couldn't move a
muscle. I was lying down, that much I knew, and the only thing
keeping me from completely freaking out was the feeling of a
solid, warm hand holding on to one of mine, heavy where it
rested on my stomach. There was a strange texture to it,
though... barely perceptible points of pressure pressing against
my skin beneath his hand.

"Oh my God," Ethan's voice breathed in a combined panic
and relief. He squeezed my hand too hard, too briefly, before
dropping it. I heard his footsteps dashing from the room, and
confusion washed over me for long seconds before I heard them
coming back in again, trailed by another set. A soft, soothing
woman's voice addressed me.

"Natalia? Hi, honey. You've just woken up from a medically
induced coma. You're going to be fine, but it might take a little
while to regain movement. You are not paralyzed, okay dear?"

I would have nodded my head, if I could have. Panic rose in my throat and my eyes flew back and forth, searching for the Ethan's face. He was here, wasn't he? He had to be. My heart flew around in my chest like a crazed bird trying to break free of a cage. Then, after a handful of agonizing seconds, his hand held mine again, and his warm, deep voice floated into my ear. Finally, finally, he leaned over me so I could see him. There were deep purple circles under his eyes, and his scruff had grown slightly wild. He looked into my eyes for a moment, and I felt the slightest twitch in my eyebrows, a tiny closing of my lids. Ethan's eyes squeezed shut in response, and a tear trickled from the corner of one. I felt his head drop to my shoulder, and everything in me wanted to take him in my arms.

I had no idea where I was, but I knew that Ethan was home. My eyelids fell closed, too heavy to keep up, but when I heard the soft female voice again, I dragged them open. Her words were fuzzy, but I'd be damned if I was going to backslide now. Another slow blink, and I forced myself to refocus on the sound of her words, commanding my brain to separate the syllables instead of allowing them to blend together.

"Natalia," the nurse said, with the tone of someone who'd been repeating herself. I blinked again, slowly, purposefully. "There we go. We're going to do a little test, okay honey?"

I blinked again, and Ethan's face, which was looking down at mine again, broke into a grin. "Did you see that?" he demanded, his voice giddy. "She totally heard you."

"Let's see," the nurse said. It struck me that the patience dripping from every word was probably not for me – Ethan sounded crazed, and annoying as hell. My heart dictated a laugh – I felt the corner of my mouth twitch up.

"She smiled," Ethan narrated, a revelation the nurse ignored. I didn't, though. I let the joy in his voice, the exuberance of the way he squeezed my hand, warm me down to my bones.

"We're going to try blinking first, okay?"

I blinked. Yes, much faster this time. I was approaching normal speed.

"How about twice, dear?" I blinked twice, though I could feel the fatigue seeping in at the corners of my consciousness.

"Okay, now let's try a bigger challenge. Can you tap your fingers on the bed?"

With gargantuan effort, mental and physical, I willed my fingers to work. Cool, scratchy fabric brushed my fingertips.

"Hmmm," the nurse said with a frown as she stared at my hand. "Might be just reflexes."

No. No, it was not. I had worked hard for that. With a grunt, I commanded my fingers to move in a rhythm. The nurse let out a laugh. "Okay then."

"That's good, that's so good, honey. Oh, thank God," he uttered. With that last sentence, the realization hit me – the strange points of pressure between Ethan's hand and mine had been rosary beads. He'd been holding them for me, just like I'd held them for my dad.

"One more thing before I leave. Now if you can't do this last one, dear, it's fine. Nothing to worry about."

I could do it, though. I could do anything I set my mind to. If the sum of my life so far had proven anything, it was that.

"Natalia," the nurse said, and I got the distinct sense I'd drifted out of focus again. I blinked, showing her that I was listening. "Try to say something for me. Say 'hi.'"

"Okay, no. She can't – she's clearly struggling just to blink and move her fingers today. It's too much. We'll try for words tomorrow."

Yep. This was really and truly my Ethan. My unsolicited safeguard and protector from anything that might stretch me too far. Under normal circumstances, I would have smacked him, or at least rolled my eyes. but given that my body didn't seem too keen on moving just now, the most I could do was a scolding, raspy whisper. It took everything in me, but after a few seconds of determined effort, I managed the two syllables. "Ethan."

CHAPTER 31

ETHAN

IT WAS RASPY, and pained, but it was clear as day. Natalia had seen me, recognized me, and said my name. I let my forehead fall on the bed beside her and let the sobs I'd been holding in since I first saw her lying in that hospital bed all those hours ago pour out of me. The deluge of tears and emotion knocked down any walls that were left between me and my devotion to Natalia. Now, I just had to hope that she would keep getting better, and that she felt the same way. The happiest moment of my life was when, an instant later, she moved her fingertips back and forth against my arm, just twice, and just a centimeter.

We were going to be okay.

Every day, Natalia spoke a little more. The first day after she came out of sedation, she was turning her head and asking for her favorite foods and drinks. Two days after that, she was staying awake for an hour at a time, asking questions about her injuries. Her memories seemed to come back along with the details I told her. The day she realized she couldn't move or flex her right leg was heartbreaking. I wiped every tear as it streamed down her cheek, promising her that she was still strong and capable and nothing was ever, ever going to change that.

One night, her still-thick, scratchy voice interrupted me as I was carefully pulling socks over her feet. The pins had just come out of her right foot a few hours ago, and her orthopedist had explained that she might have some strange sensations there for a couple of days. Since she'd just had the pin removal surgery, she needed help with her socks. It wasn't until I looked up and saw tears streaming down her cheeks that I realized she was upset.

"What are we going to do? This is impossible," she sobbed as I pulled her into a gentle hug from where I knelt on the floor.

"What? Changing socks? It's actually one of the least challenging aspects of taking care of you the last week or so, honestly." I shot her a smile, hoping she'd pick up on my teasing tone. Instead, her lower lip trembled.

Within seconds, I'd perched myself on the bed next to her so that we sat hip to hip, and gently snaked my arm over her shoulders.

"I'm pathetic. I can't move my leg. My whole body hurts. So much. Some days I can't even brush my hair."

"That's what I'm here for," I soothed.

"That's not what you signed up for," she said, letting her head fall back against the raised head of the bed. "I don't even know how you're here. Don't you have a job? That's, like, not in New York?"

"I took time off," I said. "I have sick leave. I can use it to take care of loved ones. If there's a work emergency, the internet and smart phones exist."

She squeezed her eyes shut, and a single tear rolled down her cheek. "The gym, and my dad, and everything I have to do back home...everything I want to do with my life..." she trailed off, clenching her lips closed against the words that were causing her so much pain. "What am I going to do?" she whispered again.

"Natalia Ortiz, listen to me. I know what *we* are going to do."

Her lower lip wobbled. Watching her struggle with this kind of put my suffering into perspective, and in that moment, I knew I would do anything to figure this out for her. For the both of us. Because my heart was broken, too.

"Things are going to be a little different now. It's true. But you're still you, and I'm still me."

"You're still mad at me about the stunt thing."

"I stopped being mad at you the moment I knew you were alive. That feeling got replaced with being thankful that you exist on this planet. As soon as I realized I could have lost you, Tali, I knew how stupid it was for me to get so angry with you. To treat you like that. So," I said, forcing the words out so I didn't choke on them, "I'm going to make you a promise. We're going to figure something out – a way to go forward, together. Including stunt work, if you want. Something that won't make either of us miserable. If... if that's what you want."

Even as I said it, I imagined more and more situations like the exact same horrible one we were sitting in. Natalia coming within an inch of her life for the sake of performing some stupid stunt, and me sitting at her bedside in the hospital hoping she wouldn't die and would remain more or less unmaimed. I tried to ask myself if it was something I could do and do again. I didn't know, but I knew one thing for sure. I loved her. I didn't want to live without her.

"That's what I want, if you do." I'd never seen Natalia look so uncertain. "If this freaks you out," she said softly, glancing at me through her lashes, "if you can't handle seeing me this way – I get it. I guess. But I want to make this work."

My heart sank. She actually thought I still might want to break things off. I reached up to tuck some hair behind her ear, full of sadness that she thought I'd want to leave her, especially now. She sucked in a breath, and I realized that she must have misinterpreted my sad expression. "Don't make a decision yet," she rushed out. "I've actually been doing a lot of thinking. I have... ideas. Things I want to do that I think could make me happy and keep me in Philly, running The Knockout. Because, honestly, as fun as that stunt could have been, this hurts like a bitch." She motioned to her leg, bandaged and bruised. "Plus, I don't know how my mobility will be affected. I'm twenty-five. Getting too old for stunts."

I laughed, feeling half-relieved she was saying all this. "Yeah, babe, you're decrepit."

She smacked me on the arm. "You know what I mean. And, um, I have a confession. I did a lot of thinking, about everything. About my plans for life, for my career. You know, as I was coming out of my coma?"

I winced. "Yeah?" What the hell was she going to say? That she'd wanted to break up with me for good, for not being there for her when the worst happened? That she thought I wanted to be done with her for good?

"Everything I thought of would only be possible if we do it together. And I mean that."

Relief rushed through me like a wave crashing onto the shore. I nodded my head once, then let it rest against hers. I kissed her softly, and the softest whimper let loose from her throat. It was a memory of every intimate moment we'd ever shared, and a promise of more, all at once. "Let's do it," I whispered.

"Okay," she said. "As long as you promise not to ever, ever touch my skin graft."

"Oh, babe," I said, pouting a little. "You don't mean that. I know things are rough right now, and there's not much privacy, but I fully plan on seeing you naked again sometime in our lives."

Her eyes sparkled. "You can look at it. With the lights dimmed. Just don't touch it."

"Not even during..." I waggled my eyebrows.

Natalia threw her head back and laughed. She was sunshine in this pod of fluorescent lights and alcohol-scented air. She'd just told me she wanted me in her life, and as long as she felt that way, I knew that sunshine would chase any cloud away.

A week after she woke up, Natalia had her first taste of solid food since the accident. Her intestines needed to rest after the trauma of lacerations and surgery, and she moaned as she shoveled mashed potatoes into her mouth, with me supporting her arm. Her unaffected limbs had basically returned to full capability, but she got tired quickly. Her eyes pressed shut and tears streamed down her cheeks. I peered at her with concern. "Babe, what's wrong? Is it your throat? Your stomach? Does it hurt too much?"

She opened her eyes and looked at me with the purest love I'd ever seen beaming out of them. "It just tastes so good," she said, starting to cry all over again.

That was the first time I'd really laughed since the accident.

We only stayed in New York for another week or so after Natalia's surgery. The day I took her to her first physical therapy session a few weeks later,, I held her hand while she hobbled down a ten-foot track with crutches and a walking boot protecting her leg. She gritted her teeth and grunted a little, but, beginning on that day, she didn't shed a single tear over her injuries. From the moment we left the hospital, it was like Natalia was only capable of looking forward. As soon as I realized that, I vowed to take her lead.

EPILOGUE

NATALIA

ONE YEAR Later

"Pick up your feet, Ethan Anderson!" I hollered with my hands cupped around my mouth. He was training for his first 5k ever – I was training for my first after the accident. I was still slower than he was, but I wasn't nearly as out of breath. I'd managed to stay in good cardio shape after the accident, even though my leg still protested near the end of a 4-mile run. We were nearing the end of one now, and the familiar ache was more of an annoyance than an impediment.

"Okay, babe!" he shouted, making a big show of pulling up his knees.

"Don't hurt yourself," I called back, grimacing at a pinch in my lower leg. There wasn't a day that went by without either the surgery to put the bones back together or the skin graft didn't cause me lingering discomfort, but things were getting a little better. Ethan must have noticed, even from the other side of the track, because he stopped messing around and put his head down, leaning his whole body in a sprint to my side.

In the year since the accident, The Knockout had changed a lot. We'd taken out a loan to rebuild the track that went around the outside of the lofty inside, which made us an attraction for runners who still needed to train even when Philadelphia's sidewalks froze over. I was still catching my breath when Ethan arrived at my side, scooping me into his arms. Our sweaty arms squished together, and I wrinkled my nose in a show of disgust. "Eewww," I complained as he carried me down the stairs and to the small sitting area just inside the gym's entrance – something Amalia had spent a lot of time developing.

"Graft or bone?" Ethan asked.

"Bone, I think. Just where the screws were."

In a second, Ethan was unlacing my shoe and cradling my foot in his hands, peering at my shin area. His thumbs ghosted over the patch of grafted skin that was slightly puckered and pocked – a reminder of my near-death experience that would never go away. "No swelling," he muttered. "Still hurt?"

I shook my head. "It's fine, really. Just one of those freak things."

"Still," he said, gently pulling my shoe back onto my foot. "We're done working out for the day. We have to go check out that land anyway."

Ethan was referring to a pipe dream of his that I couldn't help but get moony-eyed over right along with him. About four months after the accident, I'd decided I wanted to use my experience to help other young stunt performers. With Ethan's actuarial knowledge, I was able to put together a small course for performers just starting out for how to protect themselves on the job. It included a review of legal matters, safety considerations, how to insist on the best safety gear available, and, at the end, a small demonstration of defensive postures and movements that performers could use to best protect themselves.

After that class, the attendees had come up to me asking so many personal questions – did I know where they could learn stunt sparring? Jumping? Driving? – that I so badly wanted to answer for them. The truth was that there were places that could help you with a single skill here or there, but not a concentrated institution anywhere near Philly. The next week, I booked my first stunt-sparring course, focused on protecting your body and face that so that a performer could work as safely and long as possible without any stays in the hospital or medically induced comas or pins in their leg.

Soon enough, the entire basement of the Knockout was populated with these classes every night of the week. I sought out and hired stunt drivers willing to teach my clients a thing or two, and we rented large asphalt spaces next to the airport for driving demonstrations on the weekends. I even took groups skydiving. Through it all, Ethan didn't have a word of complaint. I never even saw him flinch.

During the nights, when we lay tangled up together at either his place or mine – we rarely slept apart anymore – he would set himself to spinning dreams. He was good at that – watching me carefully, asking me about what I wanted from the next month, or year, or five – and then floating ideas for how to make that happen. One night, as I was about to drift off, he'd murmured, "We should just open our own school."

"What?" I asked, completely floored. "The Knockout is still doing its gym thing pretty well. I wouldn't want to scrap that for a totally new business model."

"No," he'd said, chuckling softly. "A school for stunt performing. New building. New location. There's a need for it. Cheaper to live here than in New York, or LA. Why shouldn't stunt performers come to us from all over the country? Why shouldn't Natalia Ortiz's name be synonymous with stunt performing excellence and the gold standard of safety? You could be like a gateway for hiring all across the country."

"I can't leave Philadelphia," I'd stammered, unable to deny that he painted a beautiful picture.

"Wouldn't have to," he said. "There's land closer than you think. All over Montgomery county, and Bucks. Closer than you think."

"You're nuts," I said weakly. "That would never... we'd never be able to afford to..."

"Can I look, though?" He asked. "Just dig around? Get some estimates?"

I grumbled, snuggling down into his side.

"Please? I'll give you a fancy report and everything."

I'd agreed, but he'd only shown me real estate listings since. Once, we'd driven out to Bucks county and driven around the country for hours. We'd never seen anything concrete.

In the last few days, though, Ethan had been more energized than ever about showing me this land he'd found. My leg hurt like hell, and I had no Knockout classes scheduled for the rest of the day. I figured I'd go on a car ride with him, make him buy me dinner, and call it a night. So, when he squeezed me against his stinky, sweaty chest and asked again if I'd go see the land with him, I squealed and agreed, as long as we both took a shower first.

The late Spring sun was dipping down toward the horizon as we wound our way down the Expressway and then took an exit half an hour later. After a couple more turns, we were surrounded by woods. The road narrowed to a double-lane with so many dips and turns that each minute of driving revealed a new, beautiful view. Ethan consulted his phone, made one more turn, and then took us down a narrow gravel path through a field teeming with wildflowers. "Okay," he said. "This is it."

"This is what?" I laughed.

"This is where your stunt work school is going to be."

"Okay, daydreamer," I scoffed.

He gave me a faraway smile. "It's zoned for the kind of construction we'll need to do. Of course, half of it will just be concrete for the drivers, and another big chunk will be a field for the stunt jumpers to land after they jump out of planes and whatnot. You can adjust that as you see fit, you know way more than I do about what you'll need. Oh, and there will be a workshop and lab for JJ and his people, of course."

JJ had already used me as a test dummy, for lack of a better word, on some safety products for stunt work he was developing. I hadn't imagined that an actual rocket scientist like him would be interested that particular line of work, but he assured me that it was shaping up to be very lucrative. Nobody wanted a lawsuit like the one my brother had filed against the movie studio – the settlement for which could fund my stunt performance school

I stared at him. "Ethan, we don't even know how much –"

"It doesn't matter," he interrupted. "It's paid for. It's all paid for."

"What in the –?"

"I had a lot of money saved," he blurted. "My mom had a big life insurance policy. I was saving it for my retirement. But after the accident... since then... Natalia, it's like I can see my future, and your future, so clearly. We can make it happen, and we can make it good."

"You had a trust fund," I said numbly, trying to take it all in. Was he saying he had bought this land?

"There's more," he said. His words were tense now, afraid. "I don't know, Natalia. It's just that Amalia is doing such a great job managing the front desk at The Knockout, and the house is feeling a little cramped, and... well, I'll show you." Suddenly, his voice was filled with doubt. It was making me nervous.

The gravel crunched under our tires as we drove toward a tree line beyond the huge swath of land through which we'd entered. The trees, I realized, surrounded another area of land maybe half an acre wide. Perched on a small hill just beyond the trees' shadows was a small white house with a wraparound porch and black trim.

Ethan pulled up to the driveway wordlessly while my mind raced. Suddenly, his excitement from earlier in the day made sense. And because I was quickly realizing what a risk, what an adventure he was envisioning, I started to get excited too.

I popped open my door and stood, savoring the stark freshness of the air. It was green and fresh, probably hadn't had contact with a billow of smoke or puff of exhaust for days, or even weeks, before we arrived.

"The, uh…" Ethan stood outside his door. He scratched at his neck, and all of a sudden seemed to shrink into himself. He was nervous. "The house came with the land. I wasn't looking for land with a house. Like, I wasn't trying to tell you what you're supposed to want. I just thought… I don't know. Maybe we could use it. If you want. It's all up to you, Tali." His voice softened when he said my name, and I melted inside.

"Well then," I said, stretching my hand out to his, "show me."

We didn't speak as we went inside. He unlocked the front door with his keys as though he'd been doing it his whole life. Suddenly, a future flashed before my eyes. Ethan coming home from a long day at the office – to me. Me dragging myself through the front door, dirty and exhausted, after teaching young stunt actors how to jump off a motorcycle without killing themselves. Papá and my brothers walking through this door, for dinner. Maybe every other Sunday. With every step forward, my heart felt more full.

The house was empty of furniture and painted in stark shades of white, but as we moved from one room to the next, my imagination filled it. There would be a leather wrap-around sectional in the living room, and we'd put a fluffy rug in front of the fireplace. The all-white kitchen would need filling with colorful dishes and towels. By now, my hand had flown up to cover my mouth, and Ethan was watching me with a wistful smile.

"How many bedrooms?" I asked softly, finally finding some words.

He shrugged. "Three," he said. "Wanna see my favorite?"

I nodded and took his hand when he stretched it out to me. We walked up a flight of stairs to a room that took up the entire small top floor of the house. The ceiling tented in the middle, forming a perfect natural frame for the bed – the only piece of furniture in the house. I chuckled to myself. "Of course you'd make sure there was a bed here."

"It's a lot, Natalia. It's a big thing I'm asking here."

I froze in place, keeping my eyes trained on the bed. Waiting for him to say his piece.

"I want a life with you. We have been incredible partners so far, and I know we can make this dream into something bigger and more incredible than either of us ever imagined. I know you've never wanted to settle down, but I promise you, we can come and go as much as you want. Vacations. Adventures." He pulled in a deep, shuddery breath. At the same time, he tugged me toward him. I whirled around to see two skydiving jump-suits hanging on the closet door.

Then I lost all my breath. Ethan was on one knee before me, holding both my hands in his.

"What -?" I started.

"I was going to ask you when we actually used these to go skydiving. But then I thought... maybe you'd say no. I didn't want to put you on the spot. I do want you to know how serious I am, though. So," he said, on a heavy exhale, "I bought these skydiving suits, and a session. When... if... you're ready to say yes, you can book it. We can move in here first, or after, or... never, I guess." The poor man's voice shook as he rocked back on his heels and swallowed hard. He gazed out the window, and it occurred to me that he was trying not to look at me. He was convinced I didn't want this, didn't want him. It was unbelievable to me, after all the ways he had changed to make me not only able to imagine a life with him, but to desperately want one.

"I know I don't take a lot of risks in life, and being with me can be pretty boring. I know you're always going to be looking for more adventure, but I promise to give that to you in as many ways as I can. Please say you'll at least consider being my wife."

"Hey. Look at me." I cupped the side of his face with my hand, ran my thumb down his chin, as my heart thundered in my chest. "This house? This plan? Spending your savings so you can give me a chance to fulfill my dreams?"

He swallowed again, and nodded.

"That was the biggest damn risk anyone could have possibly taken." I tugged at his arms, urging him to his feet. He obliged.

"Yeah?" He chuckled, with shining eyes, gazing at me like I was the most brilliant thing he'd ever seen.

"I'm proud of you, for doing something that scared you," I murmured, moving close to him. Our bodies pressed together, and he tilted his head down so his forehead touched mine. I sighed happily. "It shouldn't have scared you, though."

I stepped back, and Ethan sucked in a breath. God, he was adorable. "Who did you call? Skydive Philadelphia?" That was the company that had taken us skydiving for Ethan's first time, over a year ago now.

He nodded, and I pulled my phone out of my pocket. I pulled up the number for Skydive Philadelphia, already in my contacts. "Hey, Tom," I greeted the owner when he answered. I smiled slyly. I would have called him about this anyway within the next couple of weeks. "I'm calling because my fiancé and I are starting a stunt performing school just outside the city, and I wanted to let you guys be the first to bid on a contract for skydiving lessons."

A grin big enough to swallow my heart, my soul, and my whole future split Ethan's face. He reached out and gripped my waist, tugging me close to him, pressing our bodies together chest to thigh as I promised Greg we'd iron out the bid meeting details in the morning. When I hung up, Ethan grabbed my phone from my hand and tossed it on the bed.

"Hey!" I protested weakly. "I wasn't done. I have a lot of calls to make."

"Oh yeah? Why's that?" Ethan growled, pressing a soft but sensuous kiss to my lips.

"I've gotta tell my whole family that we just got engaged."

"Did we? I didn't give you a ring."

"If it's not in the pocket of your flight suit over there, I swear I'll never go skydiving again." I was taking a gamble on this one, not to mention losing whatever small interest I'd had in a ring to begin with. Still, it was an empty promise.

Ethan sighed in defeat and loosened his grip on me, which made me whine a little bit. He took the few steps to his suit and pulled a sparkling diamond band out of the pocket, unhooking it from the carabiner which held it there. He made it back to me in two long strides, then dropped down to both knees. He held the ring in one hand, but fell forward just enough to let his head rest on my belly. Like they were magnetically attracted, my fingers threaded through his hair. After a moment, he looked up at me with his eyes shining once again. "Will you?" he whispered.

I bit my lower lip and nodded quickly, feeling tears prick at my eyes as well. He slipped the ring onto my finger – a perfect double-row diamond band. "So it won't get caught on anything," I mused as I held it out to admire it. I kissed him quick and hard. "Now, where's my phone?"

"If you want it, you're going to have to go get it," he said with an arched brow, looking over to the bed. I squealed, ran, and launched myself onto it. Within a second he was on top of me, snaking one hand through my hair and the other beneath my waistband. As I gave myself over to the familiar, yet still thrilling, push and pull of our lips and bodies against each other, I thought to myself that deciding on a life with Ethan was the scariest, and most worthwhile, decision I'd ever made.

The End.

ABOUT THE AUTHOR

Alessandra Thomas is a New Adult writer who swears she was in her twenties yesterday. Since that's sadly untrue, she spends her time looking back on her college years fondly, and writing sexy stories about guys and girls falling in love and really living life for the first time.

When she's not writing, you can find her with a spoonful of ice cream in one hand and the newest New Adult release in the other.

ALSO BY ALESSANDRA THOMAS

Just Love series

Just Down the Hall

Just Pretend

Just Let Go

Book of Sindal

Descended from Shadows

Reign of Mist

Crown of Blood

Picturing Perfect series

Picture Perfect

Subject to Change

Drop Everything Now